About the Author

Hazel-Anne Nair was born in London and now lives in Sydney, Australia. She is the proud mother of three superb children and has a stupendously amazing husband. She has travelled extensively, and has a master's in English Literature. It has been an ambition of hers to be an author ever since she first read *Little Women* as a child. She always hero-worshipped Jo March!

This is a work of fiction. Names, characters, businesses, places, events and incidents are either the products of the author's imagination or used in a fictitious manner. Any resemblance to actual persons, living or dead, or actual events is purely coincidental.

A VERY BENNET SCANDAL

Hazel-Anne Nair
Cover art by Frances Wheatley

A VERY BENNET SCANDAL

Vanguard Press

VANGUARD PAPERBACK

© Copyright 2023
Hazel-Anne Nair

The right of Hazel-Anne Nair to be identified as author of
this work has been asserted by her in accordance with the
Copyright, Designs and Patents Act 1988.

All Rights Reserved

No reproduction, copy or transmission of this publication
may be made without written permission.
No paragraph of this publication may be reproduced,
copied or transmitted save with the written permission of the
publisher, or in accordance with the provisions
of the Copyright Act 1956 (as amended).

Any person who commits any unauthorised act in relation to
this publication may be liable to criminal
prosecution and civil claims for damages.

A CIP catalogue record for this title is
available from the British Library.

ISBN 978 1 80016 830 5

*Vanguard Press is an imprint of
Pegasus Elliot Mackenzie Publishers Ltd.*
www.pegasuspublishers.com

First Published in 2023

**Vanguard Press
Sheraton House Castle Park
Cambridge England**

Printed & Bound in Great Britain

Dedication

This book is dedicated to my mother, who first taught me how to read; also to my family, who have tolerated me when I have been tormented by doubts that I could ever do this. And finally to Sister Margaret McKee, who made me read Jane Austen all those years ago!

Acknowledgements

During the excruciating writing and editing process of this book, there have been many people making suggestions, helping me tweak this or delete that. To them, I extend my deep gratitude.

I would like to thank my wonderfully talented cousin, Frances Wheatley, for the superb artwork!

Chapter One
Mary Bennet Bedevilled

The patriarch of the Bennet family of Longbourn, near Meryton in Hertfordshire, Mr Bertram Bennet had never quite recovered from the shock of having had one of his five daughters publicly exposed as a hoyden — and let's face it, a harlot. He had also never recovered from the sudden event of having the expense of upkeep of his two eldest daughters, Jane and Elizabeth, taken off his hands at the same time, just when he thought he would be saddled with them for life. The sensations and emotions elicited by the crashing low of Lydia's scandalous elopement and his futile attempts to track her down had left him quite exhausted, and then the following good fortune of the two extremely felicitous marriages made by Jane and Elizabeth rendered him quite giddy. He had felt he could bear no more extremes of emotion, and had therefore sought a return to that peace and quiet to which he had heretofore been accustomed, and that he so deeply valued.

In order to secure this desired state of affairs, he found it necessary to make dire threats to his two remaining unmarried daughters, Kitty and Mary, that they should live quietly at home for at least the next ten years, so as not to expose the family to any more gossip. He was adamant that they should not attend any upcoming ball, whatever its provenance. No, nor any concert, parade, or card party. He was even thinking of having them escorted everywhere they went, in order to thwart any possibility of social intercourse. This dire state of affairs continued for an interminable length of time, according to Mrs Bennet and Kitty, although Mary was relishing the peace and quiet. Previously, in the Bennet household, the usual method of proceedings resulted in Mr Bennet having no real say in matters but on this topic he remained more or less adamant. However, as time wore on and memory gradually cast a rosy glow in his mind over those tumultuous events, Mr Bennet began to thaw. Thus it was that, one night, nearly eighteen months following Lydia's scandal, and Jane and Elizabeth's weddings, there ensued a rather one-sided conversation between Mr Bennet and his wife, during which he had been forced to give way to his wife's relentless protestations over his stern social edict.

"For…" as Mrs Bennet informed him, smugly, as she sought to get her own way, "as you know, there is to be no militia quartered in town over winter."

"A fact for which I thank the Lord daily," Mr Bennet interrupted darkly, although his brief and caustic remark went unheard by his good lady wife, who was off on a cause.

Mr and Mrs Bennet's regular mode of conversation usually followed this course. She would prattle on artlessly, confident of wearing him down as water on a stone, whilst he would interject dourly, knowing full well that his *bon mots* fell upon ears as deaf as that very stone.

"However, there are still some of the Bingleys at Netherfield," Mrs Bennet prattled on. "And the Darcys will visit; and besides, I heard that the Cowpers have her brother visiting…"

"You hate Mrs Cowper. You have not given even a small nod to that lady for nearly twelve years," Mr Bennet interjected, half-heartedly.

"…with maybe some friends of his, who are lately of the Fifth Regiment, and who knows how many there are—"

"In fact, I seem to remember you stating quite emphatically, after that debacle with Mrs Cowper copying your dress, that you would rather 'die a thousand deaths than speak to that creature ever again', and I marvel at the fact that you now admit her back into your select circle of friends."

"…and with Charlotte Lucas gone, there is one less rival for my girls."

"Very well — go the damned ball, but bear in mind there is no money for new gowns. You must make do and mend."

"Oh! That reminds me! I must see about some new dress patterns!"

"Not one penny, mind. I mean it."

"Oh, there is not much time! Three dresses to be made up! Lah, if I could but get my hands on some of that lace from Brussels..."

"Just one or two shillings a yard, then, if you must. But remember — not a penny more."

It was this inevitable capitulation by Mr Bennet to his wife's demands that led to the ruination of their daughter, Miss Mary Bennet's, peaceful afternoon. This young lady sat quietly in the drawing room, perfectly content. The sun, albeit weak on this winter's day, was causing dust motes to dance in its beams and pale dappling to embroider the rugs.

Before Mary lay a large bible, several sheets of cheap paper, some pens, ink and pen rags. She was thoroughly absorbed in a most gratifying pastime; that is, engaging in itemising, for her own edification, the many statements she deemed erroneous that had been uttered that morning by the new vicar, Mr Broughton, and was using her bible as justification for her arguments. Tut-tutting frequently, she thumbed the pages of the Good Book until she found what she wanted. With each proof discovered, supporting her views, she whispered a smug little *Aha!* under her breath, and with similar studiousness she ignored whatever disproof she found. The clock ticked sombrely on the silence, and some embers fell in the fire grate. Mary wrote on, undisturbed.

Suddenly, a loud clattering of feet outside the door caused Mary to tense up. *On no*, she thought, gripping her pen too tightly and causing a large ink stain to blot her paper. *Already? It is too soon, surely?* But yes, there was the door handle being turned. She braced herself out of habit for the anticipated onslaught, thin lips becoming thinner as she waited for the noisy interruption she knew was about to occur. However, when the door was thrust open, it admitted only one half of the cadre which had hitherto constituted her perpetual torment, in the form of her younger sister Catherine, known as Kitty, now *sans accomplice*.

Kitty Bennet catapulted herself dramatically into the room. Her hair had escaped its pins and was cascading down her back, she was without a shawl, and her face was red from running.

"There you are!" Kitty exclaimed breathlessly, one hand grasping the door frame for support, and the other fanning herself vigorously.

"As you see," was Mary's terse reply.

"I'm glad I've found you!" Kitty panted. "I've been looking all over for you! I—"

"Kitty," Mary interrupted her sister, brusquely. "It is Sunday, is it not?" Mary knew, of old, that unless she halted her sister mid-flow, the following conversation would be very vapid and lengthy indeed. She fixed an irritated gaze upon her sister.

Kitty spluttered. "Of course it is… you know that!"

"And do you not, by now, know of my after-church habit?" Mary queried, sarcastically.

"Of course I do! What is that to do with anything? Oh Mary, you must come and help Mama and me…"

"No, I must not," was the cold reply.

"Oh Mary, why ever not? Don't be mean! I have been running around all over the place looking for you! You must come…"

"Kitty, if you know of my after-church habit, why did you find it necessary to go looking for me, as you said, 'all over'?" Mary was in no mood to be distracted, and wanted nothing more than to bring Kitty to the point, in the hopes of ending the interruption sooner rather than later.

"Huh?"

Mary sighed with the air of a martyr. "Kitty, after church on Sundays you know perfectly well that I go over the sermon of the day, and make notes until dinner time. Therefore, you had only to remember that, and you would have known where to find me, saving yourself both time and energy."

Kitty, who had meanwhile picked up a page of Mary's notes and was fanning herself with it, suddenly appeared to realise what she held. She looked as the paper as if it was a scandal-sheet and said: "Well, well. Poo to your endless notations and analysings!"

"If you have finished bringing the language of the farmyard into the drawing room…?"

"Wait! No! Oh Mary, do come and help! I do not know what to do!" Kitty advanced further into the room, sweeping several other sheets of paper off the table with the violence of her movements before slumping into a chair.

"Well, what is it now?" Mary softened a little, although her face did not show it. It was Sunday, after all, and having just been to church Mary was reminded that Christian charity demand she show a little compassion towards her sister, who was sorely missing her former companion in mischief, Lydia, ever since that sister had eloped with a military man of dubious character and moved with him to the north of England.

Thus encouraged, Kitty sat up straight again. "Oh, Mary! You know there is to be a ball for Yuletide… and Mama says we shall have new gowns… but Papa is adamant that he cannot afford it… and Mama says nonsense! And Papa insists that we shall have no new things to wear until he has paid back Uncle Gardiner for whatever it is that was needed when Lydia… but Mama says that it is not necessary because, after all, what is family for and that Uncle Gardiner surely don't count it, and Papa says that even if Uncle don't, then he surely does, and Mama says that Papa is just being a fuddy-duddy!"

"It's 'doesn't', not 'don't'. And am I to understand, Kitty, that all this commotion is over a new gown?" Mary's voice was dripping with sarcasm.

"Yes, and oh Mary, what shall we do? I cannot wear that old, yellow silk again! Everyone has seen it at least a dozen times! And besides, Mama needs a new one too, and she has said that you can also—"

"I refuse to be drawn into this fatuous conversation," Mary snapped, and turned resolutely back to her work, just as the door opened and their mother, Mrs Bennet, swept in.

Mrs Bennet was a small and portly woman, who was unstoppable when she was in high dramatics. Her lack of stature was made up for in the breadth of her acting abilities, which rivalled those of the most accomplished thespian on any stage. She advanced into the room with a flourish, all falling shawls and trailing lace sleeves, fluttering her hands, clutching at her throat, and inhaling lavender smelling salts most assiduously. True to form, Mrs Bennet protested and postured, sank into a chair, fanned herself violently, dabbed at her top lip with a handkerchief, gasped imploringly for water, appealed to Mary's sense of daughterly love and family duty, and altogether gave a sublime performance. The result of this saw Mary reluctantly and with a sour face locking away her notes in a bureau drawer and climbing the stairs with her Mama and sister to look over their gowns. Mary grumbled all the way, declaring that she had absolutely no interest whatsoever in fashion nonsense, and would as soon wear her brown plaid than a silk gown. She gained no reply to her terse question as to when Kitty and Mama would realise that clothes did not make the man, nor the woman for that matter, and sought support for her argument in quoting from the Good Book: "'Through tatter'd clothes small vices do appear, Robes and furr'd gowns hide all.'" Mary often resorted to these pedantic and parrot-like mouthings, and chose such passages as those that appeared, on the surface, to vindicate her personal views. However, no matter how virtuous and God-fearing Mary strove to be in her vows and opinions, she was no match for her mother when she was in a State.

For Mrs Bennet was indeed excited to the point of palpitations. Did Mary not realise there had been no parties, no balls, routs, nothing, since her darling Jane and dear Elizabeth had been married these several months past? Now that Christmas was approaching with all its tempting social opportunities, Mrs Bennet was determined to launch back into society and marry off her next two daughters in the same style and manner as the eldest two. There were times, indeed, when this determined Mama quite forgot about the third daughter Lydia's disgrace and hasty marriage. In fact, often it seemed to her that Lydia was enveloped in the same cloud of marital respectability and romance as her two elder sisters. Three daughters married! What felicity! What do you think of that, Mrs Lucas! Yes, such was her smug satisfaction at her daughters' successes that she was able, for entire days at a time, to forget completely about the looming storm on the horizon; the veritable Sword of Damocles poised to descend upon their heads — the event which was to cast them all into poverty and degradation. Such turns of phrase as these were the many histrionic forms by which Mrs Bennet referred to a fact which had cast the deepest shadow upon her life, ever since she had first come to Longbourn. Her husband's estates had always been entailed upon a male heir and thus, the Bennets having produced only daughters, the entail was now in favour of Mr Bennet's one and only male relative: his cousin, the rat-like Reverend Collins. It was a grim and lowering prospect. Despite her assiduousness in pursuing suitable marriages for her daughters, she could never forget the impending eviction from her family home.

However, on this particular afternoon, as her daughters sorted through what Mary referred to as 'a mountain' of clothing, Mrs Bennet was feeling quite sanguine and almost hopeful, now that there was the prospect of undiscovered opportunities upon the horizon. She sat down upon the edge of Kitty's bed and lay back among the pillows, indulging in a little daydream, and slipped into a half-doze, becoming more and more unaware of the conversation around her.

"How do you say you have nothing to wear?" Mary queried her sister, shaking her head at the blatant display of fashion folly before her, as their mother began to gently snore. Kitty's bedroom resembled a small clothing salon. Every surface of the bed, chairs and floor was festooned with old dresses, scarves, lace fichus, feathered and beaded shawls and yards of ribbon. Boxes lay open with their contents spilled. Various slippers and boots littered the floor. Kitty was regarding it all with despair, whilst Mary looked on it all in disgust.

"But Mary!" wailed Kitty in reply, tears springing to her eyes. "Everything is so old! Look! This is torn! And Papa says we really have no money for new things! Mama says it is all nonsense… but Mary! Papa looked so worried!"

"And so he should." Mary gave no quarter to her sister. "The state of this family's finances is a joke."

"How can that be?" Kitty was puzzled. "I mean, I don't pretend to know about money, and such like things, but… but… does the estate not provide a living? And surely, now there are three fewer mouths to feed, there is less expense?" Kitty absent-mindedly made further rips in the torn hem of her old, yellow gown.

Mary regarded her sister with something akin to pity, ignoring her mother who was, by then, fast asleep, as unconcerned as a kitten in a basket. She wondered whether she should lay all before Kitty, or whether she should allow her sister to go on as usual, cocooned in a cloud of blissful ignorance. Was Kitty, Mary wondered, able to listen to and process the grim facts, or would she just shrug and hide behind trite sayings, such as "I do declare!" and "Lord, you are so droll!" Would Kitty, in fact, have anything useful to say on the matter?

Truth be told, the only people capable of understanding the sobering financial facts had now married and moved off. Mary missed her elder sisters' conversations quite a lot. At least with them you could have a decent conversation, about important matters; France, for example, or excise duties. All Kitty and Lydia ever spoke about was fashion, gossip and boys. Never having had the slightest interest in the latest Palace scandal or what the nobility was wearing this week, Mary found she had nothing in common with the two youngest Bennet girls, and had always looked to the two eldest for company. Now she was left at home with Kitty, and sometimes was sorely tempted to give in, to feign an interest in furs and feathers, if only to have someone to speak to. Papa had retreated back behind the Great Wall of Fatherhood and Mama... Well, Mama was the greatest idiot of them all. Mary suddenly made up her mind.

"Kitty," she began, interrupting her sister's frenzied examination of her gowns. "The weddings of our two eldest sisters were a great drain on the family coffers."

"I though it must be so!" Kitty exclaimed. "But had Papa not been putting money aside for that very circumstance?" A little worried frown creased Kitty's forehead, and Mary looked at her, pityingly.

"Yes," Mary explained, "and the money was to be settled on them as an annuity."

"An annuity? You mean... to be paid every year?"

Mary decided to forgo the sarcasm this remark warranted, and continued: "Exactly. After the settlements were made, and the weddings paid for, nearly all of the money Papa had put aside had been spent. He has not even begun to address the debt he owes Uncle Gardiner."

"Mama says that needn't be paid!" Kitty interrupted.

"Kitty…" Mary was patient. "Do you not see that for Papa it is a matter of the highest honour that he pays his debt?"

"Yes," Kitty puzzled over it for a moment. "I do see that."

Marvellous, thought Mary. *There is a glimmer of intelligence at last.* "There is more," she continued inexorably, having made up her mind to now fully apprise her feckless sister of the true state of affairs of Chez Bennet. "I am afraid there is an even greater sum owed to someone now related to us by law, which torments Papa. It is a vast amount, and there is no way on God's earth for Papa to be able to pay it. It rankles him deeply."

"What can you mean?" Kitty asked, as their mother snored on.

Mary, suddenly finding it an unbearable burden and grateful for an ear into which she could spill the dilemma, found herself leaning over and whispering to her sister. With their mother now fast asleep, Mary felt no qualms in relating the entire sorry extent of the expenses borne by their new brother-in-law, Elizabeth's husband Mr Fitzwilliam Darcy, in the delicate matter of their sister Lydia's elopement with the heinous Mr. Wickham. It seemed as if, once opened, the dam could not be stopped. Mary whispered on and on, her voice becoming louder and more confident as she ignored Kitty's occasional cries of "Lord!" and "Heavens!" She told of the letters she had unashamedly intercepted between Darcy and their father during that dark time following Lydia's disappearance, when Mama had been insane with worry, and Papa furious. She spoke of sealing up the letters again and pretending not to know anything, out of her own shame and horror at what Lydia had done. Eventually, Kitty stopped interjecting completely and merely looked on, aghast, as Mary spoke of her own feelings of guilt at having had a good idea of what Lydia was up to, but not having the courage to back their sister Elizabeth, when she had begged their father to rein Lydia in.

When Mary eventually stopped speaking, Kitty stared at her, tears rolling silently down her cheeks.

"I... I think..." Kitty gulped. "I think it is a very good thing that I did not go to Brighton that time with Lydia after all!"

Mary smiled wryly. "Yes, Kitty. It was a very good thing indeed. Now, dry your eyes and do not be so downcast. Let us look at these gowns and see what can be done."

The two sisters then bent their heads together over the heap of clothing, murmuring together quite companionably as they sorted silks and whatnot. Kitty sniffed occasionally, and Mary reflected that she was sure to be rewarded for her forbearance towards her sister, for did it not say in Galatians Chapter Six, Verse Nine that one should 'not grow weary of doing good, for in due season we will reap, if we do not give up.'

Mrs Bennet snoozed on contentedly.

Chapter Two
Kitty Confused

The Meryton Grand Ball, as it was designated by its organisers, was indeed the social highlight of the year for the denizens of that prosperous market town and its surrounding countryside. Kitty was beside herself with excitement at the prospect of attending; a fact which she felt in constant need of reminding everyone. Strictly speaking it was not exactly a Ball, more an elevated kind of assembly. The community of Meryton with all its proximate denizens was, as the social season of Christmas approached, very keenly feeling the absence of several large and important families who normally would have been the instigators of such events. The fact that several of these large and important families had elected to either stay in town (as in the case of the Bingleys, much to everyone's disappointment), or at their own homes (as with the Darcys, double the disappointment!), made it very slim pickings indeed for social exchange. For this reason, Kitty vowed herself eternally grateful to the committee for seeing fit to elevate the standing of the usual Christmas Assembly to that of a ball.

A ball! Papa had capitulated after all, thanks to Mama, and Kitty had her new dress to wear. *Well, not exactly new,* she thought, as she followed her father, mother, and elder sister into the Meryton Assembly Rooms that Christmas Eve. In the vestibule of the Rooms, as the Bennets took off their cloaks and stamped the snow from their feet, Kitty looked around surreptitiously at what the other ladies were wearing, while Mrs Bennet exclaimed over the enormous Yule log burning in a fireplace, which was decorated with what she described as 'a million candles'.

Yes! Kitty was smug. The high waists on the ladies' gowns had not got any higher, nor indeed had they dropped again, and she was also glad to see that the fullness of the skirts on the various ladies' ensembles varied from very circumspect to very extravagant. She and Mary would not have anything to be ashamed of, she thought, looking down at her newly refashioned 'old' gown. *Mary was right about that yellow,* Kitty thought. *It does make my skin look sallow. This old pink thing of Lydia's is much more flattering.*

Moving into the Salon, Kitty and Mary walked across the floor to stand against the far wall, where there were already several young ladies hanging around dejectedly. *As usual, not enough chairs, or men*! Kitty observed, as she positioned herself where she could see both the dancing and her own reflection in a great mirror opposite. She thought, privately, how fortuitous it was that she was not 'indisposed' that evening. Wouldn't *that* have been the greatest irony of them all: to be allowed to go to a dance for the first time in *ages*, but not to be able to!

The music was quite lively; already there were several couples forming sets for the first dance. Not being able to spot any of her acquaintances, Kitty was just about resigned to being quite bored for the first half hour or so, when the numerous knots of ladies and gentlemen moving around the room temporarily parted in front of her, and a strange sight claimed her attention.

"Oh," said Kitty to Mary, greatly surprised at what she beheld. "Look at that! What on earth is Mama doing, talking to that frightful old Mrs Cowper? Surely not!" Then, abandoning her apathetic sister, who had actually taken out a small book from her reticule and pointedly begun reading it, Kitty moved further forward, so she could listen to the conversation. This might be worth some gossip! There might even be some malice.

It was true. As soon as they had entered the room, Mrs Bennet had indeed cornered her best enemy, Mrs Cowper. That formidable lady, ever a champion in the sport of denigrating Mrs Bennet, was staring at her foe in great amazement as she was inexplicably showered with compliments and consideration. Kitty heard her mother exclaiming such things as "What a lovely gown! Where did you have it made?" Mrs Cowper, caught very much on the back foot, could only murmur reciprocal comments on Mrs Bennet's own ensemble.

"Oh, *this* thing?" Mrs Bennet replied, nonchalantly. "Why, yes, it is the latest fashion, of course. I had it made…"

What a liar, Kitty thought, grinning a little. Mama was, in fact, wearing an old, blue silk, which Kitty had rescued from the attic. Mary had had the practical notion of taking the silver lace off another gown, which was too outmoded to be considered, and using it to replace the tired lace which already hung sadly from the blue gown. The effect was stunning, as every time Mrs Bennet moved, the fabric shimmered and the lace seemed to glitter.

Mrs Cowper, eyeing this silver lace avariciously, was torn between her desire to find out where Mrs Bennet had obtained such a gorgeous gown, and wanting to serve her the 'cut direct', to snub her completely. Compounding Mrs Cowper's discomfiture was the very public knowledge of Mrs Bennet's youngest daughter Lydia's disastrous elopement last year: indeed, Mrs Cowper herself had been one of the most conscientious persons in the neighbourhood in assisting the spread of such delicious tidings across the countryside. This juicy piece of scandal should have fed her vindictive soul for many a year. However, rather than seeing her arch enemy routed thoroughly, much to Mrs Cowper's private chagrin and the neighbourhood's gossipy delight, the two eldest Bennet girls, Jane and Elizabeth, had somehow managed to make astoundingly advantageous marriages, despite the scandal, and regardless of Mrs Cowper's publicly aired doubts as to the validity of the proposals. Thus, for the life of her, she could not understand why that awful Bennet woman was suddenly her new best friend, when for the last decade or more she had been assiduous in her animosity.

She was just on the verge of asking for the name of Mrs Bennet's *modiste*, when she suddenly recollected that standing right at her own elbow was her brother, Mr Digby Spencer, who had been bereaved of his wife only last year. Oh yes! The true object of Mrs Bennet's interest suddenly became apparent. *Oh, the deviousness of a match-making mama*, thought Mrs Cowper grimly, as she tried her best to thwart Mrs Bennet in her attempts to make eye contact with Mr Spencer. However, Mrs Cowper was no true match for Madam Bennet, who had actually managed to corner the poor man between a table and a plant-stand. Mrs Bennet was fluttering her handkerchief, plying her fan rapidly and bombarding them both with so many meaningful looks that eventually Mrs Cowper had to capitulate. *Really, Napoleon was not so invasive*, she thought crossly, before reluctantly introducing her brother to Mrs Bennet, in honey-sweet tones.

"Oh, yes. Do forgive! My *dear* Mrs Bennet, may I introduce my brother, Mr Digby Spencer? Digby, this is my *oldest* friend, Mrs Jane Bennet."

Mrs Bennet extended her hand to be kissed and shot a look of venom at Mrs Cowper for the blatant allusion to her age, but was all dulcet tones as she addressed Mr Spencer.

"So lovely to meet you, I do declare! We all had no idea!" she tittered girlishly. "Your sister has indeed been keeping you quiet! Who would have guessed that she had a brother who is so much younger than she?"

"Actually," Mr Spencer murmured, as he warded off the problem of whether to kiss or not by shaking her hand vigorously, "I am the elder, in fact!"

"And so very tanned!" Mrs Bennet flirted. "La, have you been Campaigning in Spain? Or do you work your own estates?"

Kitty, an extremely interested onlooker of this little play, thought appreciatively to herself, *I have to hand it to Mother. In one short sentence she has asked the most pertinent of questions!*

Mr Spencer, not perturbed at all by the oncoming salvo that was Mrs Bennet in full sail, detached himself from her grip before answering. "Neither! But you are nearly correct! I have recently returned to these less sunny shores from Trinidad, where I have several tobacco and sugar plantations. While, of course, I do not work them myself, I have spent many an hour riding my boundaries and checking up on my overseers."

If Mrs Bennet had no qualms about asking personal questions, then Mr Spencer certainly was not shy about answering them.

Trinidad! Mrs Bennet thought indignantly, whilst still smiling and mouthing pleasantries. She was rapidly losing hopes for this one. *Living with savages in Africa, or wherever! Good Heavens! Almost like a common farmer! And older than his sister by a good ten years, at least! Not really suitable for either of my girls, even plain Mary would balk at marrying such a senior personage.*

All of these thoughts ran rapidly in and out of Mrs Bennet's mind like mice skittering around in a barn, whilst outwardly she continued smiling and thinking Mr Spencer was a lost cause, and how best to cut the conversation short. "Lovely. How lovely," she murmured. "Now, I must excuse myself…"

"I wonder, could I introduce my son?" Mr Spencer's sudden query brought Mrs Bennet's mind sharply back into focus, and she was halted, mid-excuse, as Mr Spencer turned to draw forward a very tall young man to his side.

"I am conscious of the fact that we have, ourselves, only just made acquaintance, but I am sure you won't mind my New World manners!" Mr Spencer chuckled. "Edgar, this is Mrs Bennet, a neighbour of your aunt's. Mrs Bennet — this is my son, Edgar."

Mrs Bennet, looking up into an astonishingly handsome face dominated by startling blue eyes which were framed with masses of blond curls, took only seconds to absorb the facts of his height, his dress, his manners and his general demeanour before abruptly switching campaigns and asking, with a girlish giggle, "And may I introduce my daughter Kitty?"

It was many a long hour, or so it seemed to Kitty, before she could get away from the two matriarchs and have Mr Edgar Spencer all to herself, albeit whilst they moved in and out through the next two dances, which Edgar insisted she reserve for him. When Mr Spencer had asked her to dance, Kitty, whose card was woefully empty, had made a show of retrieving it from her reticule, frowning at it, and declaring that he was lucky! She had not yet accepted any dance partners for the next two. She was pleased to accept, especially as she noticed several partnerless young ladies glaring at her with jealousy. She had not been so excited since the time all that militia had moved into town! To think that she, out of all the other young ladies, was to have the first dance with the newest bachelor in town! She giggled at Mr Spencer's every remark and tried hard to think of something intelligent to say. Something that was not *too* smart, for goodness' sake, lest she be thought one of *those* young ladies who read books all the time, but you know — she did want to appear a little less idiotic than certain other girls who fawned on a man's every word, but who never had the least idea of conversation. What had Mary said on Sunday? What had she been on about? Oh yes! Napoleon! The war thingy! What could she say…?

An idea popped into Kitty's head. "I declare, Mr Spencer," she began, "what do you think of that dreadful man Nap—"

"Have you lived in Meryton all your life, Miss Bennet?"

Flustered at having been interrupted, all Kitty could think of to say was "Erm."

"That must be wonderful," Edgar Spencer continued without pause, "to have such a sense of belonging and community! I myself have moved around a great deal since I was a child."

"Oh?"

"Yes. Shortly after I was born, we sailed to Antigua, you see, and then we seemed to move alphabetically around the islands as my father bought and sold properties."

"Um?" Kitty had not the foggiest idea what islands he was talking about.

"Barbados, Dominica, Grenada and then Trinidad, where my mother died." Edgar rattled off the names quickly. "It was the climate that killed her, you see. Now there has been an outbreak of some kind of illness, and Father has got it into his head that we must return to England, lest we sicken as she did."

Goodness, thought Kitty. These Spencers certainly did give away a lot of information at first meeting!

"What— what kind of properties?" Kitty had taken the opportunity of the dance moving her away from him for a moment or two in order to think up a response.

"Plantations. We grew tobacco and sugar."

"Sugar?" Kitty was dubious. She thought that sugar came from Jenkins, the Provedore in town.

"Yes," Edgar Spencer continued. "The sugar you put in your cup of tea tonight might very well have come from one of our plantations, although of course it would have been refined here in England. You know, sugar is the most interesting crop to grow, for it…"

There then followed half an hour of excruciating conversation with the handsome but lecturing Edgar, during which time Kitty was treated to an in-depth treatise on the proliferation of English sugar refineries together with Edgar's intense disapproval of slave ownership. It was only after his full denouncement of the practice of not allowing the slaves to learn any phase of sugar production, other than cutting the canes, thus keeping them ignorant and dependent, that Kitty was finally able, with some relief, to extricate herself. When the dance finally ended, she gratefully moved off in search of Mary, thinking that she would ask her to teach her something of plantations in Trinadia, or wherever, so that she would have something to talk about at her next meeting with Edgar. Mary always seemed to know about everything. *Goodness*, she thought, *it is hard work getting a husband!*

It was getting late by then and the ball had moved into supper time. The musicians had gone off for a break, and the men's voices could be heard loud and clear from the card room. Kitty could see Mary, resplendent but not knowing it, in emerald green with gold, embroidered flowers, peering into the room, probably looking for Papa. Kitty thought it most likely that her father had indeed taken himself off to the card tables, there to discuss politics and Napoleon's latest antics in Europe, and she smiled at the sight of Mary edging towards the card tables in order to eavesdrop. Ah, no. Kitty shook her head: not, after all, to listen in to men's conversations about boring issues, although that was her usual occupation (when not playing incredibly long and boring concertos), but to waylay that new vicar. *Oh, la! Mary talking to a man! What fun!* Kitty thought. *Mary might be sweet on a man!* Kitty giggled, and tried hard to see what her sister was doing.

The said new vicar, Mr John Broughton, was sipping from a glass of wine and listening imperturbably to Mary as she droned on and on about some point of contention she had with last Sunday's sermon. He was a plain and stern-looking man, somewhere in his mid-thirties, dressed rather soberly as befitted a man of the cloth, but who also seemed to be sporting a jewelled pin on his neck cloth. Mary appeared to have become quite agitated by the conversation and was actually pointing a finger at the vicar's chest, whilst he merely gazed at the top of her head. He was a tall man, so he had no difficulty in achieving this.

'For the love of all money is the root of all evil: which while some coveted after, they have erred from faith, and pierced themselves through with many sorrows,' Mary was quoting triumphantly. "Expecting to be paid for work on a Sunday goes against God's teachings that His Holy Day is a day of rest!"

"Ah," Mr Broughton replied, bringing his slightly bored gaze back down to her. "But to draw from the same source as you, I would remind you that 'The labourer is worthy of his reward', and that therefore to withhold payment would also be counter to our Lord's wishes."

Good Lord, thought Kitty, *Mary might have met her match in pedantry here.*

"But in the Bible we are told not to perform servile works on Sundays!" Mary expostulated. "Those who have partaken in the recent rioting must surely realise that their outrage is misplaced. Their wages—"

"My dear Miss Bennet, those who have been protesting in London merely require their just rewards. What you are, in effect, proposing is that we either don't pay for services received, if they have been performed on the Sabbath, or that no works at all be performed on the Sabbath."

"Well, yes — no… not that people should not be fairly paid for their labours, but that, perhaps, they should not labour on the Lord's day."

"So, doctors, for example, should not work on Sundays?"

"Well, no — yes, but…"

"So if your proposal should become law, in effect, do you plan to never become ill on a Sunday, or if you do, do you plan to wait virtuously until Monday morning to call a doctor?" The vicar was inexorable in his destruction of Mary's argument. Whilst never quite allowing his voice to rise above a calm level, he nevertheless seemed able to quell Mary very effectively.

"I would forbear gladly—" Mary struggled on.

"And what of our brave militia?" Mr Broughton hammered home his point. "Shall we have them simply stand down on Sundays, and allow our more heathenish French foes to walk through Europe unchecked? Why do we not advertise this for Napoleon? He would then have no difficulty in invading England, as long as it were on a Sunday!"

Kitty moved away from them, unseen. It had become boring. Did no one ever talk about anything interesting any more? Everything was always 'the war' this, and 'the war' that. She had not heard even one piece of juicy gossip since she came into the Rooms. She was having a very boring ball. Only the long-winded Mr Spencer to dance with, everyone blithering on about politics and imports and whatnot, and no Lydia to get up to mischief with! Oh, how she missed Lydia! *She* would have known how to liven things up! They would even now be ensconced in the corner, mimicking Mr Edgar Spencer, pretending to strut around like pompous Sir William, and flirting with boys.

Kitty then tried very hard to gain some fun out of gossiping with the Cartwright twins, who were only sixteen and already very determined to be the new local beauties, but she could not help recalling how Lydia had made fun of their plain faces. "The Carthorse girls!" Lydia had gleefully tittered. And besides, they were too silly for words. Kitty found she could not stomach their ridiculous mouthings another moment.

At a loss, Kitty then wandered over to where her mother was now arm-in-arm with Mrs Cowper, but ducked away again as Edgar Spencer hove into view. Looking back, Kitty saw that Mary appeared to have lost her verbal sparring match with the new vicar, and was edging towards the pianoforte with a determined and self-righteous expression on her face, so Kitty did not dare approach her. The dance floor was filling up again, and she was partnerless. What a dreadful evening it had all turned out to be! Spotting her father returning to the card tables with a plate of cakes in his hand, Kitty thought she would get a sudden headache, and make Father take them all home early.

But something was wrong. Her father had been accosted mid-way through a door by a somewhat overdressed gentleman wearing a very gorgeous but old-fashioned pair of lemon knee breeches, teamed with a splendid coat of emerald green; someone Kitty had never seen before. The stranger had grasped her father's arm, and was preventing him from entering the room properly. Several card-players were trying to get past them, and there were many tut-tuts and murmurings of "Do you mind?" as Mr Bennet gazed in perplexity at this affront.

"I beg your pardon," Mr Bennet was saying stiffly, as the stranger glared at him in a hostile fashion. "Is there something I can assist you with?"

"Mr Bennet? Mr Bertram Bennet?" the splendidly-dressed man's voice was shrill and excited.

"You have the advantage of me," Mr Bennet bowed stiffly to the stranger.

"You are in fact *the* Bertram Bennet, of Longbourn?" the man continued, in a heavily foreign accent.

"I am that personage. Whom do I have the honour of addressing?" Mr Bennet was scathingly polite, and gave a little deprecating smile to the greatly interested crowd, which had now gathered around them as they inadvertently still barred the doorway.

"I did not think to find you here, when I have sought you far and wide! I did not think that tonight, of all nights, my quest would come to an end! What Providence caused me to investigate one last clue… what happy circumstance brought me here tonight!" The stranger's voice was choked with emotion.

"Many men are happy to make my acquaintance, but few are as— er… happy as you!" Mr Bennet rejoined sarcastically, attempting to get past his accoster. "If that is all?"

"No! That is not all! You do not know me, do you? Convenient to have such a clear conscience, to never suspect my existence!"

"My dear fellow, I have not the slightest idea to what you allude. Pray stop talking in riddles and enlighten me." Mr Bennet could be devastatingly polite when he chose.

"Very well, Bertram Bennet! It is I — Armand! Armand Picard!"

Mr Bennet merely looked at him, quizzically. "Congratulations! You must be ecstatic at the very European *timbre* of your name! It was— er... interesting to have had your acquaintance forced upon me. Now, excuse me, please." Mr Bennet attempted once more to get past the excited Frenchman.

"Wait! Not so fast! So, this is where you have been hiding! So far away and secluded! Such a good place to abscond from your responsibilities, whilst my family has borne the consequences of your folly these many years past."

Monsieur Picard's voice was deliberately loud and carrying. The band, having been warming up to begin playing again, now fell quiet and both the card room and ballroom were suddenly as still and silent as a grave. Every ear was turned towards them.

"I hardly know what you are talking about!" Mr Bennet snapped. "Why should my person and where I live be such a matter for your dramatics?"

"I suppose you thought after all these years that you were safe! But you are found, sir! Late, though it is, you are found! And now you shall be brought to take up your responsibility, to pay for your past!"

The silence in the Assembly Room was now thick and stifling. No one dared move or breathe, except for Mary, who gave a slight "Ahem" and began to play at the pianoforte. Several people turned to hiss at her. "Be quiet! I cannot hear!" The notes stopped abruptly.

"My... my responsibility?" Mr Bennet queried, warily.

"Yes! Now I have found you I shall make you pay for my sister Amelia's downfall! Aha!" he exclaimed, as the colour drained from Mr Bennet's face. "Yes! That is right! *Now* you remember my poor sister, Amelia Picard! But I intend to make you do more than remember her, for you shall be made to assume financial responsibility for your sins!"

"Financial responsibility? What are you babbling about? Financial responsibility for what — pray tell?" Mr Bennet began to perspire quite a lot as he attempted to play things down, to get away from all the shocked and greedily excited faces now staring at him. Although still largely puzzled, he was beginning to have an inkling of the foreigner's meaning, and a cold chill was playing up and down his spine. Indeed, even as he stood there, dread forming an icy grip around his heart, it seemed to him that the whole world now stood still, breathless, waiting for the next words from this excitable foreigner.

"Financial responsibility — for your son!" Armand Picard declared dramatically, as loudly as he could. Then, as true a performer as ever graced the stage, he waited for a few seconds until the gasps and exclamations of the Assembly had died down before declaiming, "Bertram Bennet, you shall pay for your son!"

Chapter Three
Mrs Bennet Beleaguered

The house was in uproar. The house was in furore. The house was a teeming morass of hysterics, tears, fainting, reproaches and breast-beating. After the bombshell had exploded at the Meryton Yuletide Ball, Mr Bennet had whisked his family home as fast as possible, ignoring all beseeching from Mrs Bennet and the two Bennet daughters to tell them what was meant by it all. Who was that over-dressed Frenchman? What had he meant by his shocking allegations? Do you think everybody heard? This last question was the one most often on Mrs Bennet's lips. She had retired immediately to her bedchamber upon returning home, having left the ball, and had stayed there all through Christmas Day and the three days following. She was gravely ill with hysteria, and thrashed around on her bed as if possessed. She twisted and turned, tore her night-cap into many pieces, threw off her shawl, pushed away her daughters, vowed to murder her husband and would not let any servant, save Mrs Hill, anywhere near the chamber. She alternately screamed and sobbed, bit her nails, shoved her fists into her mouth and lay face down, moaning.

"Why, oh why?" she repeatedly wailed. "Why did that foul Frenchman make his accusation at such a time? Oh, woe, the entire world must have heard! How could I ever…? What are we to do…? We will never hold up our heads again… We are all ruined! Ruined!"

Kitty and Mary were extremely alarmed. It was worse, by far, than when their younger sister Lydia ran away, which had been bad enough. In those days following Lydia's infamous elopement, throughout all the histrionics Mrs Bennet had displayed at that time, there had always been a little glee hiding amidst the outrage — a little gleam hidden in the corner of her eye; excitement, even, at the drama of it all and the prospect of having a married daughter. Indeed, during the entire Lydia debacle, Mrs Bennet had always maintained her hope of a good outcome, and often, whilst purportedly weeping in anguish, she had peered slyly through fingers spread across her face in order to see how her daughters were reacting. But this! This! The entire town knowing all at once that her husband of decades… decades… had turned out to be a philanderer, a despoiler of innocent girls, a libertine! And to have it so publicly advertised, at the Yule Ball! Just when she had the upper hand over Mrs Cowper! Just when she was making headway with her match-making schemes for Mary and Kitty. Just when she had been so happy over Jane and Elizabeth!

"It is just not fair that I should have such happiness torn away from me," Mrs Bennet moaned, throwing a bowl of soup across the room at her innocent servant, Mrs Hill. "Goodness knows I have had precious little happiness over the course of my married life. Goodness knows I have had little to show for my marriage… That weasel Collins is all set to inherit Longbourn and throw us all out onto the street. Oh! The certain poverty which is about to descend upon our innocent heads! Oh! How I have suffered! Oh! How I have prayed and prayed for a male child! And now, just when I thought I might hope that at least two of my new sons-in-law might help out when the dreaded day dawns… this has happened! How can Elizabeth's and Jane's marriages survive such a scandal? They will be divorced immediately… no gentleman would want to associate with them now! They will be sent home in disgrace, further burdens upon our impending poverty!"

Mrs Bennet settled in for a good lengthy wallow in self-pity. She had no thought for how the rest of her family was coping with the shocking news. She alone was the one who was suffering the most. "Yes," she muttered to herself after the harassed Mrs Hill made her escape. "It is always the same! Any chance of happiness is always ripped from me! All these years of child-raising, of being a dutiful wife! Just when I thought I had a chance of saving us all… that toad, Mr Collins! It has now all come to nothing! No one will look at Mary or Kitty now! I will be forced to beg for charity from my brother. We will probably all have to live with him, all squashed in together in his modest house! I shall be forced to take in sewing to earn a penny or two! I won't be able to send Lydia any more money, as I have often had to do when she finds herself in embarrassed circumstances with the local trades-people, in that benighted Northern town, wherever it is her new husband had whisked her to! Oh, woe! If I am not able to send Lydia any extra money, she will be cast into debtor's prison alongside her husband!"

Another terrifying thought darted into Mrs Bennet's feverish brain: there would now be no money to help marry off Kitty and Mary properly. She and Mr Bennet would be burdened with two spinsters for the rest of their lives. All, all of her friends would desert her; no doubt even Mrs Lucas would shun her completely now that her husband's perfidy was so widely known.

"Ah yes," she said bitterly to her pillow, "it was ever my lot to suffer!"

It must be known that Mrs Jane Bennet was not the kind of woman who had inner strength. Her childhood had not been one in which character is directed or nurtured, in which the child is taught self-reliance. She had been raised by a wealthy and doting father, who had given his only daughter everything her heart desired but who had failed to give her what she most needed: that being an education designed to foster intelligence. As a child she had once been curious in the manner of all small children, but whenever she had asked such questions as "Where do Africans go to school?" or

"Why do things fall?", her father had merely gazed at her indulgently. He would kiss her cheek, give her chocolate and send her on her way, adjuring her not to bother her head about complicated matters. Or he would instruct her mother to buy their daughter some new things and get her fit for marriage. She soon learned not to ask questions, not to bother Papa about anything, and to instead immerse herself in fun and fashion.

Jane Gardiner, as she was then, thus grew up poorly-educated and with a head full of vacuous nonsense. In the Longbourn attics there were trunks and trunks full of fans, gloves, stoles, gowns and laces from her glory days as a debutante. How she had taken society by storm! She had been such a beauty! Petite, with naturally curling blonde hair and a sweet face, there had been plenty of young men interested in her during her first London season. She was the toast of the town, if not exactly moving in the first circles, then certainly able to attend some of the finer Balls and Assemblies. That first season in London she had had two or three beaux hanging on her every word, including some minor Royalty. Money had been plentiful. Her lawyer father threw thousands of pounds into the quest to gain his daughter a titled husband. There had been dancing lessons, deportment lessons, French lessons. However, not all the money in the world, not all the fine gowns and French, lace gloves, nor all the badly-pronounced French phrases, were able to hide the glaring fact, discovered very quickly by anyone who spent more than half an hour in young Jane Gardiner's company, that she was practically illiterate and had not two sensible things to say.

At first, Jane's own mother had played down her daughter's lack of education, being of the opinion that her good looks, fine figure and sizeable inheritance would soon ensnare any man beyond the point of his caring what she thought about. Indeed, it did seem at first that this was going to be the case. Young Jane's debutante season in town, at the tender age of sixteen, was so successful that it seemed more than likely a husband would be hers before Christmas. There were two suitors who seemed likely candidates — the Gardiners naturally preferred young Viscount Parkes, as did Jane herself. He was tall, and handsome, and not overly intelligent himself and so not likely to quickly notice that Jane was for the most part a prattling fool. He and Jane had many dances together; he sent sweet little posies to her home, and romantically worded notes requesting the pleasure of her company at this supper, or that card party, and things went along very swimmingly.

However, it turned out that the Viscount was constrained to marry for money in order that his family home be restored. After some surreptitious investigations conducted by the Viscount's father, it was discovered that Jane's family was not nearly wealthy enough to finance the rescue of the great crumbling pile of bricks that was the Parkes' family seat, and so the budding romance died on the vine. Then, one by one as the Season wore on, all the other young men dropped away. There hung a taint of rejection over Jane Gardiner.

Jane's second London season began with an equal amount of fervour, hope, and money invested in the newest fashions and the latest craze for learning Latin, but ended as did the first. The initial buzz as Jane walked into a salon, the *frisson* of excitement as she filled up her dance card with eligible names, and the coquettish fan-flirting all came to naught. Jane now had armoires bursting at the joints with clothing, and a growing stigma of being left on the shelf. Her brittle desperation gave her chatter a manic flavour; indeed, upon one occasion, her fervent attempts at intelligent conversation led her to bore one young man half to death with a fatuous discussion of a bead-making club she had recently joined. She was out of small-talk, and her father was out of money.

The third season was a debacle. Hardly anyone noticed Jane Gardiner whenever she stepped into a salon or ballroom; there were so many other bright birds of high fashion flitting in and out! She stood, dowdy in last year's gowns, against many a wall whilst all around her the pretty girls twirled and whirled in the arms of every available bachelor. Her father was curmudgeonly, her mother apathetic, and so when the completely plain, boring and mediocre-looking Bertram Bennet came upon the scene, he was hardly noticed by the still-hopeful Gardiner family.

Unbeknownst to her, of course, Mr Bennet himself had been a little taken aback by Jane Gardiner's initial indifference towards him. Knowing that he was not exactly a buck of the first order, he nevertheless thought he was at least worthy of some attention. But this young lady, in the pretty, blue gown with her blonde hair done up in matching ribbons — why, she hardly noticed him at all. Nursing a heart freshly broken by a French coquette, and with the completely unexpected and sudden inheritance of a country estate also fresh with him, Bertram Bennet had felt something stirring in his breast; something akin to battle-blood. Bedamned to all foreign women! Before him was a passable young English girl with some money behind her, who would know what was expected of her. Also in front of him was the prospect of building up an estate, so why not offer for the girl? Offer he did; Jane could not believe her luck and practically leapt upon him, and they were married within a month.

Mrs Bennet gave a half-sob, half-sigh as she came back to the present and looked with disgust at the supper-tray Kitty had brought her earlier. It lay on the floor in ruins, along with shattered piles of lunch and breakfast dishes. No faux hunger-strike this time around; no sneaking down at midnight to eat in secret, so as to keep up the charade the next day! Mrs Bennet really was ill with despair, and gave further shrieks and groans as she heard her husband redouble his efforts at being let into the chamber. Oh, the perfidy of that man! Mrs Bennet tore at her hair and clapped her hands over her ears, so as not to hear Mr Bennet's shouting and hammering on the door.

Just listen to him, she thought, *out there now, demanding to be let in so he could 'explain' things to her! How dare he? Who did he think he was?* And then she began to sob anew, once more remembering times past and how she had grown to love him, only to have it all now thrown up into her face! For love him she did. Not at first, of course, but gradually, over the years, her feelings for him took on a life force of their own. And their marriage had started off fairly well, as well as could be expected of two near-strangers suddenly precipitating themselves into marriage and intimacy.

She fell in love first with Longbourn. Such a far cry from her father's town house, with its close neighbours and soot-covered walls. No, here was a fine manor indeed, with land and crops, and all kinds of animals doing whatever it was they did to make milk and bacon. Instead of filthy streets, and importunate vendors shoving their barrows and their dubious wares at you, there were green fields, open skies and sweet-smelling hedgerows. There were beautiful copses in which to walk; bluebells and daffodils underfoot instead of harsh cobblestones; and the glorious sound of birdsong instead of ostlers' cussing, or the discordant cries of the nightwatchmen.

It had been quite the adventure, starting out together on the journey. Mr Bennet explained that he himself had only just come into the inheritance: a geographically distant uncle had managed to die without leaving any more immediate heirs, and the estate had passed onto him as the eldest male in line. He likened each discovery he made with her by his side as a great adventure, along the lines of circumnavigating the globe and chancing upon unknown lands. Mrs Bennet and her new husband had always ridden over the estates together, at first; he learning the ways of the fields, interrogating farmers and measuring fences, and she looking on adoringly but forbearing to ask any questions. There had been a sense between them of a sort of growing together, of forging something new and worthwhile. They rode out together every day, until the inevitable time came when Mrs Bennet had to blushingly inform her husband that she ought not to ride "for seven months, or so." The babies had started coming.

Things were looking splendid. They would have boys to inherit Longbourn; they would grow old together and have a permanent home on the estates they were building up together. Well, a girl came first, and then another, but Mrs Bennet did not give up. She had boundless energy in those days and was determined that her girls would not be as ignorant as she. She made her husband hire a schoolroom governess as soon as the girls were able to sit still at a desk. She would not listen to Mr Bennet's protests that the estate was not yet in a position to bear the cost. In fact, she said, did she not have her own annuity from her father? Did that not suffice? Mr Bennet gave way.

The years passed. There were two disappointments — boys born too early and expiring shortly after being christened, and then along came Mary. Another girl. Well, what of it? Mrs Bennet, tired now with almost constant pregnancies, had not the energy to supervise the girls' education and the governess was let go before Mary had even had the chance to open a book. Catherine was born when Mary was barely one year of age (immediately dubbed "Kitty" by the eldest girl, Elizabeth, who said she mewled like a kitten) and then along came Lydia, and Mrs Bennet's hopes and health were spent. She seemed, in those days, to be permanently of low spirits. She did not notice the girls' childhood milestones, such as losing their milk teeth, or their first ponies, or Mary nagging until she got a piano and piano lessons. She hardly knew that Jane and Elizabeth spent many hours reading and trying to teach their sisters the same. She was unmoved when Kitty broke her arm; indifferent when Lydia was expelled from local day school for writing a rude word on her slate; and had no connection with her long-suffering husband except to complain at him. Mr Bennet moved into the bedroom next door, and Mrs Bennet heaved a great sigh of relief.

Then suddenly, one day, it was as if a veil lifted from her mind. She did not know what the sudden change was or how it came to her. One day, she simply sat up from her habitual reclined position on the couch and looked around herself at the drawing room, which was festooned with her daughters' sewing projects, art works and books. She looked at her five girls, all immersed in their own activities, and thought, *Well, if I can't have a boy, I'll be dashed if I let some stranger take the estate away from me! The girls must marry well, and richly, and then they can buy the estate for me and Mr Bennet! That is the only way we can be saved from that silly entail business*! And from that day on, Mrs Bennet pursued the new passion in her life, which was getting the girls married. From dawn until dusk, she plotted and schemed, studied fashion journals, commissioned dancing and French lessons, listened to gossip and generally campaigned for husbands for her girls. It was a long campaign.

Chapter Four
Mr Bennet Bested

Mr Bennet, barricaded by his wife's bedroom door, beset by the shocked and accusing faces of his servants, and abashed by the reproving looks on his daughter's faces, wondered if indeed the end of the world had come, just for him. Armageddon seemed at hand, and he had no way of extricating himself from its grasp. How could he explain himself to his wife, or his daughters, when the wife was ranting insanely from the depths of her boudoir, only pausing intermittently to hurl abuse and invective at him through the keyhole, and when the daughters were confused, angry and distant? But what was there to explain? What words could there be to mitigate the bald fact of his having an illegitimate son, living who-knew-where, hidden from even himself until now? Life was not fair. A son! He had always only ever wanted sons. And now he had one, although how to explain…?

Mr Bennet sat slumped at his desk, a well-read and well-folded letter in his hand, an empty bottle of port at his elbow, and all the cares of the world weighing upon his heart. He had had one glorious night of blissful passion in the past, and now he was paying for it. Outside, the night was serenely peaceful, as if to mock him in his shame. Brilliant stars sparkled in a sky of deepest obsidian; the owl that always saluted him goodnight obliged with a friendly hoot, but Mr Bennet saw nothing but the letter before him, and heard nothing but the voice of his own conscience. He was wracked with anguish.

He glanced at the letter. No need to read it over again. Its words, brought to him by private messenger only the day before, were now etched into his heart, deeper than any epithets on a tombstone.

Dear Sir, the letter began.

"I write to you on behalf of my poor sister, Amelia, who departed this life on the day of her son's birth, and whose sorrows and travails in this life will surely be rewarded in the next. These sorrows, you are to know, are purely the result of your own iniquity and licentiousness. Bold charges indeed, but not undeserved, you callous fiend!"

Mr Bennet reflected that even though he had only met Armand Picard briefly, two nights ago at the Yule Ball, it was obvious then, and from the style of the letter he now held, that Monsieur Picard was as fond of flowery prose as he was of dramatic speaking. He continued reading:

"It has taken me these many years to track you down, but I thank the Lord I have, at last, been successful. You may wonder at my hitherto lack of success in this matter, but believe me when I tell you it was not my own shortcomings that prevented me from finding you, but rather the actions of my sainted sister, who, for her private reasons, kept your correct name from me. For over twenty-five years I have wasted my time and money in elucidating the whereabouts of a fictitious Egan Bentley."

The letter was nearly ten pages long, tightly written on both sides, bearing many ink-blots and scratchings out, and continued in the same verbose style. Mr Bennet had waded through it so many times since it had arrived that he was now able to skip entire passages, entire pages indeed, which did nothing but extol the virtues of the dead and sainted Amelia. He skipped these passages not through boredom, but because they were now engraved upon his heart. He had not really any need to be told how wonderful, beautiful, virtuous and demure Amelia had been. He remembered her well, and certainly agreed with Armand's descriptions of her. The parts he did read over and over, however, were those devoted to more pertinent events.

"Upon my sainted sister's passing, I assumed the role of her baby boy's guardian. I have been every inch the father to him his whole life. He has been educated in the best seminaries, and has travelled extensively. My mother, the boy's grandmother, ensured there were sufficient funds to ensure that he wanted for nothing.

At this point in the epistle, Mr Bennet allowed a *frisson* of fear to play up and down his spine. If Amelia had not concealed his name quite so successfully and the family had found him...! Such contrary emotions! It was certain the repercussions would have been catastrophic for him; he was certain the powerful Picards might have exacted some awful revenge upon him. But they might have also, in some condescending way, acknowledged him as the father of the boy. Why, even now he could have been the proud father of not five but six children, one of them the all-important male heir! As he sat looking gloomily out into the darkness, he wondered at how Amelia had so successfully concealed his true name. Unbeknownst to him, Amelia's success in subterfuge was, in no small part, due to the fact that he himself had been so much of a nobody in those days that not one soul in Paris had really even recollected that he had been there. Certainly, if anyone had been asked, they would only have been able to reply: "What? That glum Englishman? Who?"

But the long-winded letter continued on, regardless of Mr Bennet's self-pity.

"My blessed mother passed away but one year ago and the truth of your name was finally revealed in the contents of my sainted sister's diaries, which my Mother had always been too grief-stricken to open, and which she had hitherto kept under lock and key. Imagine my satisfaction at discovering the truth! This truth will be brought out into the open, you foul besmircher of virtuous females, so that all will know of your perfidy, your mendaciousness, your evilness!"

Monsieur Picard was building up to his dramatic climax.

"For, sir, I fully intend to bring Thomas (for that is his name) to you, so that he may observe for himself the foul wretch who despoiled his mother and left her to a tragically short life! And what is more, Thomas now being an adult, I hope that he will demand of you himself full recompense for what you have done to his mother. I do this, not out of a sense of revenge (although the Lord knows I would be more than justified in so doing), but out of a sense of justice, that Thomas might be acknowledged by you, and might inherit what is rightfully his when the Lord deems it fit to send you to your eternal punishment!"

Clearly the Picards were under the impression that, even though — as far as they knew — the boy was illegitimate, there was no barrier to his inheritance. Perhaps the law was different in France. Perhaps they would all go away again when they had the English legalities explained to them, and his own lawyers explained that legitimacy of birth was the key factor in the inheritance. But the damage was already done. The irony was almost diabolical. No matter what French or English law might say, the boy had actually, in fact, been born legitimately! Mr Bennet knew in his heart that he would never be able to prove that he had been, extremely briefly, married to Amelia. No doubt that dreadful mother of hers had squashed all evidence. And now, with France chaotic with the devastation wrought by war, there was absolutely no way to procure any documentation.

Sighing heavily, Mr Bennet pushed aside other important letters on his desk, and extracted a few pages from the middle of Armand Picard's letter. These pages were, to him, the most shocking. Here he read and read again that the only woman he had truly, really loved, had borne him a son! A boy. It was bitter gall indeed. They had had only one night together. It was simply not fair! A son after only one night. A true heir to Longbourn. *The Fates must be laughing,* he thought. He had been married to Mrs Bennet now for nearly twenty-five years, and he had come to have some kind of affection for her. Five daughters had come, but not one living son. A boy to carry on the name and to inherit Longbourn — this had been all he wanted: something of worth in his life to assuage the earlier devastating disappointment of having had Amelia torn from him.

Instantly, Bertram Bennet was transported back in his mind to a warm, late summer's night in Paris. He was standing on a balcony, overlooking an ornate garden dominated by enormous fountains, where large tubs of lavender gave up their glorious scent to the close night air. Lanterns had lit up the scene, both in the garden and on the balcony, and music spilled out of an open door behind him. There had been the sound of people chatting, laughing, mingling, chinking their glasses together, and the clatter of cutlery upon plates. There had been a huge, yellow, harvest moon, and a woman had been weeping in his arms, while an older woman screeched invective at him. *It was only yesterday*, he thought glumly. Surely it seemed that way.

Mr Bennet remembered vividly now. "You *cochon!*" the older woman had spat at him, staring up at him through a lorgnette held in one gloved hand. In the other hand she held a smoking pistol, and Bertram's arm was bleeding profusely. "Take *that*, for your insolence! You... you... dared to presume you could ever be accepted into my family!"

"I care not for your family," Bertram had spat back, reeling a little from the shock of his wound, and grasping his new love Amelia even more tightly to his breast. "I care only for Amelia! We have pledged ourselves to each other, for life! The deed is done, and there is nothing you can do about it!"

"*Vraiment?*" the very impressive woman sneered back at him. "You think I can do nothing?"

She truly is a scary woman, Bertram had thought, taking in at a glance her imposing height, her elaborate coif, her sumptuous gown and some very serious gems hanging from her earlobes. She was also an extremely good shot, as she had only minutes before declared her intention of wounding him in the right shoulder, which was exactly where there was now a gaping hole in his flesh.

"Pah!" The woman's mouth turned down with disgust.

"Mama..." Amelia had protested feebly, half swooning in Bertram's arms.

"Quiet, you idiot!" her mother had continued, turning her wrathful glare upon her daughter. "You— you stupid girl... You have nothing to say on this matter! Nothing! You dare to come to me here, in front of all my friends, and ransom me with such news as this? You think I will do nothing for fear of what my friends may think? You are an idiot, a fool, an imbecile. What did you think, my darling daughter? That I would soften at the sight of this mediocre Englishman, and declare that all is fair for *l'amour*?"

"Mama, I did not think for one moment—"

"That is the first time you have been correct all evening!" her mother barked back at her. "You did not think! You did not think at all! You have ruined everything because you could not keep yourself intact! You *know* of my plans for you! How can any of it come about now? What decent man will want you? And if you decide to keep on with this stupid charade, then how will you and your pathetic lover keep yourselves, hmmmm? For I can assure you, there will be no money from me!"

"What are you saying?" Bertram interjected, keeping a wary eye on the hand holding the gun. "Amelia, your mother... Excuse me, Madam, but fear not, for we are indeed—"

"Shut up!" screeched Amelia's mother, somewhat crudely. "You bastard! You craven fool! You cannot possibly know with whom you are dealing!"

Bertram Bennet did not quite know what was going on, and why this woman was trying to kill him. Things were not going as planned. Amelia had assured him all would be well; the romance of the situation, the daringness! Her mother would be surprised and a little angry, but would melt when presented with their true love story! The French society girl eloping with a staid English gentleman! How charming! How exciting! But Bertram Bennet had, so far, been received only with foul language spewing from a homicidal virago. Half-swooning now, as his blood dripped relentlessly onto the ground, he desperately sought time to think whilst performing the actions of balling up a handkerchief and pressing it into his wound.

"Madam, with all the respect I can muster… I have not the slightest idea—"

"Oh, Bertram, I did not mean to keep secrets from you!" his love suddenly blurted out between sobs, interrupting what Bertram was hoping would be a most placatory speech, which would win the heart of his new mother-in-law.

"Secrets?" Bertram frowned at his new wife, wincing as blood continued to drip down his arm.

"Bertram," Amelia gulped, "you may have, by now, realised that my mother is not just any person. She is, in fact—"

"More important than you can ever believe, you slimy little English twit!" the mother had then interjected haughtily. "Keep still, do not dare to approach me or my next bullet will go somewhat lower!" and she took aim at Bertram's nether regions.

Bertram Bennet tried to be conciliatory. "Please, Madam, there is no need for further violence! I can assure you my intentions are—"

"*That*, for your intentions!" and a shot was fired into a plant pot, just to the right of Mr Bennet's left hip.

"Madam!"

"Be quiet, stupid little man! And if you must speak, be sure that you address me properly!"

"Bertram," Amelia had then joined in, with what sounded to Bertram like a rather silly giggle. "Perhaps I could introduce you properly? Er… Bertram, this is my mother, the Comptesse de la Picardy."

"Comptesse? Comptesse de la Picardy?" Bertram was aghast. "My God, Amelia, why didn't you tell me?" Bertram was not from any of the finest circles in either London or Paris, but even he had heard of the Picardys, one of France's oldest, noblest and most powerful families, said to have the ear of kings and popes alike. He was now reeling from shock, loss of blood, and this startling news. In the past forty-eight hours, he had eloped, been chased down by what he thought were armed brigands, dragged to this place by the same brigands and then forced to crash this stupid *soirée* by his Love. He had then discovered that his darling

Amelia, far from being a lady of equal status, was so far above him, it made him look like a mouse staring up at the moon.

"Tell? Tell? What is it that my daughter did not tell you, you toad? That you have befouled one of the daughters of the House of Picardy? That you will never be accepted into this family? That you are the lowest of the low; a flea on the flea of a dog, the scum at the bottom of a midden? But... I think... you are deceptive. I think you already knew who Amelia is. I think — oh yes — that you thought to get your slimy English hands on some French gold! Hmm, is that how it is?" The pistol was waved at him again.

"Mama! Truly Bertram did not know! I did not tell him—"

"Quiet, you little trollop!" The Comptesse had no soft words for her weeping daughter. She turned her head and addressed two very mean-looking men standing in the shadows. "Robert! Phillipe! Take my daughter inside!" and at her bidding, the heavy-set men came and took hold of Amelia, dragging her out of the now near-fainting Bertram's arms.

"Amelia!" Bertram grasped his love's arm, but was knocked to the ground by one of the men as easily as if he had been a reed. He suddenly became aware that his surroundings had taken on a surreal quality; the feel of the cold terrace on which he now sprawled, the sounds of the orchestra, the laughing voices, the tinkling water and the smell of some gorgeous flower on a vine, mere inches from his face, all were pressing upon him. He shook his head and tried to get up.

"Madam, I love your daughter... I did not know. She told me there would be some family opposition to our union, but..."

"What do I do with you now, hmm?" The Comptesse seemed to be thinking out loud, and spoke to an empty space above Bertram. "I could kill him — *d'accord, tres facilement* — but my poor *fille*, she may hate me more than ever before. What to do?" Shifting her gaze suddenly, she sent him a look of unbridled hatred. "You bastard, you have ruined everything! She was to marry the Duc de la Roche! Do you hear me! The Duc! Not some pig farmer from pig-swill land!"

"Madam, your Ladyship, I assure you my family is honourable. I have—"

"Family? You have family? *Merde*, probably some yokels from a yokel town! Well, then, serfs they undoubtedly are but they make it not so easy to dispose of you. Complications, hmmm. Yes. *Tres bien*, I have it. *Mais oui, c'est évident*." Making a sudden decision, the Comptesse de la Picardy declared, "Take this, then, for your payment and for your unending silence, and leave with your life!" and so saying, she tore a diamond bauble from her ear and threw it contemptuously at Bertram, who was now virtually unconscious on the cold marble of the terrace.

"Be assured... Your Ladyship, I have no intention of... I do not... you cannot..."

But at that point Bertram had lapsed unconscious, and had not awoken until the next day. And the next day, when it came, was cold. There was no Amelia. He was lying in a bed, in a shared room, at an inn somewhere in Le Havre, and his wound had been dressed. Then he had been shortly told that a passage had been booked for him on the next boat home to England. Several large and unfriendly-looking men were trying to look busy in the inn's courtyard, and Bertram had no doubt they were there to ensure his departure. The diamond earring was in his pocket, his bags had been packed. He decided there was no point in annoying those very large men, and duly took his place on board the ship. He very nearly threw the diamond earring overboard, but then thought if he sold it, he could use the money to hire lawyers or some such. Then he vowed not to rest until he found Amelia, and had her back in his arms again.

Well, that particular French farce had been well over a quarter of a century ago. Upon arrival in England, he had been stricken with a fever resulting from the poorly-attended gunshot wound. When he recovered his health, after several months of recuperation, he made enquiries, but was met with opposition at every turn. Any lawyer he engaged soon became evasive; he suspected it had something to do with the Very Large Men he kept encountering, and his money ran out. Finally, after nearly a year of fruitless searching for Amelia, a friend advised him to forget her, and to turn his thoughts towards his future. Sometimes the universe dictates coincidences, and several days after this gloomy advice, an uncle of Bertram Bennet's obligingly died. The cousin who was due to inherit the uncle's property, Longbourn, had died in the West Indies a year or so before that, and Bertram, therefore, found himself with the opportunity and means to get on with his life. It was thus, with something of a lighter heart, that he attended a few dances in London. He began to look forward to life as a country gentleman, and decided that the best way to effect this was to indeed forget the Love of His Life, find some nice, uncomplicated girl, and marry.

He had done just that and now here he was. At his desk. Married to that uncomplicated girl — a stupid, twittering wife. Ha! And a gaggle of girls. His estate entailed to the asinine Mr Collins; his life entailed to disappointment and resignation. And apparently, he was the father of an estranged son. But was it entirely compromise on his part? Had he truly, really, sought Amelia all those years ago? Had he made much effort? Yes, he had loved her. Yes, he had wanted her beyond anything else.

But why had he not fought more for Amelia? Why had he not returned to Paris and actively sought her whereabouts, instead of his passive search through friends and the lawyers he had engaged? He should have shown the Comptesse that he was not entirely without prospects. When he learned of his inheritance, he should have shoved the titles to Longbourn in her face, and demanded to see to Amelia. He should have shown her that he was more than capable of making Amelia happy. He had plans. He was going places.

But there was one sad fact remaining. One thing which, in the cold light of reason, had prevented him from doing just that. Yes, he had been blissfully happy the night of their elopement. How exciting it had been to seek out an obliging old priest whose purse was in need of replenishment! Bertram and his love had had one night only, but it was full of passion. She was everything a man desired in a woman: ardent, loving… She was so beautiful; so lively and intelligent! She filled up his heart with love and his head with swooning desire. To think that their short time together had resulted in a son! The irony… The mocking fates. Bertram sighed deeply, as a man who is reconciled to death sighs. He knew he should have returned to fight for her.

But that night, so long ago, when he was on the terrace floor, his shoulder bleeding from the wound inflicted by his love's mother, he had turned his head sideways to get a last glimpse of Amelia as she was dragged away. And in that moment, in that snippet of time which was the only thing remaining of that wonderful interlude, he had seen that she was not even looking at him. There were no anguished backward glances for Bertram. No. She was, instead, looking at her mother excitedly, and was saying, "Oh, Mama, you did not tell me about the Duc de la Roche…"

Well, Bertram thought. *So much for that.*

Bertram then thought some more. Very slowly, he got up and went over to an escritoire, which stood in a corner of the room. *Is it still there?* he asked himself, unlocking it and bringing forth a small packet, sealed with now-crumbling wax. It had been sitting there ever since he had moved into Longbourn. Hiding in plain sight. No need for further subterfuge; his dotty wife had never shown even the slightest interest in anything in his office. Well, yes. Here it was.

But would anyone believe it?

Chapter Five
Mary Bennet Managing

After several days of utter turmoil at Longbourn, Mary Bennet reflected grimly that things appeared to have quietened down. Her mother had even come out of her room, if only to ensconce herself in her favourite chair in the parlour, in order to receive visitors. There she languished, with the twin themes of spousal infidelity and her waning health ever on her lips and mind. She had a large audience for her soliloquies, for visitors came in droves. There was almost an atmosphere of *fete* in the countryside surrounding Longbourn, what with all the carriages constantly passing each other on the road to the house, and the passengers of said carriages leaning out of windows to call out the latest news to one another as they passed each other *en route*. Those who came to sympathise did so on a daily basis, commiserating with Mrs Bennet, agreeing that her husband was vile, was a libertine, a devil; whilst she, the wronged wife, was a saint, the paragon of all virtues. What she must have had to put up with over the years! How many times had she put on a bright, happy face, whilst inside she had probably been crying bitter tears over her husband's (no doubt, if truth be told!) many infidelities? It was more than shocking. Those who came to gloat did so, also with gusto, but they had less entertainment than the sympathisers, for Mary Bennet assumed the task of screening visitors, admitting those whom she was sure would (outwardly, at least) support her mother, and brusquely turning away those she was sure had come to observe their family's downfall. However, even Mary's assiduous duty could not prevent the occasional slip up, and one day, by accident, her mother had been left alone to bear the brunt of one particular matron's scathing tongue. That matron was, of course, Mrs Cowper.

The lady in question arrived unexpectedly, one dismal morning, and it said much about her eagerness to revel in her enemy's routing that she braved the weather: as she was ushered into the house by a frazzled servant, she was accompanied by a blast of exceedingly chill air, a flurry of snow and many dead leaves which had been allowed to gather on the doorstep by the no-doubt slovenly servants — another example of the type of haphazard household, it had always been surmised, run by Mrs Bennet. *Really*, Mrs Cowper thought, *if one could not keep the servants in order, what could one do with one's philandering husband? And as for those daughters...*

Mrs Cowper came, of course, with the intention of condescending as much as possible to her 'friend', Mrs Bennet, and had planned to accomplish this task by way of condemnatory comments disguised as excessive sympathy. She practically rubbed her hands together in glee. It had seemed to her, in the past, that Mrs Bennet had got away with things too easily. That shocking business with the younger daughter's elopement! By rights, the Bennet family ought to have been shunned. Instead, they seemed to have been raised up even further when the elder two daughters married so advantageously. Really, it was not fair. They did not deserve it, and she was here to redress the situation. With glee.

"My dear, dear friend!" Mrs Cowper exclaimed, sweeping into the parlour, wherein Mrs Bennet sat. Mrs Cowper's new gown, in all its magnificence, had been chosen deliberately in order to intimidate and impress with its expensive trimmings. As she entered the room, she was not completely oblivious to the fact that her gown's great volume, with its many flounces, was causing havoc, as Kitty's sewing and Mary's latest music book were knocked to the floor. In addition, an unsuspecting puppy was helped on his way by a heavily placed foot encased in Mrs Cowper's new, leather, mud shoes.

"No! Pray do not arise!" she continued in a booming voice, for Mrs Bennet, who had been lying prone upon a sofa, was now struggling to become upright and attempting to extricate herself from underneath a pile of cushions, torn lace handkerchiefs and a knitted blanket. Cutlery was also heard tinkling from somewhere within the sofa's depths. Mrs Cowper held out her hands.

"I must apologise for bringing in this mud, but really — your front door! Your staff! I suppose you are not fit enough to attend to supervising them as you should, with all this nonsense going on! You poor, poor darling! What you must be suffering!" She grasped Mrs Bennet's hands in both hers, yanking her into a standing position. A cup and saucer slid to the ground as she planted kisses in the air on either side of Mrs Bennet's cheeks. The assaulted woman could do nothing except to grasp her lace collar tightly with one hand as soon as she was released and hope that the tea stains upon it were not too evident, whilst at the same time attempting to regain control of the situation by waving vaguely at a chair and mumbling such sentiments as "Wonderful to see you… been too long… the weather…"

Mrs Bennet's lace handkerchief fluttered wildly about her face. Looking around desperately, she cast a grateful look at Mary, who had heard the arrival and had rushed into the room as quickly as she could. Mary, seeing her mother's terrified face, could only mouth "Sorry" as she moved into the room with a defiant shrug. Mrs Cowper, spotting Mary surreptitiously attempting to clear away some clutter, held out her hand as if to be greeted, made bold eye contact, and then deliberately allowed Mary to observe her gaze as it travelled slowly around the room. Mary cringed. It could not have been in more disarray, for Mrs Bennet barely allowed the servants in, remaining too distraught. Mary received another pleading look from her mother. With barely suppressed irritation, she intoned, gracelessly, "It is good to see you, Mrs Cowper. You look well. Would you take tea?"

"That would be lovely!" Mrs Cowper gushed, seating herself in the best chair. "That is, if it is not too much trouble?" She picked off a piece of fluff from the chair before glancing downward at the already overburdened tea table. Mary cursed the curdled milk, the stale bread crusts and the dirty plates littering every surface.

"Of course!" Mary rather sullenly replied. *Old crow*, she inwardly glowered, and rang the bell.

Mrs Bennet seemed incapable of making any coherent answers to any of Mrs Cowper's familial queries, and when Mrs Hill, the housekeeper, arrived at the door, looking in warily, Mary was obliged to issue instructions on her behalf. "Hill, be so good as to bring up some fresh tea for us all. And some of that fruit cake. Also the scones, if they are ready."

Mrs Hill, a battle-weary veteran of the Bennet household, merely blinked and did not display any of her surprise at finally, after many days, being able to get into the parlour. This stalwart family servant was not only an ardent supporter of the entire Bennet family, but also harboured a secret favouritism for Mary. With a shrewd look, which rapidly took in Mary's rather brittle smile, Mrs Bennet's despairing looks and the smug countenance of the visitor, Mrs Hill replied, deferentially, "Yes, Miss Mary, of course. I shall bring up the tea immediately. And would you be wanting any of that new variety of tea, which your mother ordered last week, and which has just arrived?"

It was Mary's turn to blink. "New tea? Ah, of course! Yes, indeed, the Oolong! That would be very nice, would it not, Mama?"

Mrs Bennet, sinking back down into the sofa again, merely flapped her handkerchief in the direction of Mrs Hill, and would have murmured fretfully that she had not done any such ordering, and what was Mary going on about, for goodness sake, had Mary not then shoved her back onto the cushions with some force, under the pretence of helping her, and hissed urgently in her ear, "Do not speak too much, Mama! I beg of you!"

As the ladies disposed themselves about the room, Mary reflected bitterly that she was probably never going to get back to her new music at any point within the next week. And now this! She drummed her fingers upon the table in an unconscious echo of the tune she was learning. *The old bat will probably stay for over an hour*, she thought glumly. She was, even now, attempting to drill her mother for all the salacious details, Mary realised. *Well, she won't get any out of me*!

Indeed, Mrs Cowper did not bother to remain long on the prerequisite social niceties, and very bluntly led the conversation around to Mr Bennet's iniquity, beginning with "My dear Mrs Bennet! Your husband! What a shocking blow to your family!"

Mary was incensed. How dare this old biddy come here and condescend to her mother like that! Mary felt it her duty to head her off at the pass and not give Mrs Cowper the opportunity to speak of their private troubles. Her mother looked about ready to pass out.

"Mrs Cowper!" Mary interrupted with sudden inspiration. "How is that delightful brother of yours? Such a handsome man! So well-travelled and urbane! What pride you must feel in his accomplishments!"

Mrs Cowper had the wind temporarily knocked out of her sails by this abrupt change in topic. She turned to Mary with a little bewilderment on her face. "My... my brother?" she rallied bravely. "Why, he is very well, thank you."

"And your nephew?" Mary persisted.

"He is well."

"That is good to hear. My sister did so enjoy his company at the Yuletide Ball! She expressed to me that she could listen forever to his travel tales!" Mary was all charm and smiles.

"Well, well, that is— um, lovely. But not unexpected. My nephew, you know, is an accomplished raconteur."

"That is very evident." Mary stood to relieve the returned Mrs Hill of the tea tray, and the aroma of freshly baked pastries and scones wafted through the room. She suppressed a little smirk: custard tarts, fruit cake, fresh cream and conserves from their own stores. Mrs Hill was a conspiratorial wonder.

Mrs Cowper, accepting a cup of tea and several cakes, which Mary was pressing upon her, felt that the visit was not going as she had expected. She had come fully expecting to find complete chaos, and indeed the state of the front step had considerably buoyed her hopes of finding complete anarchy inside. However, here, in front of her, was evidence that Longbourn had not, indeed, slid down into an abyss of disorganisation and immorality. Why, Miss Mary Bennet looked almost sanguine, instead of wracked with shame as she ought. Only slightly deterred, she attempted to get back on course. "Ah, yes! That fateful Yuletide Ball! How you must look back at that night with anguish!"

Mrs Bennet began making some sort of groaning noise, but Mary cut her off. "Oh, silly Mama, do wait until your tea is cool enough! You always will burn your tongue!" She patted her mother's hand with the air of an exasperated but loving daughter. "More cake, Mrs Cowper?" Without waiting for an answer, Mary heaped more baked goods onto her plate. "Tell me, Mrs Cowper, it must be wonderful having your brother back from the Indies! You must thank God every day for returning your family to you."

"Well, yes, of course! Wonderful. However, you know, I feel that whatever God bestows upon one, He is also likely to remove from another. We find often in life that if one person gains, another loses. And I speak not of mere tangible riches. The loss of reputation, for example. Mrs Bennet, your dreadful situation..." Mrs Cowper floundered a little, when she suddenly espied a rather vicious look on Mary Bennet's face, who cut off her speech with no apology, continuing her own theme, as if having a cosy chat with a valued friend.

"Kitty did so enjoy his talk of his sugar plantations. He was very adept in explaining it all to her, in such a manner that she had no trouble in then imparting this fascinating knowledge to me. But then, Kitty was always the smarter! It does seem a marvel that these little white crystals in fact grow as a plant, does it not?"

"Yes, a marvel... but... Kitty?"

"I often find, as I read the Good Book, that God works his wonders in ways incomprehensible to us mere mortals, do you not agree?"

"No. I think... However..."

"You do not agree?" Mary was inexorable. "You do not believe that God administers to our needs and yet keeps us mindful of His Omnipotence? Surely, Mrs Cowper, when you observe these tiny white grains, you cannot help but observe how fortuitous it is for us that God designed this plant in just such a way as to yield just the right sort of syrup, which can then be processed into these delightfully sweet crystals? Why, Mrs Cowper, I must confess to being a little shocked at your lack of faith!"

Mrs Bennet, unable to follow the conservation at all, looked as if she would sink back down into apathy, or fall asleep right there, or feign a convulsion; anything so as not to have to deal with Mrs Cowper right then. "Yes, yes, Mary — sugar is lovely, I'm sure it is," she mumbled, not having the energy to wonder why Mary was banging on and on about something so mundane.

Mrs Cowper, however, was not so bereft of energy, and almost dropped her plate. "*You*, Miss Bennet, *you* are shocked at me? Well, I find that most insupportable! When I consider… when the entire county knows—"

"Forgive me, Mrs Cowper!" Mary did not look at all contrite. "Forgive me for addressing a friend of my mother's in such a rude manner, but I cannot— no, I will not let this slip! Let me read this passage to you. I am sure you will gain much spiritual direction from it," and so saying, Mary picked up her bible from the side table and opened it to one of her favourite places. She then proceeded to read, at length and with a deliberately very droning voice, from the Good Book, as Mrs Bennet fell into a sort of half-sleep, and Mrs Cowper slumped back in her chair, mouth agape as she waited in vain for a break in the monotonous sermon, which was all about ingratitude, and then some other stuff about lilies of the field which did not toil but which still expected their share of sunshine; and about people who had so much, they forgot to be aware of others who lacked the basic necessities in life.

Eventually, after nearly an hour, Mary suddenly snapped the book shut, making them all jump, and disclaimed: "So, we are agreed then? Next Sunday after church?"

Mrs Cowper came to with a start. "What…?"

"Lovely! I look forward to working with you! Thank you so much for coming today! I am afraid that in my zeal I have kept you longer than is usual for an afternoon visit, but I am sure you will agree that when the Lord calls…"

And with that, Mrs Cowper, who had come to gloat and lord it over her best enemy, found herself outside on the front step (now mysteriously spotlessly clean) and climbing up into her coach, having been well and truly thwarted in her intentions, and having, somehow, promised to help out at church every Sunday for the next month, sorting out donated clothing for the poor. She looked dazed.

Mary, coming back into the parlour after having fairly ejected Mrs Cowper from the house, felt as if she had a sudden new lease on her life. Everything suddenly seemed to coalesce in her mind into a grand plan. Emboldened by her success at thwarting Mrs Cowper, Mary's mind practically teemed with ideas. *Well*, she said to herself, *I am now the eldest left at home, and I can finally — finally! — make things more orderly around here! Yes, Mama has been too indolent, Kitty is an idiot and Jane and Elizabeth are gone. It is time to redress the situation!*

Glancing around at the dishevelled room, and ignoring her mother, who was timidly asking why she was staring in such a ridiculous manner, Mary clapped her hands together with force and decision.

"Mrs Hill? Mrs Hill!" she called, gathering up tea things as she waited impatiently for the long-suffering servant to appear. When that redoubtable woman entered the room, she was both astonished and gratified to at last be given permission to enter the parlour and "give things a right going over." Mary, muttering under her breath about "Cleanliness being next to Godliness", then astonished Mrs Hill even further by following her to the kitchens, a place she had rarely visited before, and demanding to see the week's menus. Laundry lists were then scrutinised, overdue accounts snatched up and sorted, ready for her father to attend to, and a lazy yard-boy admonished firmly.

While she organised and sorted, ordered and admonished, Mary experienced a real glow. She hummed happily to herself. This... this was proper! A house was but an extension of a person's character, and a person's character reflected their soul, she told herself righteously. Some of the servants had been taking advantage of Mrs Bennet's hysterics and Mr Bennet's sloth. Well, it would cease immediately: she would take things in hand herself. She herself would run the house smoothly and the servants would all benefit from her direction. She would also see that Kitty would be instructed daily in Bible Studies. At last she was not the middle daughter any more, the one least noticed, but a person to be respected. Her mother would be a pushover, Kitty would complain bitterly but would eventually acquiesce and her father probably would not even notice. Yes, it was time!

Taking little notice of her mother, who had been all the while tottering unsteadily behind her, twittering and wringing her hands, Mary then strode up the stairs towards the bedrooms. Flinging open a door, she startled poor Kitty so much that the girl leapt up off a chair, causing all her dress patterns, which she had spread around her like a paper crinoline, to flutter around her to the floor like leaves in a whirlwind.

"What do you—" Kitty began, but Mary was not to be halted.

"Kitty!" Mary stated firmly. "Put aside that trivial and vain pastime! You will not get a new dress now until your birthday, unless you re-fashion an old one. Instead, I will tell you what you *will* get!"

Kitty looked wary, both alarmed at the sudden whirlwind standing in front of her, and excited at the thought of a possible present. "What? What shall I get, Mary?"

"You will get a clean room! And you shall clean it yourself. Now! Pick up all those clothes and order them properly! Look at this shawl! Laundered only yesterday and you have thrown it to the floor! It is already grubby because... because..." Mary made a disgusted face, "Because your puppy has disgraced himself on the rug! And the shawl is in it! Pick it up and give it to Anna."

"Anna?"

"Anna, the laundry-maid, you imbecile. Are you that lofty and removed from the world that you have no concept of who works for you? I expect to see a vast improvement in the state of this room by tomorrow morning, young lady. I cannot abide slothfulness! Then, and only then, if I am satisfied with the improvement, we shall go into Meryton and do some shopping, and take luncheon in the King George Arms."

"But you do not like shopping!" Kitty expostulated, glancing in shock behind Mary to her mother, who was wringing her hands and declaring, "My poor nerves! I cannot be seen in public. People will stare, and talk!"

"Kitty, I shall forbear the evils of material possession in order to save this family! And Mama, you *can* be seen in public, and by God, you will!" Mary was implacable. "You will put on a good face. You will look as if you had not a care in the world, and we shall act as if we do not believe one word of those dreadful accusations. We shall act as if it is all a lie, even though we know different."

Mrs Bennet and Kitty were both dumbfounded in the face of Mary's new demeanour.

Mary continued mercilessly. "Because if we do not, then we will be forever ridiculed, forever shunned and made the subject of salacious gossip. Is that really what you want?"

There was silence. Mrs Bennet was deeply shocked at Mary's sudden forcefulness, and Kitty knew not what to say in the face of this terrifying termagant.

"Because I can tell you now, my chances of making an advantageous match have always been very slim. In truth, I do not really mind, for I do not relish the thought of giving up my independence to some prancing fool, who believes himself to be my intellectual superior. However, given that it behoves me not to be a burden on this family as I grow older, I have determined that I will not remain a spinster, growing more and more impoverished as the years pass me by. I shall find myself an amenable, pliable sort of husband, despite all the ridiculous shenanigans I have had to put up with over the years! Kitty, you must also must be looked after. Therefore, and to that end, you will both assist me in attempting to salvage whatever good name we may have left. This means, Kitty, that you will comport yourself with decorum and dignity whenever we are in company, and hope that, in time to come, people will forget how you used to make an exhibition of yourself with Lydia, and only remember that you are the younger sister of Mrs Fitzwilliam Darcy and Mrs Charles Bingley. And this also means, Mama, that you will stir yourself sufficiently to run the household properly, with me as the director, so that never again need I be mortified by the state of our home and that society, should they call, will not have even the smallest modicum of suspicion that stories of my father's supposed past sins are true."

Mary took a breath after this very long speech and Mrs Bennet, beginning her swooning postures and fluttering hands again, expostulated feebly. "Why do you lecture me so, Mary? Oh, what I suffer! You have no idea…"

"You may suffer all you like in private, Mama, but as I said to Kitty, decorum and dignity will be our mode of behaviour when in company. So, Kitty, begin with the state of your room, and your character will follow. I will help you organise your belongings once I can see the floor. And Mama, there is one more thing."

"W…what is that?" Mrs Bennet was truly terrified of Mary now. She had never had more than sullen irritation from her in the past, but here she was now, ordering her about like a drill sergeant and planning her and Kitty's futures!

"You will take a bath."

"A bath?" Mrs Bennet ceased her histrionic hand-wringing.

"Yes, a bath, dear Mama! Do not be under the misapprehension that I have not noticed it has been nearly a week! You are beginning to have an odour not unlike that of the puppy!"

****

The next day, the entire population of Meryton was scandalised at the sight of Mrs Bennet, Miss Bennet and Miss Kitty Bennet, parading along the High Street as bold as you like, busily perusing items in all the shop windows, followed by a manservant who bore several packages. It was a tough act. In every store they entered, they were very well aware of the sudden silences, the whispers behind hands, and the cold glances. It took all of their collective courage to converse intelligently with shop personnel, to order ribbons, scrutinise cheeses and squeeze loaves of bread. However, the three Bennet women strolled around town as if they had not a care in the world. And if, at times, Mrs Bennet's charade wavered slightly, it was quickly covered up by Kitty, who got into the spirit of things rather rapidly, declaring it was just like putting on a play at Christmas time, only more fun, as she had not had to memorise any lines.

The trio then went to order some more tea because, as Mary explained glibly to the tea merchant, they had had such a social time of it lately that all their stores were nearly already spent. The merchant was confused, as he knew there was some kind of scandal going on involving, yet again, the Bennets, but here they were looking quite blithe! After sampling a new tea and ordering two different varieties, they smiled pleasantly at all the ladies waiting to be served, making enquiries after children's health and spouses' activities. Then they made a great show of looking at dress patterns in two different modiste's establishments, undeterred by the fact that they seemed to have forgotten to make prior appointments. No, declared Mary to one proprietor, it was all their fault: they should have sent word. But no matter, they would just study the new patterns while the other ladies (of which there were many) were attended to. Mary then put on a really good act of being interested in Kitty's exclamations over new styles, talking in a rather louder voice than normal.

Mrs Bennet, her arm firmly grasped by Mary, managed to nod and smile at friends and acquaintances, only attempting once to bring out a lavender-scented handkerchief and hold it to her mouth. At that moment, inexplicably, Mary's grip upon her mother's arm tightened, and the consequent irritated look upon Mrs Bennet's face was interpreted by those who saw it as being nothing but her usual discontent with the sales people.

After loudly ordering the servant home with the packages, they then declared their intention of having some high tea, and proceeded to the King George Arms. Once again, they seemed to have failed to send word, and the hotel was exceedingly busy. However, upon Mary's encouraging words, they accepted a table in the busier part of the hotel, and were seated in full view of all who passed. Mrs Bennet was then prompted to order quite an extravagant repast, of which the Bennet ladies appeared to enjoy every mouthful. Mrs Bennet, indeed, had the sort of mind that is easily distracted, and after scoffing down three or more scones, heavily-laden with double cream and raspberry jam, some cucumber sandwiches, a large slice of fruitcake and two cups of coffee, felt heartened enough by the success of the morning to look around herself with interest. She spent several minutes observing to the girls, in what she had always imagined was her discreet voice, that Mrs Cartwright, over there, looked exceedingly plump. Do you think she was expecting... again? A passing matron overheard this, and turned to her.

"Mrs Bennet! How lovely to see you. Yes, I do believe you are right! Shocking, with the youngest not yet two years of age!" the matron confided to Mrs Bennet.

"Oh, my dear. You are so right! So many daughters, too! How many is it, four? And three boys, you say? And so plain, all of them!"

The two gossipy ladies then put their heads together for a few moments, casting sly looks at the oblivious Mrs Cartwright. Then, as if suddenly remembering something, Mrs Bennet's confidante became a little wary, and looked towards the door.

"Well, it is lovely to see you out and about! You look— um... well, considering!"

"Considering what?" Mrs Bennet demanded, querulously.

Inwardly, Mary groaned. *Don't start, Mama*, she pleaded silently. It had been going so well.

"Well— um... one hears things, you know."

"Reports of my mother's... ill health... have been much exaggerated," Mary interrupted, with a smile.

"Indeed?" the lady was doubtful.

"Yes. It always amazes me that people have so little to do they must listen to gossip," Mary continued. "Unfounded gossip, at that."

"Quite. Unfounded, as you say. Well, I have detained you too long. Enjoy your— um... excursion." The lady left, and the three Bennet ladies let out long sighs of relief.

Mary was gradually beginning to relax. It seemed they might get away with it. Who knows — in time... She shook her head, and inwardly admonished herself. No, it would take a great deal of time, far more than she could suppose, for society to forget this scandal. She groaned. *Oh, Papa... What have you done?*

But Bertram Bennet, Mary and Kitty's Papa, and Mrs Bennet's much maligned husband, had seized the opportunity of having everyone out of the house. He was, even as they lunched, on a horse, galloping very fast in the opposite direction, towards London.

Chapter Six
Anne De Bourgh Decamps

Lady Anne de Bourgh, of Rosings Park in Derbyshire, was seated in an armchair as overstuffed with horsehair as the room in which she sat was crowded with furniture. She was sitting almost atop a huge, log fire in a cramped drawing room and fanning herself rapidly but surreptitiously as she tried to edge her chair away from the flames, which threatened to ignite the flounces on her rather old-fashioned frock. She was surrounded by numerous cushions and one or two knitted blankets, and these latter items she was attempting to quietly cast onto the floor. She was not, alas, unobserved by her hawk-eyed mother.

"Anne! Anne, I say! You look very flushed. Are you well? I am convinced you cannot be well! Darcy, don't just stand there: your cousin is in distress. Assist her." And so saying, Lady Catherine de Bourgh ordered her nephew, Fitzwilliam Darcy, quite bossily as he crossed the room and bent down to ascertain if Anne did, indeed, need assistance.

"Take that shawl and place it back over her shoulders!" Lady Catherine continued. "Give her some water; mix in some wine... not that much: she cannot digest it, you know. For heaven's sake, Darcy, have a care... Bring that footstool— not like that... really..."

Anne de Bourgh, glancing wryly up into her cousin's face, merely murmured, "I am quite well, Fitz, if only somewhat hot!" Her mother's ministrations did not diminish, however, and so, out of long habit, Anne stayed silent as a bell was rung, another shawl fetched, and Darcy dispatched to find some restorative draught from her maid. Only after all of this was accomplished was it possible for Anne to direct attention away from herself, by addressing her cousin's new wife.

"We have interrupted your playing, dear Elizabeth; please continue."

Elizabeth Darcy, at the pianoforte, attempted to continue with the lively piece she had been playing, but was shot down by Lady Catherine, who declared that all that infernal racket had given Anne a headache, and that she, Elizabeth, should have been more considerate. Could she not play something more soothing? Or was music hall style her only repertoire? A conspiratorial smile then passed between Elizabeth and Anne, as the latter shrugged and retreated back into her shawls.

Elizabeth gave up playing and left the pianoforte reluctantly, for it was far superior to any instrument her father had been able to afford at Longbourne, and she greatly admired its tone and resonance. She resumed her seat on the sofa next to her long-time friend Charlotte Collins, who had married Lady Catherine's protégé, the

Reverend Collins — he of the Longbourn entail fame — and cast a longing look at the ornate clock upon the mantlepiece. Would the evening never end? These mandatory quarterly family visits to pay homage, as Elizabeth put it, to her husband's domineering aunt, Lady Catherine, could only be endured with large amounts of patience on the part of the ladies (and wine on the part of the men). Elizabeth felt the absence of her milder sister Jane's meekness and forbearance keenly; qualities which abounded in Jane but which were often sadly diminished in herself. Elizabeth shrugged mentally, and knew that Jane would gain much enjoyment when she read of this evening in one of Elizabeth's very lively letters. In fact, she longed to have a quiet hour or two in which to sit down and write, but in the meantime yet another stultifying evening had to be endured.

Lady Catherine had resumed her haranguing of no one in particular and everyone in general. "Mrs Darcy, you must practise more on the pianoforte, you are gone quite lax. You have every opportunity to be diligent in your music, now you are free of your family who, heaven knows, took up much of your time in the past. Free, I must also say, of that influence in the field of music which has in the past held you back. Much as she likes to think she can play, your sister — what was her name? Margaret…?"

"Mary, Lady Catherine."

"...has really no talent to speak of. Well, what can one expect, with five of you to learn. You probably had not sufficient time at the piano, competing as you, no doubt, did with them all. Of course, you had only the one instrument, whereas here at Rosings we have three pianofortes and a harpsichord or two. And certainly, my nephew has one or two at Pemberley. Really! There is no excuse for your lack of practise!"

Elizabeth sipped her tea and glanced sideways at Charlotte Collins, who was next in the firing line.

"Mrs Collins, your posture is disgraceful! I cannot abide sloth. You will damage your spine. Sit up straight. One can always tell character by the rigidity of the spine. Those who stoop are, no doubt, lax also in their habits. Anne has a noble posture, but her health does not allow her to be erect for too long. Mr Collins, look to your wife's posture, she will benefit from your instruction in this regard."

The Reverend Mr Collins, hapless husband to Charlotte, made a feeble attempt to explain that his wife found it difficult to sit up straight due to her delicate condition, but was terrified into silence as Lady Catherine began a more violent diatribe.

"Do not mention *that* in my daughter's presence, Mr Collins! I am shocked! A young lady of her tender years! Anne, do not listen!"

"Really, Mother, I will not faint if we talk about Mrs Collins' condition. I am not entirely ignorant!"

Anne's murmurs were lost to her mother's strident tones.

"Ladies of quality do not even hint at such things! I cannot think where you can have come under such a detrimental influence as to feel that it is a fitting topic of conversation for *this* drawing room!" Lady Catherine drew a deep breath at this point, and glared pointedly at Elizabeth. Fitzwilliam Darcy, having observed that Mrs Collins was very uncomfortable, began arranging another footstool for her, and thus did not catch his aunt aiming a barb at his wife. He did, however, see the glare directed at Elizabeth. He moved to his wife's side and placed a restraining hand upon her shoulder, with good reason, for Elizabeth had taken up the challenge.

"I do not take your point, Lady Catherine," Elizabeth spoke forthrightly, not at all cowed.

Lady Catherine turned her full attention upon Elizabeth. "Well! It would seem that there has not been sufficient time for the deleterious influence of your family to dissipate entirely. If you do not take my point, then you obviously have a far less well-bred notion of what is suitable conversation for mixed company! Well, no matter. I am sure my nephew will work with me to assure your improvement."

This remark caused Elizabeth to splutter in her tea cup, and even the usually placid Anne was moved to protest. "Mama! You are too unkind!" But she was not heard amid the raised voices that ensued, for Darcy could not let the remark pass by without protest, and

Elizabeth, relishing the thought of defending herself, had begun a rebuttal.

Seeing that her mother was distracted, Anne moved her chair, at last, away from the overpowering fire and stood up to make an escape. She longed for a breath of air that was not infused with lavender or violets, and was almost at the door, when it opened suddenly to admit an under-footman, who almost collided with her as he entered, bearing a silver tray with a letter upon it.

Glancing in awe at the heated discussion within, the over-whelmed servant decided not to enter the lion's den and instead addressed Lady Anne.

"Beg pardon, my Lady, but this has just arrived by urgent courier from Longbourn." He then practically thrust the letter at Anne, and fled. Anne took the letter immediately, but not before her mother spied it. A letter arriving in the middle of the evening was just enough to deflect Lady Catherine and steer her onto a new course.

"What is that you have there? Anne? Bring it to me at once, if you please."

"It is a letter for Mrs Darcy, Mother," Anne replied, moving back into the room and over to where Elizabeth and her husband stood side by side under the onslaught.

"For Mrs Darcy? For her? You cannot be correct. Depend upon it, it is a mistake. Give it to me at once," Lady Catherine called imperiously, snapping her fingers impatiently, her tone of voice implying that such a lowly personage as Elizabeth could not possibly have anyone of note writing to her.

"No, Mama, it is most definitely for Elizabeth," and Anne gave the letter to her, casting a look of sympathy mixed with curiosity at her as she did so. The letter must contain news of some import.

Elizabeth Darcy took it, and with a slightly trembling hand, opened it immediately. Thoughts of all kinds ran through her head. She well remembered the last time she had been given such an urgent letter. She had been with Mr Darcy also at that time, and thought then that the news it brought must alienate him from her forever. This time, she was far surer of him and his steadfast nature, but still such a delivery could only bring ill tidings. She read the letter with her husband's dark head held closer to hers. Together, they gleaned its contents.

"What is it, then? Tell me at once! Really, such impertinence! To be having your correspondence redirected to Rosings, as if you dwelt here — it is the height of impudence!" Lady Catherine was adamant she would find out what was in the missive. "Darcy, come!" She snapped her fingers again at her nephew. "Bring it!"

"I regret, Lady Catherine, that the contents of this letter are private. However, they are such that I must travel to Longbourn as soon as possible. My mother has need of me," Elizabeth addressed Lady Catherine, outwardly calm but inside undergoing a torrent of emotions. Her father! What? Allegations of infidelity! What? It could not be true!

"I do not believe what I am hearing! What can be so private, pray? You are a guest in my house. I have every right to know."

"Desist with your demands, Aunt. It is not for you to know," Darcy snapped suddenly in his wife's defence.

There was a short, shocked silence. Lady Catherine sat up straighter, her ram-rod spine seeming to conduct icy contempt into her voice.

"I see," she said, her voice as steely as the most honed rapier. "I see that your... association with this person you call your wife has coarsened you. I see that after only a short term of cohabitation with that woman, she has managed to induce you to forget all your family pride and responsibility!"

At this, Elizabeth strode angrily across the room to stand in front of her antagonist, but her husband got there first.

"Aunt! That is beyond everything! I have in the past overlooked several insults you have offered to my wife, under the guise of helpful hints, but I will not let you insult my wife any longer!"

"Don't be ridiculous, nephew! As head of this family, I only seek to correct and improve!"

"But you are not head of this family, really, are you? Technically, I am. But that is beside the point. I will not stay in this house a moment longer than necessary. Since you seem to have such antipathy towards my wife, I shall remove both of us from your vicinity at first light." Darcy was inexorable.

Lady Catherine blinked. Never had anyone spoken to her like that — never!

"Come, Darcy," Elizabeth tugged on her husband's arm. "Do not engage with your aunt in this manner! We shall leave, but you need not be on bad terms with her."

"Be quiet!" Lady Catherine snapped her fan at Elizabeth. "I do not need the likes of you to fight my battles for me!"

"The likes of me?" Elizabeth queried, her voice now trembling with anger. Mr Darcy's ire was also evident from the thin line of his lips.

"You see how insolent she is?" Lady Catherine appealed to the room for support. Mr Collins sat on the edge of his sofa, aghast at the turn of events, quaking from head to toe. His wife seemed to find to great satisfaction in alternately pleating and un-pleating the hem of her shawl, and hoped fearfully that they would not be the next in the firing line.

"Do you see how she addresses me, and questions me as if I were not her superior?" Lady Catherine continued. "Such effrontery! To think where she was a mere year and a half ago, and how she now dares to flare up at my remarks!"

"You cannot suppose I would allow you to speak to my wife in that manner," Darcy angrily turned Elizabeth away from his aunt. "Your insinuations and constant attempts to belittle her have not gone unnoticed by me."

"And you cannot suppose that I will tolerate this—this upstart wheedling her way into this august family and then having the impertinence to keep secrets from me!"

"The contents of that letter are private and it is for Elizabeth only to decide who shall be privy to any information it might contain. However, if you had any — even the slightest modicum of humanity, or even the slightest hint of empathy for others, you must surely realise that a letter at this hour of the night can only contain dire news. However, it seems that, as usual, you have seized upon anything you can to continue your constant condemnation of my wife." Darcy was white hot, but his voice remained calm.

Elizabeth, now quite afraid of what her husband might say or do, laid a hand upon his arm and attempted to mitigate the situation. "Come, husband, that is enough. We shall leave as you say first thing, and—"

"Yes, leave you shall! Any time you wish!" Lady Catherine reached for the handbell, as if she were about to call to have them evicted.

"The fact that you order us to leave, after we had already declared our intention of doing so, merely reinforces my opinion that you have descended into senility," Darcy was so enraged, he hardly cared what he said.

Anne de Bourgh, another appalled observer of this argument, could only stare at her elder cousin in shock. He must be very angry indeed, she thought, to allow her mother to disturb his usual urbane demeanour and to forget everything he had ever been taught about respect for one's elders.

"Fitz…" she began, not knowing what she would say, but only hoping to convey to him how very much she understood him at that point.

"Anne!" Lady Catherine suddenly remembered the existence of her daughter. "Anne! Do not speak to them lest you, too, become … contaminated by the blight brought into this family by the Bennets! At least I can ensure that you will be spared further exposure to such a shocking departure from everything that speaks of good breeding, by insisting that you must leave this room at once, before too much damage is done and before your very morals are compromised. We must also take care that you never have anything more to do with such a creature as that, starting immediately. Come now, and go to your room!"

But Anne, with a rare moment of rebellion, was not to be so ordered.

"No," she declared simply.

This single word, uttered not loudly, but quite forcefully, by the meek and normally biddable daughter of the house, had the sudden effect of sending everyone mute.

Mr Collins coughed and looked longingly at the door. Charlotte Collins cowered into a cushion. Elizabeth Darcy turned amazed eyes upon the perpetrator of this remark, and Darcy himself shot a look of acute appraisal at his young cousin.

"What — did — you — say?" Lady Catherine stood, her shoulders drawn back to emphasise her height, bosom heaving, the ostrich plumes in her turban waving menacingly, and her walking stick thundering on the floor with each syllable.

"I said no, Mother. I will not leave the room, for I perceive that Elizabeth might have need of me. Neither will I be bullied into severing my connexion with her. She has done no wrong: she merely denied your intentions to snoop into her private affairs."

There was a long, long, silence.

"I see. It is too late." Lady Catherine drew a long breath, and let it out slowly. "She has already poisoned your mind against me and imbued you with the less savoury aspects of her character. You are now the sort of person who has forgotten all upbringing, all education. You are now as common as the lowliest shop-wife who screeches at her parents and denies them their rights. I am both disgusted and heart-sore."

"As you say, Mama. However, I will not be bullied any further. I also will not cause you any more disgust at my presence than necessary. Fitz, will you have room for me in your carriage on the morrow?"

"Of course, cousin. And all the room you need at Pemberley, and for as long as you need." Darcy, albeit amazed at his cousin's sudden courage, was ready to stand by her side.

"Then it is settled." Anne took Elizabeth's arm, and walked to the door with her. "I shall be going away, Mama, and shall stay away for as long as I must in order to give whatever assistance my cousin-in-law requires. Good night."

"I see how it all is now. I see what has been happening under my very roof!" Lady Catherine was not really convinced Anne would leave. She thought she did not have the backbone. "I have been a careful nurturer of my only living child, and now a viper has come into my nest to steal her away! Fitz! You must see what your wife has been doing!"

"I see nothing of the sort. You, however, will always see exactly what you want to see." Darcy was not impressed with his aunt's ludicrous accusations.

"Anne! You are not well enough to travel, you know that." Lady Catherine now had a tinge of panic in her voice. "What nonsense. You can be sure that… that *she* is not that discommoded! It is all nonsense and attention-seeking. Must you be swept up in the dramatics? Must you throw your health to the winds? Surely it cannot be that important. That type of family, you know, is always in the midst of some kind of hysterical crisis or another! If you wish to have an excursion, we shall seek medical advice first, and then perhaps, when the weather improves, we shall see about a sedate journey to Scarborough, perhaps, for the sea air."

"No, Mother. I am going to Pemberley tomorrow with the Darcys."

Lady Catherine was now convinced that Anne was having a brain-attack. "You cannot be serious. I am sure even Elizabeth will admit there is no need for these histrionics, whatever the news is."

Elizabeth fired up again at that expression, and wanted to know what Lady Catherine meant by "even Elizabeth", but Anne held them to their course by simply replying, "I feel some time away is for the best, and I wish to be of service to my dear cousin-in-law."

"Mr Collins! Do not sit there like a stuffed parrot. Tell Anne that she must not travel." Lady Catherine called for reinforcements, but the petrified vicar only made some peculiar strangled noises, and grasped his wife's arm tightly, as if she could protect him.

Lady Catherine, now becoming desperate, then turned to Charlotte, a person she never addressed unless it was to make some remark intended to let her know exactly how lowly she was in comparison to her own exalted self. "Mrs Collins! Tell Mrs Darcy that if she will only let me know what the news is, I am sure that with my superior connections and resources we can soon sort that matter out, and that there is no need for her to make away with my daughter."

Mrs Collins did not answer, either out of fear or circumspection, and soon thereafter Lady Catherine's voice followed Anne, Elizabeth and Darcy as they left the room. Her admonitions of "Really! Such effrontery!" and the such, mingled with the noise and hullaballoo of Darcy calling for his valet and the ladies' maids together created a fearful racket. As they each ascended the staircase to their rooms, they could hear Lady Catherine announcing loudly, "Foolish girl! Very well, I shall allow her a little taste of independence, but mark my words, the first sniffle she gets she will come running home to me! No doubt the beds are not properly aired at Pemberley, now that there is a new mistress! She will catch cold and come home to her Mama, you will see."

****

The next morning, there was no sight of Lady Catherine, but the others' travel plans proceeded forthwith.

The letter and its contents had been thoroughly dissected by Darcy, Elizabeth and Anne. Elizabeth was understandably distraught, and could only shake her head tearfully as Anne tried to think of some way to ameliorate the dreadful news. Perchance it was all a ludicrous mistake. The French gentleman had the wrong person. Bennet was a common name. Or, possibly, it was merely an attempt at extorting money from an innocent man. Perhaps there was no illegitimate son, but maybe there had been an affair that Elizabeth's father had broken off, and now the lady wanted revenge... Unfortunately, it was felt that the question of why it had taken the Picards so long to exact revenge only led credence to the whole story.

As the trio rode in the Darcy carriage towards Pemberley, the conversation turned around and around in a great circle. The matter of the possible existence of an illegitimate son of Elizabeth's father segued into the matter of Anne's rebellion, which returned inevitably to the matter of the illegitimate son. Elizabeth spoke calmly to Anne about not burning bridges, about keeping the lines of communication clear between herself and her mother, and about allowing things to calm down and then writing a firm but apologetic letter. Anne spoke to Elizabeth about possible outcomes, about getting to the bottom of the matter and about being sure she would have all her support during the troubles.

Darcy, restless and chafing at the forced inactivity as they proceeded slowly to Pemberley, became broody. All that was decided was that they would travel to Longbourn as soon as possible, spending only a day or so at Pemberley to re-pack their trunks, and that Anne would also accompany them. He longed for more decisive action. He was also in somewhat of a quandary as he felt that Anne, being thrust suddenly into the bosom of the Bennet family — heaving as it was with this new catastrophe — might just discover her newly-found liberation overwhelming, and thought that there was surely some other way to test one's new independence. Indeed, he expressed doubts as to whether it was circumspect for Anne to travel to Longbourn with them, but his opinion was not held up in the face of his wife's and cousin's decision. Seeing that the ladies had several deep discussions to get through he felt *de trop*, so he stopped the carriage and ordered his horse be untethered. He then rode off at a great pace, his face inscrutable, to try and shake off the restlessness which threatened to depress him.

Although usually a man of action and quick decision-making, Darcy was also able to acknowledge when it was best to wait, so after galloping off his fidgets, he was content to trot alongside the carriage silently. His thoughts were kept to himself. One thing, of which he was certain: he would no longer allow his aunt's insinuations to be aired in public. He would insist she keep them to herself, since there was really no hope of changing her mind. So far, Lady Catherine did not appear to have broken her own code of 'Family First', but then she hardly considered Elizabeth to be part of the family, so it seemed as if, to his aunt, all bets were off. He was certain that Lady Catherine's hatred of Elizabeth stemmed from having had her ridiculous schemes for him to marry his cousin Anne, thereby resurrecting an ancient yet long defunct Darcy-de Bourgh dynasty, well and truly thwarted. He was also sure that Anne's apparent defection had unhinged her. He did not know how long it would be before she aired her views in public, and that he would not allow. And as for Anne… Well, he always suspected she had more to her than was apparent. Darcy sighed, acknowledging that he might be called upon to once again gallop off and extricate his wife's family from scandal. He did not look forward to that. At least their departure from Rosings that morning had gone without hitch. There had been no sign of Lady Catherine and all was quiet. At least it was a blessing she did not know what was in that letter. Small mercies.

Unbeknownst to the Darcys and Anne de Bourgh, however, there was a very valid reason for Lady Catherine's silence. Far from being in the dark, Lady Catherine had, by devious methods, managed to ascertain exactly what was in that letter from Longbourn. Even as the trio placed mile upon mile between themselves and Rosings, Lady Catherine held in her hand an exact copy of it, obtained by way of having her house-keeper steal the letter in the middle of the night. Lady Catherine's discreet and reliable secretary had then been woken and ordered to copy it before returning it to its original place in Elizabeth's reticule. Lady Catherine smirked at how easy it had been, but then, it was ease that came from long practice. It said much of Lady Catherine that she often employed such underhand activities in order to achieve her ends, and also that she kept the sort of staff in her employ who willingly performed such duties without comment. Thus, Lady Catherine was content and gleeful. She foresaw that the public disgrace and humiliation of the Bennets would sow the seeds of disgust in her nephew for his wife and her lowly connexions. She foresaw that he would begin to regret his misalliance, and looked forward to the inevitable conclusion of an application to the High Court for a divorce. She felt sure that society would forgive the scandal, under the circumstances, and once the public hullabaloo had died down, Darcy would console himself with his one true love: her daughter Anne. Simple. Lady Catherine's eyes glittered. *Simple*.

Chapter Seven
Bertram Bennet Bushwacked

Bertram Bennet, briskly avoiding a foetid puddle by stepping around it, only to come to grief in an even slimier pool, which had just been ejected from an upstairs window, looked around himself anxiously. None of the grime-encrusted buildings he had passed had numbers on them, and none of the streets seemed to have any names attached. He began to feel that he had been rather foolish to have come to London. Even as he turned up his collar against a biting wind, snow began to fall in light flurries, mixing with the ordure and filth lying in the gutters. All around him, people in dirty clothes or rags pushed and jostled past, and he was sure several attempts had already been made to lift his pocket-book.

He thought he would cross the street to see if the address he sought was on the other side, but the constant traffic of vegetable carts, coal drays, dilapidated carriages pulled by broken-down horses, and street urchins, was a palpable deterrent. All around him the noise was deafening: street vendors called out constantly, unemployed men yelled obscene comments as he passed, cart wheels rattled on uneven cobblestones, and the street walkers, tired from their nocturnal activities, accosted him half-heartedly as he tried to get past. Pushing away one particularly insistent lady of the night, who reeked of gin and some undefinable body odour, Mr Bennet thought again to himself, why had he come?

When the hired horse and carriage had dropped him there that morning, Mr Bennet had had high hopes of a successful mission. Indeed, acting upon the advice of the landlord of the Duck 'n Cider — an inn of reasonable tariff and only slightly questionable cleanliness, where he had taken a room — Mr Bennet had felt that it would not take him very long to find what he was looking for, which was a speedy passage to France. In fact, the Landlord, one Mr Jem Haddar, had assured him that shipping agents were as thick as thieves upon the ground of 'St Giles', where he now found himself. However, he could now see that, regardless of whether this exaggeration was even half-way true, he was not about to discover his quarry easily. Indeed, the fact that St. Giles was one of the more notorious neighbourhoods in that writhing, stinking, foetid labyrinth of filthy streets, known as The Rookeries, could not have been known by the slightly overweight and completely overwhelmed country gentleman, who now trotted nervously along, peering dubiously into buildings mostly comprising gin shops, whore houses and abandoned windowless shops. Mr

Bennet was perplexed. The landlord had seemed so helpful, and as luck would have it (or so he said), he had a brother who owned a horse and buggy for public conveyance. The landlord had called to his brother to "take up this gen'man to St Giles, and don't you be gammin' 'im!" in such a friendly and helpful way that Mr Bennet had started out on his mission with high hopes of finishing by lunchtime, and with much self-congratulation at not having had to appeal to his wife's brother, Mr Gardiner, for assistance.

The buggy driver took him up with alacrity, for he could see a fat fare coming his way, and after only a few devious twists and turns in order to ramp up the cost, deposited Mr Bennet at the top of a dingy street, with the admonition that if he went straight ahead now afoot, he'd come to St Giles sure enough, but "I stops 'ere cos I durs'nt go no further." He also added, as Mr Bennet paid him, that if he ran into difficulty he could always ask for 'Black Frank', who would see him right, no worries.

Mr Bennet, stepping down from the buggy, at first regarded his new locale with a fair amount of trepidation, but stepped forward after only a few minutes' hesitation with all the outward appearance of a confident man. Operating under his usual but often misguided belief in the goodness of all human nature, he felt sure that he would come to no harm if he himself offered no harm to others. This belief was sorely tested. All of his polite enquiries were met with guffaws and downright obscene comments, and he was now certain that several ruffians were following him. After nearly two hours of fruitless asking, resulting only in edifying comments, he felt it prudent to leave but was reluctant to do so without finding his quarry. In addition, as the morning wore on and he trudged the streets uselessly, it became apparent to him that his erstwhile sedate habits of reading and gentle walks to church and back had not best fitted him for the marathon he was now enduring. His shoes were thin and his coat even thinner. Somehow, the vision he had had of himself meandering into an office, making his enquiries, laying down some cash and leaving again after a half-hour or so with his mission complete seemed ludicrous in the light of his aching feet and damp shoulders. Also, although geography was not his strongest point, he was now certain that the neighbourhood he was in was nowhere near any dock at which he could embark on his proposed voyage. Even stretching the point by believing that upon the nearby malodorous branch of the river Thames there was a smaller boat, which he could hire and which would take him to Tilbury Docks or to Dover, seemed ridiculous now, as he dodged yet another street cart.

He decided to turn around. Stopping off in London had been a mistake, but his bank was there, and he had not wanted to wait the tedious two weeks or so it would have taken for letters to go back and forth. On second thoughts, he reflected that in the light of his failure he had better leave London as soon as possible and go to

Dover directly. He could probably sell something of value at the harbour to pay for his passage. Yes, that was the better plan, he decided. If the family should make enquiries as to his whereabouts, the bank would naturally be one of the first places they would visit, and since he did not want them to have any inkling as to where he had gone, it was probably better that he leave no clues.

He began to retrace his steps. He was sure that if he walked back down these few streets, and maybe if he crossed that road over there and walked just a bit further, he would find himself once again in a more salubrious district, and would be able to hire a carriage to take him back to the inn. However, once again the lack of street signage was confusing. Turning another corner, he collided with a large, smelly man, who admonished him to "Watch it, you soddin' cove." With a murmured apology, Mr Bennet turned again, but the man began to follow him. Glancing anxiously over his shoulder, Mr Bennet quickened his steps, and took another turn down a street, which he fancied was more or less familiar. The man continued to follow him. Now feeling seriously alarmed, Mr Bennet walked even faster, but quelled the impulse to panic and run. It was probably nothing. The man was probably just going the same way, that was all. However, after a few more turns, he was certain the man was after him. He then did, indeed, begin to run, conscious of the man's heavy footfalls closing in on him from behind. He looked around fearfully. There was no shop he could duck into. People he passed made no attempt to get out of his way. Indeed, as they milled around and blocked his path, they seemed to be abetting the ruffian who was now closing fast upon the hapless Mr Bennet. The snow turned into a sleeting, freezing rain, and Mr Bennet could see no escape. He was sure to be nabbed from behind, probably cudgelled to death for his meagre pocket-book, his body rolled into the gutter to lie in the filth and squalor until it rotted. He almost sobbed with his exertions to get away from the footpad. His life could not end like this!

A rough, heavy hand came down upon his shoulder. He braced himself for the attack and thought fleetingly of his family.

"'Ere! 'old on, Mr Johnny Raw! I ain't about to draw yer claret, nor am I like to lift yer pocket." Mr Bennet was spun around, and looked up into a square jaw, a dirty face and a lowering brow, all topped by a filthy cloth cap.

"Unhand me, sir! What do you want? I shall call the Watch!" Mr Bennet struggled gamely in the clutch of his assailant.

"'Old yer 'orses! I ain't about ter nab yer one! What I wants to know is, what does the likes of you need in The Rookeries? This ain't no place for a genn'um like yerself. When I saw'd you, I thought to meself ye was after a Haymarket girl, and thought ye was a regular flat, to be thinkin' ye'd find the sort of abbess around here that would be suitable-like fer ye to do business with.

But then I gets ter thinkin' that yer just a cursed rum touch, and that mebbe I can get you on the right road… Am I right?"

Mr Bennet, not sure that he understood more than half of this declaration, comprehended at least that the man still grasping his shoulder seemed to be not about to rob him, or not immediately, in any case. He then had a flash of inspiration and thought that maybe he could bribe him to take him back to the Inn.

"Um, thank you. Yes, my good man. I do seem to be a little lost. However, I am not looking for a… lady from Haymarket but am seeking an address, where, I have been told, I can buy a passage to France, and where I am assured anonymity is to be had." Mr Bennet took out his kerchief and wiped the sleet off his face.

"Passage to France?" The man was amused. "Wot fer? Don'tcha know that 'alf of France is coming over 'ere?"

Mr Bennet was taken aback. "Half? Coming over here? Really?"

"Don'tcha know nuffin'? Blimey, the man's a regular chaw bacon! It's cos of Nappy, and 'is 'avin' overrun all o' France!"

By this, Mr Bennet understood the man to be alluding to the fact that the war-mongering, self-styled Emperor Napoleon, having recently escaped from Elba, had returned to Paris and had declared himself Emperor once again. Mr Bennet knew, of course, that the Beau Monde, having been lulled into a false sense of security by Napoleon's banishment, had been once again vacationing in droves in France and Italy. It would have to be a complete ignoramus indeed who did not know of the subsequent panic when Napoleon escaped, and the ensuing debacle as hordes of scared English people (and those with suddenly Anglicised names) fled to the ports, trying to get passage to England.

"But I have the most pressing business there!" Mr Bennet stated baldly. "You cannot possibly understand! It is imperative that I get to Paris, as soon as possible. Now, let me go!" Once again he attempted to throw off the detaining hand, which was the weight of a ham, at least.

"Now just you 'old yer 'orses! Ain't no need fer yer to get all anxious-like. Mebbe I can be of assistance, fer a little bit of the ready?" The man rubbed his thumb and forefinger together in the universal sign for money.

"How could you possibly assist me?"

"Well, now, I ain't known to make a complete mull of things. I reckon I'm right clever in a lot of stuff. I'm wot yer might call a Jack of All Trades, bein' as it were a groom, an ostler, and a bit of a sailor. Right now I'm groom at the Duck N' Cider, a doss which you be layin' yer head at tonight, if I'm not mistaken."

Mr Bennet looked at the man. Did he seem familiar? Was he indeed a groom at the very inn where he was putting up? If so, then this fellow had followed him here! With intent to murder and rob, no doubt! It was too much to assume coincidence.

"So you followed me here?" Mr Bennet asked, outrage in his voice.

"Reckon I did, but not so's I could turn you over. Nope, I said to myself this morning, when ye was makin' yer enquiries, that ye was about to get done. Couldn't understand why ye would be wantin' to come here. Then I figgers, see, that this be the only place a man could get a ride to France, what with all them reg'lar ports closed an' all. Then I figgers it must be real important to ye, but ye don't look like ye'd be able to get around with yer head still on yer shoulders, if you get my drift."

Mr Bennet acknowledged his failure. "But what do you want?" he demanded.

"Well now," and at last the man took his meaty hand off Mr Bennet's shoulder. "H'if you will h'allow me to interduce meself… I am Jack Dobbrey, temp'ry groom when in England, and Jacques D'Aubrey, temp'ry ship's mate when in France. A man of many talents, ye might say."

Mr Bennet looked at Dobbrey dubiously. "A man with two names? How extravagant!"

Dobbrey shrugged. "A man's got ter make a livin' ain't 'e? I goes where I'm needed, and I makes me own way. Now then, seems to me a man such as yerself, wot 'as a right pressin' need to get to France, might be in need of a man such as meself."

"Indeed?"

"Indeed it is, guv'nor. Soon as I 'eard you talkin' to Jem at the Duck n'Cider, I thinks to meself that 'ere was a man who might need my h'expert 'elp. Now then, it also seems to me that ye might be in a bit of a fix right now, wot with ye bein' here all alone, and not havin' any money, like."

Mr Bennet's hand flew to his pocket. Damn! His money purse was gone.

Dobbrey smirked a little. "Saw that cove a while back relieving you of it! So, seein' as you ain't got sixpence to fly with, and seein' as you ain't got no choice, I reckon the best ye can do right now is ter let me get ye back to the Duck n'Cider, and then see if I don't come up with a plan to get us both to France, on the quiet, like!"

Mr Bennet had to admit he was defeated. It was certain he had no other choice. He had already most decidedly ruled out enlisting family help, as he knew he needed to keep things very secret. He therefore had no other recourse than to trot along beside the large, smelly Dobbrey as he confidently led the way through the maze of odorous streets and alleyways. Once they were clear of certain areas that made even Dobbrey look anxious, a carriage was hailed. Dobbrey spoke in a strange kind of patois to the driver, who consequently took a much more direct route than the earlier driver. As they bounced along the ill-kept streets, Dobbrey kept up a long and rattling account of his past exploits; an account which was, no doubt, intended to assure Mr Bennet, who sat in the carriage leaning backwards with his kerchief held to his nose, of his suitability and aptitude as a travelling companion, but which was so filled with cant and colourful turns of phrase as to render him unable to comprehend more than half of it. What he did comprehend, however, was that Jack was not enamoured of his present employer, was further less enamoured of horses, and actually needed to make an exit across the Channel rather hastily, on account of some trifling difficulties with the law.

Further information, regarding his regular activities on the waters between France and England, revealed that his occupation in the past seemed to have involved slipping into France extremely quietly, under cover of fog and darkness, and running various contraband items, such as brandy and lace, back to England for a profit. Before the mismatched pair reached the relative safety of quieter streets away from the Rookeries, Mr Bennet somehow found that he had hired the talented Dobbrey as a sort of travel agent. Apparently, Dobbrey was to take him along on his next run, which was to be in six or seven days' time. In addition, Dobbrey was going to procure such items of clothing for Mr Bennet as would seem to fit his new character as rum smuggler, was going to secure newer, better lodgings for the interim for his new and very trusting employer, and was going to help him get around in Paris, when they got there, and to assist him with whatever quest Mr Bennet had. All of this aid, Dobbrey assured Mr Bennet, was for a very reasonable sum; hardly worth considering at all. Mr Bennet had no recourse but to go along with his new friend.

What a turn of events, he thought. A few short days ago, he had been in his beloved library at Longbourn, and now he was consorting with criminals and smugglers! Life had never been so exciting.

****

Dobbrey appeared to be as good as his word, even if delivering on his promises entailed somewhat dubious methods. Mr Bennet was both highly amused and scandalised at some of the new things he was learning in the company of his new factotum. Their return to the Duck n' Cider caused no small amount of consternation to the landlord, Jem, who clearly did not expect it. Mysteriously, Mr Bennet's things had already been packed up in a small bag and were waiting at the back door. The landlord expressed innocence with a shrug of his shoulders, stating that he was sure he had heard Mr Bennet instruct that it be so. Mr Bennet was both puzzled and outraged. How could he have told the landlord he would be leaving that afternoon, when he had only just found that out himself? After a short exchange of personalities with Mr Bennet and Jack, Jem slunk off into the dark, back regions of the inn. The shifty-looking character who had been about to take possession of Mr Bennet's belongings went with him, and Jack summoned a carriage, waving away Jem's hopeful brother with a few more epithets of a colourful kind. Dobbrey had assumed command.

Once installed in an inn of far more pleasant appointments, and with far less nefarious staff, Mr Bennet was amazed at how quickly things were progressing. At Longbourn, he had been used to the much slower pace of the countryside. There, either he or Mrs Bennet gave the orders to the slow-moving but faithful Mrs Hill, who would over the course of a day or so filter the orders, more or less, down the ranks to the lower staff, who in their turn would get things done eventually. If anything urgent cropped up, it was addressed in only a slightly less leisurely manner. Here in London, however, events moved at a very rapid pace, as evidenced by the constant stream of traffic arriving at and departing from the Prince of Wales Arms. Indeed, although it was a far classier establishment than the Duck n' Cider, it was also far noisier, what with ostlers constantly changing over horses, coach drivers calling loudly for ale and cakes, passengers alighting and embarking, and the never-ending business of carting luggage, allocating rooms, cooking, and the washing and airing of linen. Mr Bennet had never in his life been so close to the daily business of housekeeping, which occurred right outside his bedroom door and often requited his active participation. He learned much about bleaching linen, rubbing down horses, cooking, and tapping kegs of ale during his short stay there, as Jack organised their excursion across the Channel. Mr Bennet's clothes were sold to pay for a new set made of homespun wool and sturdy boots of no beauty but great usefulness. The rest of his things were stored in a back room of the inn, along with several barrels of contraband. It seemed that, despite its lofty name, the Prince of Wales inn was not above trading in fine French brandy and Flemish lace.

Mr Bennet was getting used to the new, faster pace of life, and soon knew the names of the various coach drivers and the bitter rivalry between them. If asked, he could have discoursed quite knowledgeably about the even more bitter rivalry between the Prince of Wales and the Green Man, an inn on the opposite side of the road. Although bereft of his books, he felt that here was education enough! Salting pork, decanting wine, banishing bed bugs and conversing freely with those of the lower classes constituted a type of freedom he had never known. He thought of Longbourn frequently and had many pangs when he contemplated how his wife must be suffering but more often than not, if he thought of his home at all it was to think how he would relate such-and-such an event to Mary, or write of so-and-so's idiosyncrasies to Elizabeth. He also discovered that, in his guise of non-descript inn worker, he was told things that no gentlefolk would ever impart to another. Here was a fine lady, on her way to Brighton, who informed him quite candidly, as he helped load her baggage, that her husband, the rat, would be along shortly, and if he should happen to be with quite another different lady, he was to send word to her at once! And here was a fine gentleman, who kicked his wife's dog when she wasn't looking and asked Mr Bennet bluntly if there was a pond nearby in which to "drown the crappy thing".

Such was the parade of people passing by. Mr Bennet saw lords and ladies, clergymen and commoners, raw schoolgirls and bluff farmers, all scurrying hither and thither, travelling around the country, and all intent upon their own private businesses. It seemed amazing to him that there was more life in one day, here, than in an entire season at Longbourn. He began to feel slightly contemptuous of his previous life. How narrow it had been, and how constrained! There was only one moment in which Mr Bennet's equanimity was challenged, and that was when a coach drew up, its horses all a-lather, and as fate would have it, Captain Carter of the Seventh Horse Guards, alighted from it in a great hurry. This officer was well known to Mr Bennet: he had dined at his table, lost at cards to him, borrowed one of his books, and frequently danced with Jane or Elizabeth at a ball in Meryton. Mr Bennet stood, transfixed, certain his subterfuge was found out and his quest come to an end.

"You there! I say, my good man!" Captain Carter called out.

Mr Bennet made a half turn, trying to pull the brim of his straw hat down further.

"Yessir?" he drawled, as convincingly as he could.

"Get my horses away as soon as possible, and give me a new set. And not those same sway-backed nags you palmed off on me last time, but a decent pair! I'm in a hurry! And fetch me some cake and ale… What do I have to do to get decent service around here? Go across the road?"

"Aye, sir, right away sir!" Mr Bennet watched in awe as the Captain looked directly at him, without recognition.

"Snap to it!" And the officer swept inside the inn, leaving Mr Bennet gasping for air as he sighed with relief. He was not recognised! Incredible! This was a salubrious lesson indeed for Mr Bennet, and one he never forgot in the years ahead of him. He was not recognised by the officer, a frequent guest at his own table, because to him, the 'stable boy' at the inn was invisible. He was a nonentity. Not worth knowing. Clothes really do make the man, he mused ironically. How many times in the past had he done the same? Not really seen the men and women who called him 'Master' and whose lives depended upon him? It was a sobering thought. Soon enough, however, this new education came to an abrupt end. Jack Dobbrey informed Mr Bennet that the day after tomorrow was the time when a run would be made, and that they would be assisting certain men in their efforts to avoid excise duties on highly desirable French goods, in exchange for a free passage across the Channel.

And thus it was that Mr Bennet was on horseback once again, heading off to the small seaside village of St Margaret's, just north of Dover, to meet up with men with blackened faces, in a boat with a blackened sail and muffled oars.

Chapter Eight
Mary Bennet Muddles Through

Mr Bennet had been gone for five, long weeks. His wife, bathing a little more often and being bossed around by her daughter Mary a lot more often, had resumed her habitual complaining and moaning, informing all who would listen that Mary had become a veritable termagant! She was bullied day and night! She was brought to tears at least twice a day, as she was constantly hectored and harangued, and it had come to the point where she dare not even leave so much as a shawl or a knitting needle out of place for fear of incurring Mary's wrath. The unjustly vilified Mary cared not for her family's complaints. She was very thoroughly enjoying her new role of Commander-in-Chief, and ran Longbourn with near-military precision. The servants, including the nearly-pensioned Mrs Hill, had at first revolted, but when faced with being turned out without recommendation had decided *en masse* that capitulation was more prudent, and sprang to their new timetable with alacrity, albeit with many a grumble. However, after a week or so of the new regime, even the doddering old Benjamin, Head Gardener, had to admit that things were actually easier now that they were running more efficiently. Gone were the old days of doubling up on tasks, of wasted time due to unclear orders, and sinful wastage. Meals were planned weekly; groceries and other provisions ordered in timely fashion; and work rosters refashioned in such a manner that each servant had their equal share of leisure time and less-arduous tasks.

Mary positively glowed with pride in her accomplishments. Before, it had seemed to her that the family had always been teetering on the edge of chaos and anarchy. Housekeeping debacles had occurred with distressing regularity. Staff often quarrelled bitterly with each other, to the detriment of the productivity of all. However, with the new roster in place, tensions had all but been eliminated. Now, thanks to Mary's tireless efforts, one knew by the meal on the table and the linens on the bed which day of the week it was. Alarms and crises were banished, efficient calm and cooperation became the order of the day.

Whilst Mary organised and ordered, Mrs Bennet was keen on keeping up their new pretence that Mr Bennet was away for a protracted stay in Brighton, for his health, and was also keen to resume the usual countryside pursuits of gossiping and morning calls. Mary had to capitulate in this, as the rumours caused by their departure from the social scene were only slightly less injurious than those caused by Mr Bennet's abrupt departure. Mary had thus to endure many a morning call from their neighbours, and was dismayed at the convention which held that each call paid to them had to be returned within a fortnight. Consequently, the steady stream of visitors to Longbourn, although unpredictable in its regularity, did not abate and Mary, having been caught out only once, and that by the carping Mrs Cowper, soon learned to be flexible in her catering arrangements. A stock of tea was always at hand, and cakes and pastries baked thrice-weekly to feed visitors. They even entertained at a small dinner, attended by the Lucases and the vicar, Mr Broughton, although Mary, having been given short notice, found herself bereft of a fish course. This was in itself not unusual, as Meryton was far from the coast and fish was not easily procured. However, as her mother had issued the invitations unbeknownst to her, Mary felt that a little more forethought and planning could have averted the problem. Mary had subsequently refused to send the staff galloping off around the countryside on a panicked quest for flounder, and had herself devised a fish chowder with some pickled herrings. Mr Lucas declared it to be excitingly different, Mrs Lucas demanded the recipe, and Mr Broughton ate two helpings before sonorously intoning that it had been delicious.

This new vicar was, most annoyingly, a frequent visitor to Longbourn. Mary, irritated at being interrupted one time too often, made the mistake of allowing him to peruse her new timetable, in order to hopefully forestall future interruptions.

"For example," she pointed out to him one day, opening a large notebook and indicating a meticulously-drawn set of squares, each labelled according to the day of the week, with further labels showing times of the day, "you can see that on Tuesdays, at three o'clock, both my sister Kitty and I are free for leisure, and that we usually spend that time in quiet reading or contemplation of passages from the bible." Mary hoped he would take the hint, and curtail his visits to these times on Tuesdays only.

Mr Broughton was a very fast reader, albeit a slow talker, and had taken in at a glance the little squares dictating such activities as 'needlework', 'overseeing accounts', and 'piano'. With a quizzical air, he asked, "And how does your sister like such regimentation?"

"She likes it very well," Mary replied. "I feel she has improved her mind greatly by reading along with me. Of course, she has her lapses. Only the other day she was engaged in drawing silly sketches of new gowns and the like, instead of—"

"Not silly to her, no doubt," Mr Broughton had interrupted.

"...instead of practicing her piano, as decreed." Mary quelled her irritation with him. He was, after all, a man of God.

"And does her playing improve?" queried the vicar, with a slightly deprecating air, which effectively quelled Mary and brought the conversation to a halt.

Such was his habitual manner with Mary (and he made visiting often just as much of a habit), that the almost daily sight of Mr Broughton's portly pony trotting around the bend in the driveway, carrying its increasingly portly master, was a source of much irritation to her. There could be no escaping him; he would come just after breakfast, or around noon, or in time to be invited to dinner, and maintained unpredictability in this matter. Mary loathed his visits, and also detested the usual weekly round of morning social calls the family made for the sake of keeping up appearances, escaping this duty whenever she could.

However, one fine day, her mother became very querulous when Mary assayed her usual excuses, and so she had grudgingly accompanied her mother and Kitty to the Cartwright's. On this occasion, she had been attempting to at least gain something worthwhile out of the afternoon by reading from the book she had secreted in her reticule, and had been seething in a corner at what she considered a "monumental waste of time", determined to abstract herself from the inane conversation, when a servant announced the arrival of Mr Broughton. *Oh God, even here!* Mary despaired. She looked up in irritation, but hoped to pass the afternoon unnoticed by Mr Broughton, as there were several other callers in the room already, and she was in a corner, half hidden by a gossiping couple. However, after first observing all the civilities, the vicar perversely spied her immediately and deliberately drew her into the circle of gossips. He first admired Kitty's new sketches and then asked Mary's opinion of the dress patterns Kitty had so cleverly devised. Mary, not knowing or caring about the relative merits of cambric versus muslin, was one who barely knew how to dress for the season. The fact that spring was "only weeks away... We must make haste to procure new walking dresses!" declared breathlessly by one of the Cartwright twins, was of even less import to her than the doings of an ant, and her reply amply demonstrated this.

"It is of no matter to me!" she snapped.

"But it ought to be," continued the implacable Broughton. "Your interests are, perforce, of matter to Kitty, and it seems that in return hers ought to be to you."

There were several pieces of this sentence demanding attention but Mary seized upon the most obvious. "Perforce?" she almost seethed. "Perforce?"

Mr Broughton nodded. "Perforce indeed... or so it would seem to anyone having had the privilege of viewing your list of daily activities, which you most kindly showed me last week. Upon almost every day you have allocated, somewhat arbitrarily, exactly what pastimes Kitty must engage in. Reading, piano, sorting clothing for the poor... It is no wonder poor Kitty has had recourse to sitting up late at night. There must be no other times in which to satisfy her own interests."

At this point, Mr Broughton, who had been gazing around the room with a supercilious air, met Mary's bewildered face full on, his own expression conveying a hint of contempt. Mary was rendered almost speechless. Kitty had been sitting up late? This was news to her. Why hadn't she known that? How did *he* know? What business…? The effrontery of the man! So intimately interested in their private doings! He must be severely quelled.

"I wonder at your busy-body attitude, Mr Broughton. It is no concern of yours how Kitty spends her time. Why do you care? And how do you know she sits up late at night?" Mary was working herself up to a goodly hot temper, despite her efforts to be as forbearing as a Christian should.

"Ah! I am the sort of person who takes to heart Genesis chapter four, verse nine, and believe that I am always my brother's keeper, and when I see another person in distress I know it is my duty to do what I can. I wonder you do not notice what is obvious me, and would be also obvious to you if you would but be less concerned with yourself and took more time to observe others," Mr Broughton replied.

"How dare you suppose that I have no concern for my sister?" Mary practically shrieked, so great was her indignation. "Everything I do is for her education and improvement! If you could have seen her disastrous handwriting before I took her education in hand! And her mind has been vastly improved since I began directing her reading away from the sensational novel to the more—"

"If you had real concern for your sister, you would note that she is very tired from sitting up late at night; a fact you could have easily deduced for yourself if you had noted her increased consumption of candles — an issue I overheard your respected mother lamenting. In addition, Kitty does not look happy."

Mary's mouth gaped unattractively for a moment or two. This man was too much! He may be a servant of the Lord, but really! She felt all the outrage of a person who finds that someone has been snooping into her private affairs, and all the self-justification of someone who has been caught out by that snooping. She knew that Kitty had been using more candles, but had not even for one moment stopped to consider why. No doubt it was to draw her silly fashions, she scoffed to herself. No wonder she was hiding it from her.

In an effort to reclaim her position, Mary said "You allude, no doubt, to Kitty's artistic endeavours? You may be assured I am perfectly well acquainted with them," and she lifted one eyebrow haughtily at him, before turning away.

"If you were acquainted with them at all, you would see that her endeavours are noteworthy indeed. She has a good eye for both style and colour," was the last thing Mary heard as she flounced across to the other side of the room.

And this was not the only time she was sorely tested by Mr Broughton. In fact, he seemed to pop up at the most inconvenient times. It seemed to Mary that wherever she went, there he was; unfailingly polite but supercilious, always with a criticism disguised as concern, assisting Kitty with her purchases in a shop, presenting her mother with a new hymnal, or insisting upon carrying Mary's basket of vegetables from the garden for her. When she rather artfully suggested, once, that he was sacrificing too much of his own time to her family, he replied that he felt compelled to assist them where he could, stating that he hoped to be even a small part of their lives, and that since they must be "feeling the lack of a male in the house", they could look forward to enjoying his solicitations for many a day to come. Mary fumed.

Inevitably, Mr Broughton made himself obvious when the Darcys descended upon Longbourn. They arrived one fine morning in a handsome chaise drawn by four, very nice chestnuts, Mr Darcy riding alongside on a glossy black stallion, and with a larger wagon following, which contained all their baggage and retinue. There had been many delays prior to their arrival, despite their dramatic exit from Rosings following Darcy's argument with his aunt. Elizabeth had been unwell, and Anne had succumbed for a while to her old lung ailment, and so it was quite a few weeks later when they eventually arrived. Naturally, letters had flown back and forth, and Elizabeth chafed at every delay. Although Mary and the family had been expecting word from them almost daily, in the end they had but two days' notice of their arrival. However, the visitors were dispersed efficiently around the house to their various accommodations by Mary, who was eager to put her new household management skills to the test. She was pleased she was able to allocate bedrooms and order meals with great efficiency, and within an hour or so of arriving, her sister Elizabeth and her husband Darcy, and her cousin-in-law Anne, were very comfortably situated in the best guest bedrooms.

Elizabeth remarked immediately upon the change in the household wrought by Mary, giving praise where it was due. In the old days the house always seemed in turmoil. Now, even though there was no good news and in fact things were considerably worse, given Mr Bennet's decampment, the house was at least running smoothly. The public face exhibited by the Bennet ladies was much approved of by Mr Darcy, to whom reputation was everything. And although the lie concerning Mr Bennet's whereabouts, that he was sojourning at a health retreat following a long illness, was decried by him, he acknowledged its necessity. Elizabeth Darcy was also a great help in soothing their mother, who fretted daily about their father's absence. She spent many a long hour listening again and again to her mother's wailing over the dreadful accusations of that "primped-up Picard." Nobody wanted to point out to her that Mr Bennet's disappearance lent only more credence to the whole story, and seemed rather to emphasise guilt than innocence, while Elizabeth was patience itself as Mrs Bennet alternately bemoaned her husband's perfidy, and gloated at the thought of parading her illustrious daughter, Mrs Elizabeth Darcy (of Pemberley!) in front of all the town's matrons (particularly Mrs Cowper).

Anne de Bourgh was charmed by Longbourn from the very first moment of her visit. It was such a happy house! She was astounded at the family's free and easy manners. Here, windows were thrown open to admit fresh air; here, furniture was for lounging on, and not for show; here, one could speak one's mind without censure. Indeed, she was such an easy guest, so helpful with Mrs Bennet, that Mary hardly knew she was there. Anne took it upon herself to befriend Kitty, who was overwhelmed by her new and very stylish friend and who skittered around nervously in her wake. Mary was gratified at having her mother and sister thus distracted and occupied, as it freed up more of her own precious time for reading and reflection.

The only fly in the honey, in her opinion, was Mr Darcy, who asked annoying questions all the time, looked at all the books, strode around the farm as if he owned it, and countermanded several of her orders to the farm manager. The farm-workers' ready obeisance to him made Mary fume even more. She thought that there would have been no such traitorous behaviour from the staff had she been a male. Further annoyance came on the second day, when Mr Broughton popped up so close to dinner as to make not inviting him to stay downright rude. Mary knew that Mr Broughton had timed his arrival to perfection, but anticipated being able to palm him off onto Mr Darcy for the evening, so then at least it would not be a total waste of time. However, dinner had first to be endured. Mary had already had a trying time in the kitchen convincing the staff that the world would not end if dinner was served later, at half past seven, rather than at their usual time of six o'clock, in light of Mr Darcy's preference for town hours. She well remembered past battles with the cook over Mrs Bennet's insistence that they shift their main meal from noon to the evening, due to that lady having gleaned that this was the new done thing in great houses. Mary did not relish the thought of yet another hysterical kitchen drama as she ordered the meal. The very first time Mr Broughton had dined with them, a slight kitchen conflagration had caused the meal on that occasion to be pushed back to about seven-ish, anyway, and since, on subsequent occasions, Mary did not want Mr Broughton to think that they did not always keep such modish hours, she always had a little battle with the kitchen staff. In the end a compromise was reached, with the meal, after all, making its appearance at seven.

Mary had nothing to be ashamed of in the content of the meal: the first course she had chosen was mutton soup accompanied by a dish of asparagus and one of chicken pie, and the second course comprised a haunch of venison, several capons and a whole baked trout surrounded by various vegetables in two or three sauces. Dessert was to be a plate of magnificent apple pastries and a rhubarb pie, decorated with an artistic flourish depicting a tree, and accompanied by Longbourn's famous clotted cream and brandy sauce. Because of her preparations, Mary's good temper at dinner did indeed bode well for the rest of the evening, for Kitty had promised not to reach across the table in their family style but to wait and see if a dish was offered, and her mother seemed rather sanguine after two pre-dinner glasses of sherry. Mary felt almost capable of tolerating Mr Broughton, were it not for his annoying habit of monopolising the conversation and of always repeating what other people said as if the thoughts were his own.

It was in this manner of wanting to appear learned that Mr Broughton introduced the subject of crop rotations, a topic he had recently been told about by one of his parishioners; he now felt it was his duty to present all the facts to the assembled company. In fact, he spoke as if this tried-and-true farming technique was a novel innovation (his careful phrasing making it seem as if some, if not all, of this revolution was due to his own perspicacity) and not as if it were a common practice. His monologue made him impervious to the wry looks being exchanged between Mr and Mrs Darcy, and by the time the first course had been removed, Mary felt she would scream if Mr Broughton made just one more self-important remark.

It was not a very convivial meal, despite Elizabeth Darcy's gallant attempts to jolly things along. Conversation mostly revolved around various topics of interest to country folk — not enough rain, too much frost, on and on, with resolute attempts by Mr Broughton to return to his favourite subjects. It then turned to the health of Meryton's oldest inhabitant; a doughty old dame of whom Elizabeth had fond memories. Mary had just visited the lady only that day and was pleased to inform the company that the said lady, Mrs Finchley, was much better following her recent fever, and that Dr Markham felt that she would rally nicely. However, before anyone could reply to this information, Mr Broughton interjected in an important voice.

"Dr Markham, our esteemed physician, feels that our dear Mrs Finchley is doing much better now. Yes, he feels that a full recovery is most likely."

"Thank you, Mr Broughton," Elizabeth turned to the vicar with a slightly sarcastic smile, "for keeping me up to date with events in my own home town!"

Mary fumed even harder. Wasn't that what she had just said? Why was Elizabeth fawning upon him? And why did Mr Broughton assume such ownership with Meryton? "Our Dr Markham" and "Our Mrs Finchley", indeed! Such effrontery from someone hardly in the country six months! So incensed was she that she did not see the look of high amusement passing between Elizabeth and her husband. She also missed Mr Darcy saying, "Yes, thank you, Broughton", rather in the manner of someone dismissing a servant.

The evening ended after dinner with the two gentlemen joining the ladies as fast as Darcy could manage it. It seemed as if the ladies had only just retired to the salon, when Darcy threw back his glass of brandy in one gulp and hurried Mr Broughton through. He told Elizabeth, *sotto voce*, that five minutes in that bore's company was five minutes of his life gone down the midden, and tea was brought in as quickly as possible. Nobody suggested music or cards. Mary fiddled with her fringe, and Kitty yawned, not too subtly. After another half hour of Mr Broughton lecturing the ladies on embroidery threads, he led the company in evening prayers, if for no other reason than to prolong his visit, as Mary thought. Blessedly, even the longest evening must end, and it was with enormous sighs of relief from all concerned that the vicar finally left.

Mr Darcy left for London a few days after this. He felt he could be of more use by seeking out the errant Mr Bennet, and since he abhorred inaction he felt he may as well ride into town, and might even be able to bring him home; if not, then at least find out what he was up to. Besides, he had recently been told that the vicar's visits were irritatingly unpredictable, but nevertheless frequent, and therefore surely another was due soon. Consequently, he left the ladies of the Bennet household in the capable hands of his wife, whom he believed was chiefly responsible for the changes at Longbourn. Mary was quite glad to see him go, and as soon as Darcy's horse disappeared around a bend in the driveway, lost no time in informing her sister Elizabeth that she was grateful for her help, but that she had things well in hand, thank you very much. Elizabeth replied that she could see that for herself, but Mary was feeling too prickly to hear the praise.

A few days passed, with Elizabeth mostly tending to their mother, and Anne lending a lively air to the household as she playfully teased both Kitty and Mary alike. Mr Broughton called once or twice, to see how the ladies were coping now that they were once more without a man. Mary contrived to always be busy whenever his horse appeared, and he was left to be entertained by the other ladies. One morning, after nearly a week had passed, when spring was trying very hard to get her head up, Mary was in the kitchen conservatory looking over some herbs. A storm the night before had broken a few windows and hail had killed off many plants. Tut-tutting to herself, she was completely absorbed in calculating the cost of some new glass panels, when she was arrested by the sounds of her mother's and sister's voices, coming through from the garden walk outside, where they passed unseen, but not unheard.

Mary was about to step outside to request her mother come to view the damage, when the content of their conversation became apparent. She stopped dead in her tracks, unseen by the others.

"Now, Mama," Elizabeth was saying, "we do not yet know what her answer will be."

"La, how can you say so? Of course she will accept him! Is there any other choice? And it is a good match. She will be comfortable for life!"

"Mama, do not run on so! Although I am sure it is a very good offer, we must wait for Papa…"

"Oh, Lizzie! Do not mention his name! He has abandoned us completely. What else are we to do? Mr Broughton has assured me that we can all stay with them once that… that… cockroach Collins has inherited, and really it seems to be the best solution! Who knows when, or even if, your father will return!"

"But Mama, to have had the nerve to apply to you, rather than to Papa! What is anyone to think? Mary will—"

"Lizzie, Lizzie, Lizzie! Do not torment me any further! He made such a sensible case of it. To be sure it is not quite the thing, but sensible, you know! What else can we do? This marriage will allow us all to live in peace and security. If your father does return, then he will be pleased with the match, I am sure, for he said to me once he did not hold out much hope for a suitable match for her. And what is there for anyone to cavil at, if he asked me, rather than her father? And if your father does not… does not return, then we are not cast off, but will have a home."

"I understand you, Mama, but really! As if you were ever to have been cast off! But I rather wish he had applied to Darcy, as would be correct if Papa were indeed... er... no longer with us, but I cannot help but think that he should have waited—"

"But how long must we wait? Where is your father? For all we know he is dead, dead!" and here Mrs Bennet gave herself over to a good cry, with Elizabeth holding her up as she attempted a swoon.

"Mama, come, come! I am certain Papa shall come home soon. For all we know, Darcy has found him, and they are returning even now! And..."

Whatever Elizabeth was about to say then was lost to Mary, who stood frozen in the hothouse, absolutely aghast, with crumpled marjoram seedlings in her hand and horror on her face. Mr Broughton had applied to her mother! What incredible effrontery... The man knew no modesty. And the arrogance — the utmost, outright arrogance — to presume to ask for her hand in marriage! For that could be the only possible connotation put upon it. Whenever a gentleman was said to have applied to a lady's father, matrimony was the only possible reason, so much so that "applied to her father" had become a cypher for "about to propose marriage". Marriage! To him! To that pompous, egg-headed, know-it-all, swaggering, pompous, jumped-up... 'pompous' came to mind for the third time. Mary was speechless with rage. What had she ever done to make him think, for even a moment, that she would marry him? She was sure she had given no sign. In fact, she was positive she had done the opposite. To think he would come here, certain of his answer... Well! Mary thought of all the times over the past few weeks when he had presumed authority over the household staff. *He has taken advantage of Papa's being absent*, she silently railed. Well, Mary knew that she did not ever want to marry, but if by some small happenstance she was obliged to give up her freedom, he would certainly not be her choice of husband! And to have waited until Mr Darcy had left was all of a piece, Mary was sure. The prosing bore did not want to press his suit with Darcy around. Well, let him come and ask! He would get an earful!

Mary spend the rest of the morning in alternating states of impatience for it to all be over, and dread that Mr Broughton would come and propose. She rehearsed again and again what she would say. Contemptuous phrases such as "Never! I shall never marry you!" warred in her mind with dignified refusals such as "I regret that I cannot marry you, Mr Broughton, as I am sure we should not suit." She could not decide whether to refuse him with gleeful ridicule, scornful derision, or sarcastic truths. Pacing up and down the very garden path from which she had learned of Mr Broughton's intentions, Mary eventually settled upon a mixture of all three: "I regret, Mr Broughton, that I have no wish to marry anyone who supposes himself to be my intellectual superior, who criticises my every deed and who is so patently boring," was what she decided to say. She actually began to look forward to it.

The day wore on, and Mary attempted to keep busy. Kitchen matters occupied her for an hour, and then an altercation between two roosters dictated what was to be served for dinner. Kitty and Anne de Bourgh returned from their jaunt to Meryton, the family partook of a light luncheon of fruit and cheese, and Mary spent the afternoon with a book in her lap and an ear on the carriageway for the sounds of a horse approaching. However, dinner came and went, with the bellicose rooster as the star attraction, and tea was brought and drunk. Mary gradually began to relax, although she knew it would be but a fleeting respite. He was certain to come on the morrow, but by then she would have had more time in which to compose an even more scathing put-down. She looked forward to his visit now, not with dread but with happy anticipation at seeing his face as he was refused.

The next day came with the expected showdown. It was close to luncheon and Mary, now very calm and composed, was sitting at her pianoforte marking off some music, while at the same time keeping an eye on the carriageway. Eventually, she heard Mr Broughton's pony's hoofs on the gravel and observed his arrival. Mary put away her pen and book, and turned towards the door with a haughty expression on her face. However, he did not immediately come to her, although she was sure he had glanced up at her in the window as he approached. Odd. She supposed he had been waylaid by her mother and thus she walked across to the door to listen intently. There was no sound of him. Accordingly, she sat back down at the pianoforte and picked up her pen again. After almost fifteen minutes, he had still not come. Perchance he was still talking to her Mother. She was just beginning to think she should go and find him, to expedite the inevitable, when the door suddenly opened. Mr Broughton was announced, and he swaggered into the room with his usual superior attitude, full of confidence.

"Miss Bennet, I trust I find you well?"

Mary nodded curtly, standing up and then bobbing down in the shallowest possible curtsey. "Mr Broughton," she acknowledged. With exaggerated care, she closed the pages of her music, and turned to him with a slightly bored expression.

"Miss Mary, I am confident you already know the purpose of my visit?"

"I do indeed, Mr Broughton, and let me start off immediately by saying that, whilst I am cognisant of the usual platitudes a lady is expected to mouth in situations such as this, I wish to assure you—"

"Then it is only left to me to ask you to wish me joy…"

"I can never marry you, as you are very far from my ideal of a husband, and…"

"…for Kitty has made me the happiest man alive."

"…and furthermore, I would far rather live in poverty than—"

"And we wait only for June to join ourselves…"

"What?"

"What?"

There was silence as they stared at each other for several moments, and then a look of derisive and triumphant amusement came over Mr Broughton's face, while Mary suffered under the spread of deep red embarrassment across hers. She could not believe it. Mr Broughton had proposed not to her, but to her sister instead. To Kitty. Not to her! What on earth was going on? She was dying of mortification.

"Miss Bennet, I hope you can wish me joy, for Kitty has today made me the happiest man alive. But I interrupted you: you were saying something about somebody being the last something or another?" Unbelievably, Mr Broughton smirked at her.

Damn, he was fast at recovery! "No, pray… Mr Broughton, I wasn't saying… I only wished to…" The more Mary spluttered, the redder her face became. There was no way he had not heard what she said! She could die! She hoped the roof would cave in, a storm lift her up and carry her off, or a crevasse to suddenly open up under her.

"You were about to congratulate me," Mr Broughton held out his hand, and Mary could do nothing but shake it. She tried to avoid his eyes, but could not help herself. When she looked at him, she saw the contempt in his.

"I shall bid you *adieu* then, Miss Bennet, or may I now call you sister?" He left.

Mary sank down into a chair, her head reeling. Mr Broughton had not been interested in her, after all, but in her idiotic sibling. Really! To think he preferred Kitty over her! What was it with these canting, sermonising vicars with passing her over for one of her sisters? First of all, Mr Collins, after having been refused by Elizabeth, had turned outside the family and opted for that simpering Charlotte Lucas, and now Mr Broughton! What was he thinking? But wait… Had she really wanted Mr Collins for herself? No, she had never wanted to marry, she was sure of that. Mr Collins had been but a fleeting possibility, brought on by the growing conviction that life as an old maid in an impoverished household might not be to her taste. But Mr Collins had never looked at her in that way, and she had been piqued. And now it seemed that all her rehearsed refusals of Mr Broughton were not now needed, and had never been needed, in fact!

Mary felt as if she had been dealt a terrible blow. She was both angry and chastened. She did not want to marry, but still, it seemed as if no man wanted her. Maybe she didn't want to marry only because she knew in her heart she could never attract a man? Sour grapes, indeed. She had never felt so confused. Rejected by two different men at two different times, even though she hadn't really wanted their advances; hurt at being deemed unworthy of a marriage proposal, but scorning those who could propose; contemptuous of all men, yet dismally aware she was not capable of attracting one. She felt dizzy and sick, and sought refuge in her bedchamber.

Chapter Nine
The Bennets, Brighton-Bound

Mrs Bennet was euphoric at the thought of having another daughter safely married, and to a man who would see them all through their old age, at that. She wondered briefly if she could have similar success with Mary, but once glance at that daughter's stern countenance, her hair caught up in an ugly cap as she sat at the pianoforte, plodding through yet another concerto, made Mrs Bennet realise Mary would die an old maid, a spinster, a blue-stocking. She sighed. Well, four out of five wasn't too bad! She decided not to give up on Mary entirely, but after a few more minutes of casting around in her mind for a suitable match, she gave up.

No matter, there was a wedding to plan! She mentally clapped her hands together in glee. Now, the dress should be of muslin, maybe that delightful new shade of sky blue, and maybe sprigged over with tiny pink roses. Ah, a June wedding — what felicity in terms of available blossoms for the church! Pink roses for the bouquets, of course, and white to decorate the pews. Kitty's shoes must be ordered and the wedding clothes looked over. She would get Hill to bring the trunk out of storage - she couldn't remember if those Egyptian cotton nightgowns were given to Kitty or to Mary... no matter, Mary would give them up if need be. She had no use for such lovely night attire. And not to forget the pearls bequeathed by her own mother. Five gorgeous strands, each one bought at the birth of each of the five girls. Nothing to sniff at there. Oh, she wondered if the wedding luncheon should have champagne, or was it too early in the day? Not for country folk, of course, but the Darcys and Bingleys might think it a little *de trop*. And there must be an entire side of venison with at least six sauces, and salmon, as well as trout, and the pastries must be ordered in... Should she have each little tartlet decorated with a love heart and an initial? Mrs Bennet did not quite trust cook to be up to scratch with the type of delicacy she had in mind, and so she resolved to send to London for the essential treats.

In this manner Mrs Bennet prattled on; making lists, losing them, starting new ones, suddenly remembering details and forgetting important people on the guest list. Mary was no help; Mrs Bennet was sure she was sulking. And Kitty! Kitty? Oh, how silly she had been: she'd ordered the banns to announce the betrothal of Miss Kitty Bennet and the Reverend Broughton, but it should have been Miss Catherine Bennet, of course! Time to put off that childish nickname... She would be Catherine from now on, as befitted a vicar's wife.

Kitty had herself felt for some considerable time that she didn't care to be Kitty Bennet any longer, as that only reminded her of the days when she and Lydia ran amok around Meryton: Kitty and Lydia, Lydia and Kitty — it even had a musical ring to it. Now she was to be Mrs Catherine Broughton, and Catherine was a satisfyingly dignified name which would lend her gravitas in her new community. Kitty sighed tremulously, and passed a hand across her eyes. She tried hard to follow her mother's scattered thoughts as the wedding was planned, but no one had ever been able to keep check when Mrs Bennet took the bit between her teeth and ran. Therefore, Kitty sat meekly, and listened half-heartedly, and agreed to place settings, fruit platters, the scoop of her wedding-dress neckline, the length of the train and the hymns to be sung. If she had any preferences of her own for what was, after all, to be her special day, she was silent about them.

Mr Broughton now visited on a daily basis, as an affianced husband ought, but his possessive manner towards Kitty and his proprietorial airs around the house were too much for Mary to tolerate. She escaped as often as she could, slipping out through the kitchen entrance or ducking behind doors whenever his irksome presence was heralded. However, there were far too many times when this was impossible and she had to bear, in silence, his knowing looks and sarcastic smirks. That dreadful day when she had thought him about to propose to her, and not to Kitty, was burned into her brain! It lay between them; a barricade of shame for Mary and a weapon of torment for the vicar. It seemed to Mary that Mr Broughton alluded to it as often as once a visit, and took great satisfaction in watching her squirm, as the rest of the family remained oblivious. Once, he had even had the nerve to read aloud to them, one evening after dinner, the subject matter being an excerpt from a classical novel he had found. The passage was an amusing (to others!) description of a misunderstanding between a lady and a soldier in Ancient Greece, when the lady had thought the soldier about to propose and feared for his life lest her father find out. The assembled company laughed long and loud at the climax of the story, when the soldier revealed that the object of his love was, instead, the lady's cousin, who had been unwitting of his intentions. Oh, how Mrs Bennet revelled in the comedy of the situation! And how very much did she appreciate the lady's discomfiture, adding that it was poetic justice, served to one who had been so conceited. And how Mary did seethe and grit her teeth. Mary was suspicious that the Greek fable did not exist — she felt herself rather well-read in that area — and her fruitless search for it only confirmed her belief that it had been made up by the vicar for the express purpose of torturing her. She hoped to be wrong, for it supported her views of Mr Broughton's sly character, and she wondered how Kitty might cope with such subtle cruelty in the future. But then she thought, viciously, that Kitty was too stupid to understand sarcasm.

Kitty herself had not much to say on any occasion that saw Mr Broughton at the house. She was silent at dinners, hardly eating anything and contributing even less to the conversation. When Mrs Bennet asked her querulously one evening if she had not liked the food, Kitty almost cried with vexation.

"I cannot remember if I am allowed to reach across the table, or not! Or if I can only do that when I am married! And the only dish within my reach was the potatoes!" and she burst into tears. It seemed that Mr Broughton had been lecturing Kitty on more refined table manners. In the evenings, Kitty sat with a little prayer book in her hands, almost twisting the spine off, and stammering a little when her affianced husband asked her if she had memorised certain passages yet. It seemed Mr Broughton sought to control what she read.

If not torturing her prayer book, Kitty was getting into a muddle with her embroidery threads, and despairing of finding a suitable pattern to follow. It seemed Mr Broughton liked only ecclesiastical patterns, and thought flowers were frivolous. She was also directed daily into appropriate subject matter for her sketches; quaint rural scenes and still-life studies were approved, new dress designs were not. In fact, so indecisive was Kitty over whether or not Mr Broughton would approve of this pattern or that colour that she eventually froze into inaction completely, thinking that doing nothing was better than doing something wrong. She ceased her drawing, put away her Bible and stowed her embroidery away in a drawer. Instead, she spent many an hour just sitting and staring off into the distance, as if she alone were privy to some unknown land.

It was in this attitude of a rabbit caught in the glare of a game-keeper's flare that Mary found her one morning, sitting on a bench in a pretty bower in the garden, with a sodden handkerchief on her lap.

"Kitty? Kitty? What do you do here all alone and so quiet?" Mary queried.

At that, Kitty appeared to come back to her senses. She gave a little start and turned towards her sister with a stricken look on her face.

"Kitty! What on earth is the matter?" Mary was alarmed, and her voice was uncharacteristically caring as she beheld the look of utter despair upon her sister's face. Mary felt something in her heart crack.

"M-Mary! You gave me a start! It's nothing, nothing! I am just... Mama says it is wedding jitters! Ha, ha! Only three weeks to go!" And on this last syllable, Kitty's voice gave way to uncontrolled sobs. Clutching Mary's arm, Kitty gave herself over to hysterics, alternately sobbing and screeching incoherently.

Mary sat down next to her sister on the bench, patting her somewhat awkwardly on the shoulder; the role of comforter did not come easily to her.

"Kitty. Kitty, don't despair. I am here." Mary spoke with real feeling, as she suddenly realised she knew what the problem was.

"M-Mary! What shall I do?" Kitty almost shrieked, tears streaking down her face and her breath coming in huge gulps. "No, no, it is wrong! Mama said it will pass. I am only—"

"Kitty, hush, hush! I know what is wrong. You do not wish to marry Mr Broughton, do you?" Mary asked her gently.

At those kind words, coming from where she least expected them, Kitty let the dam go.

"God, no! Mary! He is so boring, and prosy, and always telling me I am wrong, I cannot do anything right. He says I am to sell Grandmama's pearls when we are wed; we are to live simply with no carriage. He says that when Papa is dead, he shall put you and Mama in the blacksmith's cottage, because you'll be living on his charity, and I must give up my annuity to him to do with as he sees fit and he talks on and on about children and my duty and his mother will live with us and I am not to see my friends!" Kitty collapsed onto Mary's bosom, sobbing her heart out.

Mary had never known what it was to have someone so bereft and so distraught relying upon her for comfort, and she relished the unfamiliar stirrings of protectiveness surging through her. She patted Kitty's shoulder rather roughly and declared passionately, "You shall not marry him if you do not wish!"

"You see I must! Mama says so! Elizabeth says I can do whatever I like but that is all right for her to declare independence, like the colonials, for she is wealthy and besides Mr Darcy does not—"

"No, Kitty, you do not have to: I shall make sure of it." Mary had a sudden qualm, thinking that Mr Broughton was sure to accuse her of retaliatory interference, but quashed it, assuring herself that nobody listening to Kitty's hysterics could remain untouched.

"B-But Mary, what am I to do?" Kitty raised her head, a little hope beginning to dawn.

"We shall have to tell him you do not wish to marry him," Mary stated calmly.

"Cry off! Good God, I will be branded forever! I cannot do that to the family!"

"Kitty, do you really think that anything you or I do now is going to be any worse than what Lydia did?"

Kitty paused for a moment, thinking. "Lydia's elopement was... was pretty hoydenish, was it not?"

"Hoydenish? That is an understatement. What Lydia did nearly brought the entire family into ruin!" Mary attempted to jolly Kitty along a bit more.

Kitty responded with a little giggle. "It was dreadful! I thought Mama would die of shame!" And then these thoughts depressed her again and she continued, "So, you see, I cannot do that to Mama! She cannot bear another scandal!" Fresh tears ran unchecked down Kitty's blotched face.

"Shush, shush now. It is not really a scandal; ladies do often change their minds. It is not done for a gentleman, of course, but ladies may cry off if they wish! The invitations have not yet been sent out."

Kitty sniffed. "Do you really think I can get out of this? Oh, Mary, I would do anything not to marry that man! I think… I think he is a bully, and I think he is cruel. Oh… not in actions, but in the way he talks, you know?"

Mary did indeed know. "We shall tell him together, if you like," she offered, contemplating with glee the look on his face when he was told he had been rejected.

"Would you? Would you be with me when I do it? Oh Mary, I am sure I can do anything with your help! You always know what to do! But what about Mama?"

"She'll get over it; just like she got over Lydia and— Papa. She is stronger now than she looks and will gain much satisfaction in playing the victim."

"Do you really think so?"

"Yes, I do. Come now."

The two sisters put their heads together and planned the announcement.

****

As luck would have it, Mary and Kitty's brother-in-law, Mr Darcy, returned to Longbourn that very next day following a very protracted and fruitless search around London for his quarry. Their sister Elizabeth had been apprised, of course, of the latest unfolding drama in the Bennet family saga, and waited until she and her husband were alone in their room to inform him of it, with a little trepidation at what his reaction might be. She need not have worried, though, as he merely laughed and said, "Thank God! Kitty finally shows some sense. To think of the years of Christmases and family gatherings ahead of us with that pontificating fool as a member of our family, swaggering around as if his cloth gave him more rights than my birth. I shudder at the very thought of it. We have had a lucky escape."

Elizabeth was a little amazed at her husband's speech — not that she thought he would decry Kitty breaking the engagement, but that his feelings of self-worth had been challenged by the sanctimonious vicar. It would seem that her husband's position in society had been under attack from the rebel priest, who had been making it clear to him that he viewed hereditary wealth as sinful.

"Do you know, that canting clod-hopper actually advocates redistribution of wealth among the masses? Not content with my usual charitable donations, he feels I ought to eschew Pemberley and all its trappings and turn it into a house for unmarried mothers!" Darcy continued.

Elizabeth laughed. "Oh, Fitz! Really! And does he also think we should set up a sanctuary for Welsh mining ponies?"

"Or maybe we should give away our jewels and take up a trade? But to get back to the point, how is Kitty going to tell our friend she does not want him?" Darcy queried.

"She is deathly scared to," Elizabeth admitted, "although Mary stands by her side."

"Do you know, in times such as these, I do believe that it is proper for the lady's father to break the news. I also believe that a proxy can stand in for your father."

"You are right, dear husband," Elizabeth simpered coyly. "Would that we had such a one... But who could we ask?"

"Minx. Then I shall not do it unless you ask nicely."

"Who is Mr Nicely? Another suitor?"

"Vixen! Ask me to do it," Darcy demanded, advancing a little into the room, a smile lighting up his dark eyes.

"Oh, dear husband, I ask you to tell me who we can get to tell Mr Broughton the bad news," and Elizabeth backed off a little, her own eyes dancing with laughter.

"Hoyden! You may do it yourself!" Darcy made a dash for her.

She fled to the other side of the bed, shrieking with mirth.

****

Of course, Darcy did the deed on behalf of Kitty. Mary held her hand as they stood together, facing Mr

Broughton, with Mr Darcy on one side and Elizabeth on the other.

The Vicar, no fool, knew immediately what was going on. "I see there has been a coup," he jeered at them, before Darcy could speak.

Darcy was cool. "Your military cant implies an overthrow of authority. I know of no such authority here except mine own in the absence of Miss Catherine's father."

"Cut to the chase, Darcy. You are about to make apologies on behalf of the lady, I presume?"

"You are correct."

"I see." There followed a long moment, while Mr Broughton glared at the assembled company. And then, "This is your doing!" he spat at Mary.

Darcy would not allow Mary to answer. "On the contrary, Miss Catherine has a mind of her own, and her mind is not inclined towards you. I regret to inform you that she no longer wishes to be affianced to you."

"This is all of a piece! Miss Mary has been poisoning Kitty's mind against me, no doubt as a sop to her mortification at being rejected by me!" Mr Broughton had decided to go out fighting, and to take as many with him as he could.

Mary felt the ground ought to swallow her up right there and then as she saw the startled looks on the others' faces.

Darcy took one quick look at Mary's pale face, instantly garnering the truth of Broughton's accusation, and riposted immediately. "You seek to divert attention from yourself, and lay blame on others. Miss Catherine has decided you and she cannot suit — that is all. I see no evidence of any other reason, and frankly find your allusion to Miss Bennet very offensive."

Mary felt she could have kissed him.

Mr Broughton paused, and then abruptly changed tactics. "Come, come, my dearest Kitty! What is all this?" His voice was all honey and sugar. "If you have misgivings, you should come to me with them. I only ever strive for your happiness." He took a few steps towards Kitty, hand outstretched as if to grasp hers, but Kitty shrank back, and that one small action on her part was enough to convince all present that Kitty was terrified of the man and was not simply indulging in missish qualms.

"Leave her alone!" Mary sprang up between them. "You have intimidated her for the last time."

Mr Broughton turned such a look of hatred upon Mary that she nearly shrank away also, but she stood firm.

"Intimidation? Is that what you call it? When I have only ever sought to guide, educate and protect? To fit her out for life as a vicar's help meet? I find your insinuations quite ridiculous!"

"You mean you seek only to control, brow-beat and enslave!" Mary was white hot with anger.

"Enough!" Darcy stepped in. "This conversation is fruitless. "You had better act the gentleman, Broughton, and accept the *coup de grace* with equanimity." No one missed the stress Darcy put upon the word 'act', and all correctly interpreted the insult as it was meant.

Mr Broughton stepped back, and drew his gloves back and forth between his hands. Mary thought for one moment he was about to slap Darcy across the face and force him to call him out. She wished he would!

"Very well, then. I see the family has turned against me. Well… I take my leave of you all. I hope you do not come to regret this day." Mr Broughton then stalked out of the room in an extremely dignified manner, while Kitty collapsed onto a chair.

If there was one thing about which Mary was wrong, it was her prediction that her mother would weather this new storm as she had the others. At being told the news that Kitty was no longer to marry the vicar, Mrs Bennet fell into such a decline that everyone was seriously alarmed. This time there were no hysterics, no screams or breast-beating, no loud lamentations; instead, she merely said "Oh" and then went to bed. She did not eat and it was a real depression of appetite, rather than a false hunger strike as in the past. Dr Markham was sent for and he looked grave. He had expected to find his patient as he had often times in the past; that is, thoroughly enjoying a good wallow in self-pity. He had anticipated prescribing the usual weak laudanum draughts, and thought to himself, *Here we go again*. However, after examining Mrs Bennet, he shook his head and told the family he was certain she had had a blow to her mind as powerful as if it were to her body. He felt that it was the straw that broke the camel's back. Kitty was prostrate with contrition, sobbing and saying it was all her fault and that she would marry Mr Broughton tomorrow, but her sisters soothed her conscience, saying she was not to be blamed; even Mama would agree that marriage to that bully was not to be borne, and that their mother would get better in due course.

Kitty continued to sniff and gulp, and in order to assuage her guilt she became a regular bedside nurse, bathing her mother's brow with lavender water, smoothing her pillows and coaxing her to eat. In any other circumstances, Mary would have been pleased to see how mature her sister was becoming. A week passed and still Mrs Bennet ailed. Dr Markham was seriously alarmed at her blank expression, her low, flat voice and her lack of appetite. He ordered her to sit in a chair at the window, in the hopes that the early June sunshine would light up her heart. Mrs Bennet wilted.

After two more days, Dr Markham made a decision. A complete change of scene was called for, as every aspect in the house and its surrounds served only to remind Mrs Bennet of her daughter's recalcitrance and her husband's disappearance. Brighton was proposed. Elizabeth and Darcy applauded the idea and immediately took action in seeking out a suitable house to rent for the summer. Darcy, of course, offered to bear the cost, and Mary was eventually talked into accompanying her mother and Kitty to that seaside resort. Mary quailed at the expense, Kitty went into transports of delight, and the servants were ordered to shut up Longbourn.

Eventually, after a few weeks of Mary fretting over books and becoming mollified when Elizabeth pointed out that there were several excellent book stores in Brighton at the Seven Dials (a well-known haunt of academics), and Kitty fretting over shoes and clothes and becoming ecstatic when Elizabeth gave her an allowance for shopping, the arrangements were made. It was only then, when everything was a *fait accompli,* did the family inform Mrs Bennet of her impending holiday.

Mrs Bennet conceded apathetically, and in due course the Bennet entourage was ready for the journey down to Brighton.

Darcy had meticulously planned every stage of the trip, even down to meals and rooms ordered at the posting houses along the way. Trunks were packed and re-packed. Kitty wondered if she should leave room in her trunks for all the new clothes she would buy. Mary's trunk was heavy with books. Mrs Bennet took no interest. Finally, the morning arrived and the cavalcade of carriages — three in all — left. The Bennets travelled in one coach, the Darcys and Anne de Bourgh in the second, as they were returning to Pemberley, and all the staff and baggage in a cart.

Mrs Bennet, still rather pale and inclined to blank moments, leaned back in the coach and listlessly watched the countryside pass by. Kitty sat as one glued to her seat, exclaiming at every view. She dutifully announced every milestone as they passed it, read out the name on every signpost, and went quiet for only a few moments, during which time she appeared to be waiting for something. Then, she suddenly leapt up out of her seat and declared: "This is the furthest I have ever been from home! How wonderful! At last, at last, oh at long last… I am going to Brighton!"

Chapter Ten
Miss Catherine's Couture

Although Albert, the Crown Prince of Wales, was once famously accredited with making the London-Brighton run in just under five hours, the Bennets did not have the advantage of his sporting, high-perch, phaeton carriage, drawn by two sixteen-mile-an-hour horses, nor were they able to squander enormous amounts of money (even if it was Darcy's) on having postilions ride ahead to clear the way. Instead, they took five days to travel the distance from Meryton to Brighton, although it was not a hardship at all. Their accommodations along the way were wonderfully comfortable, the people they met made ample fodder for gossip, and Mary felt her mind expand a little — she also had not ever been so far from home. When they arrived in Brighton, on a beautiful afternoon towards the beginning of July, they found that their lodgings were as good as any they could hope for. Mr Darcy, whilst having decided on behalf of his family not to accompany the Bennets to Brighton, had not stinted on his generosity, and had secured for them a rather grand residence on the Marine Parade, perhaps as a sop to his conscience. Kitty exclaimed in breathless tones over the uninterrupted views of sea and sand from every front room, and Mrs Bennet almost rose up out of her torpor as she beheld the sparkling and happy scene before them, for the beach was dotted with gaily-striped bathing pavilions, merry little boats bobbed up and down on the blue sea, and people thronged in every direction. Mrs Bennet stated she had never seen so many people all together in one place: elderly people being pushed along in bathchairs by attendants, children out walking with their nurses, horses trotting up and down bearing dandies carrying telescopes, and ladies of high fashion promenading coquettishly.

The house was fully staffed, even including a French chef, so there was nothing for anyone to do but enjoy themselves, which each did according to their own tastes. Kitty soon discovered the Stein with its elegant shops and providores, the dressmakers, milliners, lace and ribbon makers, shoe makers, and dear little tea shops. She also discovered a new form of exercise, walking along the Promenade after nine o'clock at night, when all the *ton* were out and about and where one might catch a glimpse of the Prince Regent himself. She declared that sitting around after dinner was not healthy, and that a pleasant stroll or two might aid digestion. Mary thought she was transparent and often refused to join her, for she had her own new pleasures to enjoy. She was ecstatic at the pile of new books beside her bed, borrowed from either Donaldson's or Fisher's libraries, and severely resented any moment not spent in either one of these excellent venues. There did not seem to be enough time in one day to read, for Mary also knew it her duty to force their mother into going out as much as possible. After all, they were supposed to be there for her mother's health.

Luckily each of the libraries had amusement for all of them: Kitty to ogle fashions and giggle over gentlemen, Mrs Bennet to view everyone critically and enumerate those rather tenuously connected to people they actually knew, and Mary to observe human folly in all its forms. The absent Mr Darcy's generosity was also evident by him having bought several tickets for the ladies to various musical soirées, which were weekly events held at both libraries, and also to card parties at the Old Ship, an inn which enjoyed great favour among the upper class. There was also an assembly or two, although sadly, without a male escort, the Bennets did not feel they should go.

It was at one such genteel musical event, where the Bennets were enjoying a champagne supper, when a gentleman suddenly approached them, exclaiming, "Why, Mrs Bennet, and Miss Mary and Miss Kitty! Delighted to renew our acquaintance!"

The ladies turned and beheld none other than Mr Edgar Spencer, accompanied by his father, Edward Spencer. They had not seen either of the gentlemen since that dreadful Yule Ball when the awful scandal had erupted around them. Mary and Kitty had suddenly pink faces, and made their curtseys rather abruptly, but

Mrs Bennet apparently had no such qualms. "Why, Mr Spencer! How lovely to see you." Although not quite her old self, Mrs Bennet was regaining interest in life. "Since we had not seen you for such a long time, we thought you had decamped back to Trinadia."

"Trinidad," corrected the younger Spencer, and then, "You, of course, are already acquainted with my aunt, Mrs Cowper? And my father, Edward Spencer?"

Since Mrs Cowper had momentarily been hidden behind the two gentlemen, she had not at first been observed by Mrs Bennet, whose smile faltered for a moment as a rather rude word popped into her head, but she was all affability as she greeted her old friend, who was just as aghast at the encounter as she. After the usual pleasantries and exclamations of regret at having not seen one another for so long, Edgar Spencer left the three elders to their own conversation and turned to the sisters. He seemed genuinely pleased to meet up with them again and clearly wanted to have some friends around, for he engaged them for half an hour in really lively conversation, while his father looked on and his aunt and Mrs Bennet made a pretence of bonhomie. Kitty did not think it was the same person she had met at the Ball, for he was really quite amusing as he spoke of recent events on the Continent. In fact, he seemed very much more at ease on this occasion than he had before, when he had been all stiff and formal. The little party broke up as the musicians prepared to resume their performance and Mrs Bennet and Mrs Cowper exchanged addresses.

"Oh, my dear Mrs Bennet," gushed Mrs Cowper, "let me give you my card. You will see from it that we are quite comfortably accommodated here in Brighton."

Mrs Bennet took it, saying, "Why, thank you! Well now — Coulter's Row: yes, a very comfortable area indeed. Pray, allow me to give you *my* card."

Mrs Cowper, accepting the proffered card with a supercilious air, blinked hard when she saw the Bennet's vastly superior Marine Parade address, but attempted to regain lost ground when she made promises to catch up, maybe at the Prince's Pavilion, if the Bennets were invited?

Mrs Bennet assured Mrs Cowper that they had their invitation "somewhere", but couldn't say which day they were going. "So many engagements, you know!"

Mrs Cowper then expressed her feelings of sympathy. "Oh, my dear — I know! We are so much in demand! I hardly know if we can make the time for you!"

Each family then returned to their seats for the second half of the concert. Mary was glad that the awful social bit was over and that she could again be "transported by the music", and Mrs Bennet bashed Kitty's ear about Mrs Cowper's condescension, demeanour, and manner of dress. At the end of the evening there was another awkward moment, when both parties had perforce to stand together as they waited for their coaches. Mrs Bennet offered to take the Cowpers up and Mrs Cowper responded with "I was about to offer the same, dear friend!" Eventually, each family waved goodbye with fixed smiles and false friendship on the faces of the elder ladies, and with the younger ones calling out promises to meet up. Mary scowled but looked forward to having more free time if her sister were to be engaged elsewhere.

If Mary thought that her time in Brighton was then to continue as before, she was sadly mistaken. Having friends in town now meant they were obliged to resume the awful rituals of paying calls, meeting for lunch, and shopping excursions. Edgar Cowper was a regular visitor and became Kitty's lap dog. He always carried her parcels for her, or escorted her to tea shops, or generally made himself useful. Mary thought he had lost that peculiar accent he had had when they first met him. She almost approved. Kitty seemed a little ambivalent towards him, and did not pay him very much more attention than she had to any other young man of her acquaintance, although she did exclaim to Mary, one afternoon, that she found him quite amusing, and could not think why she thought he was such a prosing pedant before.

Mary laughed, and said, "Oh Kitty, you do not now think him so boring because you were once affianced to the world's worst bore! Anyone would seem lively compared to the vicar!" Kitty agreed, and the two sisters laughed together in a very conspiratorial way.

The Bennets were soon overrun with friends. On another summer's afternoon, as they were walking along the Marine Parade in the direction of the bathing machines, they were suddenly startled by a loud squealing sound. Out of the blue, two identically dressed young ladies launched themselves upon them, laughing in delight, embracing them tightly and depositing kisses upon their cheeks. In amazement, Mrs Bennet and Mary beheld the Cartwright twins, dancing around energetically, each twin twirling Kitty in turn.

"Betty! Letty!" Kitty was astounded to see them. "You are here! How wonderful! When did you arrive?" Kitty had apparently forgotten she once thought them silly.

"We just arrived! Oh, how marvellous to find you here!" The twins included Mary in the general remark. "Where are you staying? We should get together! Oh, what fun!"

Although it turned out that Betty and Letty Cartwright were not staying at quite so fashionable an address as the Bennets, it did not daunt them as it had Mrs Cowper. In fact, these two young ladies were quite well known around their home town of Meryton as being irrepressibly cheerful and jaunty. Not well-endowed with looks, they nevertheless made good with what they had, being tall with slim figures, and having honey-blonde hair which they wore *au naturel*, clear complexions and straight teeth. They always had the latest fashions, enjoyed regular deliveries of all the modish ladies' journals, and were *au fait* with all the latest rages. In addition, their father was a minor Royal, and had money, both Old and New — a fact which greatly enhanced their attractiveness.

When Lydia had been home, she and Kitty often made fun of them, particularly their names. It seemed that, when the twins were born, their parents had decided to honour each of the twins' grandmothers, who were both deceased. Consequently, one twin had been christened Elizabeth and the other Letitia. It was not certain if Lydia had been the first one to call them "Betty and Letty", but Lydia certainly did have fun promoting their interchangeable qualities. The twins did not help by dressing, acting and speaking alike. It was suspected they often swapped names, also. It became a local joke and one could not help appending their names as one: 'Betty-Letty'. Now, though, Kitty regretted her past cattiness towards them, although she need not have worried. The twins either chose not to remember or had been oblivious to it. Certainly, the young ladies now proposing many fun outings to Kitty had changed since their schooldays, when Lydia had called them the 'Carthorse girls'. They were vivacious and energetic, and Kitty readily agreed to their schemes.

The weather held out marvellously, and there were many picnics and carriage rides, and they often walked down to the newspaper office to intercept the arrival of the latest ladies' journals or news of the war as it arrived from Dieppe. In all of these excursions, Edgar Cowper was an eager participant, and often proposed schemes of his own. He had brought with him his own chaise-and-four, and was always driving the girls out to some place of beauty, or perhaps a ruined castle. It appeared he also shared Kitty's artistic talents, and Mary certainly admired the pencil sketches he made of Brighton life. In Brighton, some of the sterner inhabitants (those who decried the Prince Regent and his set of cronies, and especially those who had not been admitted to his circle of friends) felt that many of the young people of the day emulated the Prince too much in terms of loud behaviour, drinking, gambling and outrageous fashions. This disapproval was not heeded much by the younger set, and was particularly not viewed in much regard by Edgar Spencer, Kitty and the Cartwrights, who seemed to delight in being extra noisy or animated whenever they espied doughty dowagers looking at them disapprovingly. Edward, in particular, turned out to be a very good sort, always ready for a lark and anxious to appear to be "bang up to the mark", as Kitty put it. The four friends became somewhat of a fixture around town, and even led the way in one new fad.

It came about that Edgar, not being able to ever tell the twins apart, had the notion to call them both simply "Cartwright", military style. Betty and Letty were well-pleased with this as it scandalised those who overheard them. Soon the foursome became Bennet, Cartwright, and Spencer — "As if they were a shop!" declaimed Mrs Bennet, indignantly. This amused the young people further, and soon enough others followed suit, with half the young people in Brighton dashing around town calling all their friends by their surnames alone.

Only upon one occasion were they ever called to account, and that was by Mary Bennet. She could see her sister running amok in the old style and decried it. She feared all her good work was being undone and took it upon herself to accost Edgar and upbraid him for leading the young ladies astray. Edgar was both appalled and indignant at Mary's concerns and accusations. He explained things very nicely to Mary, stating that it was all just fun and why should she poke her nose in? Mary was not daunted and asked him what his intentions were by Kitty.

"None other than to have a friend," Edgar replied.

Mary then accused him of duplicity, saying he was so completely different from the young man they had met last Christmas that he was either pretending then, or was pretending now, and which was it? Edgar turned a serious look upon her.

"I am duty bound to eventually return to Trinidad," he explained to her, "and I merely wanted to enjoy life a little before I shackle myself to the plantations and all that dreadful weather!"

"Be that as it may," Mary replied severely, "you may not lead my sister around and encourage her to behave so hoydenishly. She will get a bad name."

Over the next few days Mary did not see a change in his behaviour, but took comfort from the fact that

Kitty did not seem to have lost her heart to him and treated him only as she would a brother.

It seemed there was always something claiming Mary's attention. When not having conniptions over Kitty's activities, Mary was trying to coax their mother into taking more exercise. The doctor had thought that Mrs Bennet would benefit from this, but other than walking down the Promenade every day, a matter of no more than five minutes' exercise, Mrs Bennet avoided exertion at all times, taking a chair whenever possible. Mary had hoped that she could encourage her to walk further along the sea front and get more fresh air.

"But I cannot walk!" exclaimed Mrs Bennet one morning, when she was cornered by Mary about this. "It is so hot, and I am so tired. I cannot sleep, such palpitations! And my legs ache abominably; I feel feverish and then cold and then hot again. If you only knew what I suffer!"

Mary thought this was probably true, as her mother did indeed look tired and ill. A local doctor was consulted, and concurred with the previously often-given advice of their family physician that Mrs Bennet try to take more exercise. Again, Mrs Bennet demurred. Again Mary insisted and the only day she was able to encourage her mother to walk nearly ended in disaster, with Mrs Bennet swooning after only five minutes.

"I cannot breathe in this heat!" she moaned.

Kitty, having assisted in bringing their mother home, was fanning her face and applying cool lavender-water.

"No wonder you are hot, Mama!" she suddenly exclaimed. "Your clothes are so thick - all this brocade and lace! Such long, heavy sleeves, and if you will pardon me, Mama, your undergarments are so heavy!"

"My undergarments?" Mrs Bennet was outraged. "Do you expect me to wear no corsets? Ridiculous child!"

"No, Mama, do not be silly! Of course you must wear corsets, only... only... you have so many layers, and your skirts are so full. If you would but wear some lighter material..."

"Would you suggest I look ridiculous as I parade around in a young girl's costume? With my arms exposed? Stupid girl!"

But Kitty merely talked over her mother, saying, "You do not have to expose your arms, Mama! Of course that is not done by... er, older matrons. Only, do you not think, if you had a gown made from, say, muslin instead of that brocade, you could feel cooler? See..." Kitty swooped down to pick up a sketch book, "Here, in this design of mine, the sleeves are still to the wrist, but of such a light fabric it would be much freer for you. The pattern I have drawn is quite novel, I think, for one can adapt it in such a way as to have long or short sleeves, for younger or older ladies. In addition, you can see that wearing more modern gowns with the higher waistlines means you do not have to wear such constricting corsetry. See?"

Mary, who had been looking on half-sneeringly, was about to scoff at Kitty's designs, as usual, but was arrested by the sense of what she was saying. She was correct: Kitty had designed an elegantly simple gown which could be made up with either muslin or cotton, and high-waisted, as was the fashion. The sleeves either ended at the wrist, with a little frill, or could be made quite short with a little puff. In addition, Kitty had designed each gown in such a way that it could be made up with extra panels which could be embroidered or left plain, to give the gown a more formal look. In other sketches, of which there were plenty, Kitty had drawn up more gowns, some with little flowers, or plain blocks of colour for older ladies, or even light checks, which she declared were "for that picnic-in-the-country look".

Mrs Bennet was gazing admiringly at the patterns. "Kitty! How divine! Look, Mary! Oh, if I could but have new gowns made up like this, why, I would be ever so much cooler! I did hear..." And at this point, she lowered her voice, as if there were people around to be scandalised, "that some ladies of quite high *ton* do, in fact, wear a shorter corset, with only one chemise underneath."

"Well, Mama," concluded Kitty, "if you wish, we can get some new fabrics tomorrow, and make them up. The Cartwrights have their own seamstress, and I am sure we can send to Meryton for her, but in the meantime I am able to sew very well, as long as it is not boring embroidery!"

Mary was actually quite enthusiastic over the plan. She thought she could help out and also expressed amazement at Kitty's industry. "And Mama, once you are properly attired, you can take more exercise, for the heat will not be a problem!"

"La, how you girls do bully your poor Mama!" Mrs Bennet expostulated, but only feebly, for the thought of new gowns was very exciting. "However, I am very happy to dress myself in Kitty's fashions."

"No, Mama," enjoined Kitty. "From now on, I am calling them 'Miss Catherine's Coutures'."

Chapter Eleven
Mister Bennet, Bootlegger

Mr Bennet sat on a plank at the stern of a small boat, his boots tied around his neck and his stockings stuffed into them. His feet were ankle-deep in water, which threatened to swamp the boat, and he was bailing as fast as he could, his arms aching with the strain. Although it was a summer's night in June, it was quite cold. There was dense cloud cover and no moon, no stars to see by, and he could not figure out how the others knew which way to steer. His companions consisted of his new factotum Jack Dobbrey and some other ruffians who seemed to have names such as 'Smelly', 'Smiler' and 'Grunt'. Jack Dobbrey had introduced himself as 'Black Jack', and Mr Bennet as 'The Squire'. Nobody on the boat seemed to be bothered by Mr Bennet's appearance, nor were they overly curious about him. After a few more moments, or hours as it seemed, of bending, scooping water, and heaving it over the side, one of the men called out to Mr Bennet, saying, "All right then, Squire? Keeping nice and dry?"

"Indeed, I am quite all right. And although I cannot feel them, I am sure my feet are also fine. I have heard that bathing one's feet in cold sea water is beneficial for gout," Bertram replied, wryly.

"Right, then. See if you can look a bit livelier and haul them there pots on board."

Mr Bennet observed that Jack and the others had stopped rowing and were now peering over the side of the boat, anxiously scanning the choppy waters. This was not what he had expected smuggling to be. Somehow, he had a vague notion they would be aboard a jaunty and fast sloop, dashing ashore on some rocky beach in France, hoisting bales of silks and kegs of brandy on their shoulders before escaping from the excise men by the skin of their teeth; all a little romantic and daring. In contrast, he was bucketing water out of a sinking rowboat in the company of wanted men.

"But you told me not to stop bailing, lest the boat sink," Mr Bennet objected. "See, the water is still coming in."

All of the men sniggered at this, but Jack quieted them, and then told him, "Ah, that's juss what we tell greenhorns, on their first run. See, this 'ere bung is open a little! It's like whatcha might call an initiation rite. The water comes in at the same rate you bail it out."

Mr Bennet appreciated the joke, even if his chest and arms did not. "I see. Then I am glad to be the object of your amusement. Pray inform me if you want a song, or a jig or two."

Jack grinned at him, and then said, "Well, Squire, mebbe later. Fer now, you can get a-hold of this 'ere rope, and pull up these 'ere barrels."

Mr Bennet turned around and saw that the others were all now intensely staring into the water, scrutinising the waves. Just then, a rope did indeed become momentarily visible, and one of the men quickly took hold of a long gaffer's pole with a hook at the end. Deftly catching hold of the floating rope with the hook, he began pulling on it firmly and hissing for help. As the rope was gradually pulled in towards the boat, Mr Bennet thought it must be hampered in some way and indeed, at the other end of the rope were tied two small kegs. *Ah, brandy*, he thought. *This is more like it.*

Jack began to explain. "Our compatriots over the ditch drop these fer us, and we come n' get 'em when there's no one around. Nice n' safe, y'see. No one 'as ter hang on ter the stuff fer too long."

And ingenious, thought Bertram. Any boat engaged in smuggling would be watched very closely for suspicious activity. A long trip across the Channel and back would be highly suspicious, but in this manner each boat was only making half the trip — a distance that might be covered by honest fishermen. Indeed, stashed at the prow of the boat were several nets and lines to add to the deception. He spied another small rope bobbing on the surface, and finding his own gaffer's hook, found it was not that difficult to snare the floating ropes. He began to pull up contraband along with the other crewmen.

"Never thought I would be engaged in such nefarious activities," puffed Mr Bennet. "I always thought I was a law-abiding citizen."

"Well, it ain't really breakin' the law. This 'ere cargo be bought and paid fer, all right and tight. It's just that it's banned goods, being as what it's French," Jack explained.

"All the same, I really thought I would be on my way to France right now — not breaking the law."

"Needs must when the devil drives," Jack retorted. Sometimes his accent slipped. "And anyways, it's the price of yer passage across the Ditch."

And it was a price paid three times more by Mr Bennet. Each night they went out on their excursions, taking advantage of the dark moon, and each night he thought he was going to France, but when they repeatedly boarded the same small boat, time after time, he felt daunted. He knew they could not sail across the Channel in such a tiny vessel. On the fourth night, however, he was eventually rewarded. At first Mr Bennet thought it was business as usual, as he and Jack were taken aboard the same boat with the same crew as before, but this time, quite puzzlingly, there was genuine fishing activity. Mr Bennet thought he could not stand it any longer. His feet were waterlogged and his clothes never felt dry. Besides, being up all night and trying to sleep during the day was having a deleterious effect upon his constitution. He coughed too much, and he was so weary he actually forgot to think about Longbourn and his family. Upon this night, however, when he was hauling in a net heavy with cod, he thought he saw something odd ahead on the sea. It was a large, black shape, darker than its dark surrounds, and looming upon them ominously. The shape drew nearer and nearer and eventually resolved itself into a much larger vessel than their own. Someone beside him gave off a low whistle, and an unseen crewman across the water whistled back. Jack then spoke in a low voice, in French, and was duly answered.

"Who is it?" whispered Mr Bennet with some excitement.

"Don't whisper; whispers carry further than low voices," Jack instructed.

"Well, who is it?" Mr Bennet complied.

"It is the captain of our luxury boat to France, *mon ami!*"

****

There was no name visible on boat that conveyed them to France and her sails were darkened with black dye. Because it was considerably larger than their previous vessel, it carried considerably more crew, but every person was French and very stand-offish, thought Mr Bennet, as he made several attempts at conversation, only to be ignored with blank looks. He felt very unnerved, for the terrifying mid-air transfer across ropes from one boat to the other was extremely harrowing for a man of Mr Bennet's tender upbringing, and he did not feel capable of very much more physical activity. Therefore, he tried to find a quiet place to sit. He was conscious of being very much in the way as the crew scurried about, doing incomprehensible things with ropes and sails and rudders — perhaps they knew he was just a passenger and could not be bothered to make the acquaintance.

Jack Dobbrey, or Jacques as he was now called, scoffed at this. "But no," he said in a heavy French accent, "it is just that they do not understand a word you say."

"But I am speaking perfectly good French," Mr Bennet objected.

"Your opinion of what constitutes perfectly good French, and what is actually perfectly good French, are two points of view never destined to meet," Jacques laughed.

Mr Bennet blinked at his friend's sudden transformation from rough Londoner to native Frenchman — quite a well-educated Frenchman at that. "What do you mean?"

"*Mon ami*, it is just that your accent is so abominable, but like all Englishmen, you think you are bilingual."

"I see," huffed Mr Bennet. "As for yourself, you seem to be quite— er... flexible with your own accent. Perhaps you could give me a few pointers?"

Jacques shrugged in a very Gallic way and replied, "*D'accord.* We have plenty of time."

This was true. Their boat tacked up and down, up and down, changing direction at a whim of the Captain, or so it seemed to Mr Bennet, and never actually going anywhere. Sometimes the coast hove into view, and sometimes they headed back out to open sea. At all times a man was positioned on deck with a telescope, making cryptic remarks to the Captain, such as, "Madeline be alight, but not Annette. Marie... alight, *ah non*, she has gone out."

Mr Bennet spent the time learning from Jacques how to say three or four phrases in perfect French. Jacques thought that his pupil could manage *'Vraiment?'* and *'Je ne sais pas'*, *'Mais non'* and *'D'accord'* with a passable French accent. Nonetheless, he felt that it was best if Mr Bennet appear taciturn and not attempt any other linguistic feats.

"If you cannot answer with one of these phrases, then you must shrug, look contemptuous, and maybe spit?"

Mr Bennet drew the line at spitting but agreed to be the strong and silent type.

After nearly two days of this extremely frustrating delay, the daylight hours of which were spent fishing and the nights scanning the shore for lights, Mr Bennet finally asked of Jacques what on earth the Captain was doing.

"We are waiting, quite literally, for the coast to be clear. It is a regrettable but necessary delay. You see, certain houses along the shore line are friendly to our trade and light their front windows with lanterns according to set patterns. I have not been able to learn the patterns, for they are very secret, but in essence when certain of the lanterns are on and others off, it is either safe or not safe to land."

It was true. While some lights remained on the entire time, others blinked on and off through the night, which was why they made no progress at all during the day. Eventually, just as Mr Bennet thought he would go mad with frustration and possibly jump overboard, the correct sequence miraculously appeared and the entire ship's crew suddenly broke out into frenzied activity. Before Mr Bennet could say "*Comment votre pére?*", he was once again in a small row boat, rowing to the distant shore with considerably stronger arms than when he first tried it. Jacques accompanied him on the trip, their worldly goods packed into two valises between them.

As they neared the shore, Jacques bade Mr Bennet to make no sound. Silently, they rowed the small boat towards the shingled beach, jumped into the cold water when it was shallow enough and waded ashore, hauling the boat up with them. From out of nowhere a dark figure suddenly appeared, giving Mr Bennet the fright of his life. He almost yelled out in alarm but just in time saw that the man was only there to toss a tattered fishing net, encrusted with barnacles, over the boat they had now dragged half way up the beach. Without a word, they sat down upon a rock to put on their stockings and boots, and then the unknown man led the way up the beach to where there was a small dwelling with a stable attached. The man gestured to the stable and upon entering, they found it to be quite dry but very odorous. Mr Bennet nearly quailed when he thought that this was their accommodation for the night. However, it seemed that their lodgings were not even going to be as luxurious as that, for inside the stable, hidden on the back wall behind an enormous and bad-tempered Percheron, was a little hatchway leading down a rickety ladder into a cellar, which was in fact their board for the night. The cellar housed many bales and barrels, and a straw pallet which was their bed, it seemed. Their silent helper then handed them a small packet each, containing bread and hard cheese. Jacques thanked him quietly, and they then had a brief conversation together.

"We'll stay here tonight," Jacques informed Mr Bennet, after their host had climbed back up the ladder. "We will get going in the morning. Best get some sleep, if you can."

Mr Bennet, looking around himself by the light of a small lantern, observed his surroundings with wry humour. Windowless, crowded, smelling strongly of horse urine and dung, he proclaimed the room "Charming."

Jacques grinned. "*Bijou*, is what they call it!"

Mr Bennet thought back to his relatively comfortable bunk on the boat they had just left and thought that things could not possibly get worse. A rat began to nibble his cheese.

The next morning, Mr Bennet assumed his persona of grumpy and taciturn Frenchman who, apparently, was now an onion and garlic seller, off to the markets with his wares and his brother Jacques. However, before they set off, Jacques demanded that Mr Bennet finally tell him where they were going and what the trip was all about. "I detest being in the dark, you know, and if I am better informed I can serve you better, *non*?"

Mr Bennet had been dodging this question of Jacques' ever since he had met him, still believing that the least number of people who knew what he was doing, the better. At the beginning of his adventures, he had had some vague and chivalrous notion in his head of being heroic, of dashing off to France dramatically, locating the proof of his son's legitimacy and flinging it onto a table in front of his amazed and adoring family. He thought that, in this way, he could redeem himself and win back his family's, and society's, respect. Unfortunately his escapades in London, together with his more recent adventures, told him now that if he wanted to get anywhere at all he had better recruit allies. He had sadly misjudged the political climate in France and his ability to track down the proof he wanted, and he now acknowledged humbly that he needed all the help he could get. Accordingly, the sad little tale of lost love and elopement was told, along with the more recent events at the Yule Ball.

"I see," replied Jacques, when the story came to its end and Mr Bennet stood there, looking a little sheepish. "You say you fell in love with a lady of high standing, you eloped with her, her mother found out and had you dragged back. She shot you, and then bought you off? Hmmm. Are you sure you are not French?"

As Mr Bennet bristled at this, Jacques continued. "I make joke, but I need to actually know the name of this family, if there are any relatives still living and where we might find them, *mon ami*."

"Sadly, my love died in childbirth, although I did not know that until lately, and her mother died quite recently," replied Bertram. "The only relative I know, still living, apart from the son Thomas, is one Armand Picard."

"Armand Picard?" Jacques' voice was sharp.

"Yes, that was the name he gave when he made his dramatic appearance in my home town last Christmas."

"Vraiment?"

"It was quite the opera," Mr Bennet continued. "The people of Meryton and surrounds had, heretofore, thought the school nativity play the height of drama. To continue, the Picards, or Picardys—"

"Picardy?"

"Yes, Picardy. Do not interrupt, my good fellow. Anyway, I think they might have paid people to burn the marriage certificate, but I regret I really do not know what happened. In any case, to learn that I was the father of a son born of this union—"

"You say you married the lady?"

"Yes, did I not say so? You see, I need to find the priest who officiated at the ceremony, else I and my family are ruined. This young man who is my son is, in fact, my true heir, if I can only prove legitimacy. Apparently he was born a few months before I even met my present wife, Mrs Bennet."

"A male heir? So there is property?"

"Yes, indeed. We are not nabobs, you know, but Longbourn does well enough. To continue, the estate is currently entailed to my cousin Mr Collins, who is married now and who will naturally assume ownership when I pass. I cannot see my wife and remaining unmarried daughters turned out of their home!"

"Unmarried daughters?"

"Yes, two are left at home but three are married. Anyway—"

"Your story grows more interesting with every passing moment. You have land and unmarried daughters. Well, well! It seems to me that we ought to find the official marriage certificate, to prove legitimacy of this son of yours, and proceed from there."

"Of course, that is my intention, did I not already say so? In fact, it seems to be my only option. However, there is always the possibility that the Monsignor who officiated at the marriage ceremony might now also be dead, for he was of considerable antiquity when he married us. In any case, I must get to the church where we were married: there must be a record somewhere, even if the original certificate is not to be found."

"Monsieur Bennet, let me have the facts stated clearly. Are you telling me you married into the Picardy family?" Jacques interrupted in a very excited voice.

"Have you not been listening?"

"*Mon dieu*, why did you not say so? This becomes very intriguing, *tu sais*. Armand Picard is quite famous in Paris, although he is now a wanted man, and maybe very difficult to find. But the most important point, *tu sais*, is that you married a noble-born lady."

"Why is that so important?"

"Because, as you married a noble born, the Monsignor who officiated at your marriage may have sent notification to the relevant records office, as well as keeping a copy in the church."

"That's marvellous!" Mr Bennet exclaimed, when the full import of this statement made itself known to his tired mind. "So there *may,* in fact, still be an official record, even if the actual certificate is gone! We must go to the Records office and search for it!"

"*Mon ami*, do you not remember that France is now at war with England once again? Paris is overrun with the military, the French aristocracy is being killed off on a daily basis, and English families are being hunted down and imprisoned as spies! And there is no guarantee at all that the Monsignor sent notification to the Records Office! To go off hunting for what may or may not exist —why, this is so dangerous it is lunacy!" Jacques suddenly wanted nothing to do with the plan.

"But it's my only hope!" groaned Mr Bennet. "My family will be ruined — is probably already ruined — if I do not prove legitimacy of my son! I have the receipt for the Monsignor's fee, but it is not helpful; it merely verifies that I paid the sum of five francs to the Monsignor, without specifying what for. No, I need the Certificate of Marriage also! Or at least I need a copy of the records. Without it, I cannot prove my story! The entire countryside will forever brand me a libertine who fathered a child and abandoned him. Oh, good God, this is worse than that thing with Lydia! It cannot be smoothed over and there isn't enough money in the world to buy off Armand Picard, for he promised to make me pay!"

"But to enter the capital itself! No, no and no! I cannot do it, and I will not let you do it, either!"

"Then I must revert to my earlier plan." Mr Bennet seemed deflated. "I must find this marriage certificate alone. Perhaps Picard has returned here to France, he might know…"

"You are clutching at straws, *mon ami*. Did you not hear me say that Picard is a wanted man? Even if he has been so foolish as to return home, he will be extremely difficult to find! No, to be certain he is hiding out in England still."

"But I must try! He might have some family knowledge of the certificate's whereabouts! And why is he wanted?"

"Well, Monsieur Bennet, your friend Picard is an English sympathiser, and has been rather active in… um… certain anti-French pursuits."

"Really?" Mr Bennet replied, wryly. "A Frenchman spying for the enemy? How unusual!"

"Do not be so deprecating, my friend. There are many Frenchmen who are loyal to France but who mourn to see it laid waste by that Corsican who proclaims himself Emperor of All!" Jacques looked around guiltily, and lowered his voice. "As I said before, Monsieur Picard may not even be in France, not if he has any sense. I did hear he had married and was—"

"Then my only recourse is to find my marriage certificate by myself," Mr Bennet stubbornly declared, returning to his original point.

After a moment, Jacques made a decision. "Very well. I know where to go. I will take you there. But you must not be merely taciturn on this trip — you must be dumb. Yes, you are dumb from battle-weariness. You cannot speak, and I am your caring brother. After two days only in Paris, we will leave again. Do you agree?"

Mr Bennet nodded.

"And also, if at any time during that two-day period I find it too dangerous, we will leave. Agree?"

Again Mr Bennet nodded.

"*Tres bien*. Then we go now, and sell our onions!"

****

Paris in 1815 was chaotic. Nobody had expected Napoleon to return, but return he did. The city was full of confusion: a chaotic cacophony of exultation from Napoleon's supporters, and mass panic by the Royalists. Battalion after battalion of French soldiers descended upon the city, clashing daily with the officials from every nation, comprising the Coalition forces, including Austria, Great Britain, Prussia and Russia, all of which had been jubilant at Napoleon's defeat and exile. There were a thousand babbling voices at every turn; a thousand hysterical refugees crowding into every boat, and it seemed, a thousand conflicting stories regarding Napoleon's armies, who were either ravening hordes from hell or angelic liberators, depending upon one's point of view.

Into this mix of mayhem and chaos Mr Bennet and Jacques D'Aubrey catapulted themselves. Paris was bedlam as English travellers fled in dismay at Napoleon's return. *It had been rather precipitous of them all anyway*, thought Mr Bennet, *to return to Paris so soon after Napoleon's defeat.* But English people had always had a love-hate relationship with France and many English people wanted to see the remnants of the revolution for themselves. Indeed, many were there merely to pick over the remains of noble French houses, as gold, paintings and even aristocracies went up for auction. Now that Napoleon had returned from exile, the English were fleeing as fast as they could and making their way *en masse* to the ports, brandishing money as their protector. Many French also thought it prudent to escape; those who had been supporters of the Monarchy, and those ultra-royalists who now suddenly found themselves in grave danger as Napoleon swept in once again.

Being an Englishman in Paris was therefore fraught with danger and Mr Bennet complied with Jacques' instructions not to open his mouth. In addition, any and all able-bodied men were being press-ganged to swell the ranks of Napoleon's armies, as Napoleon did not want to repeat the mistake of under-estimating the Coalition. Although Bertram did not think he was soldier material, being neither young nor fit, he was still petrified of the recruiting gangs roaming the streets and alleyways every night. There were also spies everywhere: Prussian spies, Russian spies, British spies, all suspicious of everyone and everything. Paris was thus a great place for excitement, but certainly not safe for anyone.

"The only good thing," Jacques explained to Mr Bennet, as they secured lodgings for themselves in a modest part of the city, "is that there are so many factions around, all with secrets and hidden agendas, and the city is so crowded, that we shall probably blend in quite well."

Mr Bennet shrugged but remained silent, mindful that anybody could betray them. He was beginning to have a very healthy respect for his factotum, and also to suspect that he was more than just an itinerant jack-of-all-trades. He seemed to know more than he should. His French was faultless, as was his English: he had no contrary accent in whichever language he spoke; a fact that led Mr Bennet to wonder which nationality he actually was.

"There is, however, a great complication," Jacques continued. "For a brief period, maybe for two years or so, it was law that marriages could take place only in the canton of either party, but after that period the law was revoked and marriages could be performed in any local town again, as it was when you married your lady, I think. Certificates were therefore sometimes issued in the canton, and then sent to be held in Paris, or sometimes the opposite with certificates originating in Paris and then sent to the local canton, but no one now seems to have a consensus on where records should be kept. Certainly, back then, there were no clear guidelines as to whether or not notification was to have been sent to Paris. The problem is, if notification was not sent, then you need the certificate. And if the certificate still exists, was it issued in the canton or in the town where you were married? Can you remember which it was?"

"Of course not," Mr Bennet replied, worriedly. "I hardly paid attention to that detail. I was excited, there was a piece of paper…"

"Then, can you remember the name of the town where you were married?"

"I remember it well: it was St. Vincent-sur-la-Croix," replied Mr Bennet.

Jacques shook his head ruefully. "*Merde*! We cannot travel there ourselves, for this region is now a major encampment and training centre for the new French army! It could have been anywhere else!"

"Then we must go to the Records Office and find out, at least, if there was a Notation of Marriage."

"*Non*. We shall not be going anywhere near any official buildings, I can tell you!"

"We are talking in circles," Mr Bennet interjected. "From memory, St. Vincent-sur-la-Croix is only about twelve miles from here. Surely we could hire some horses and go there and back in one day?"

"*Mon ami*, if we rode anywhere near this place our horses would be commandeered, as well as our persons! No, we must find some other way."

Jacques paused to consider their options for a short while, and then continued. "Very well. It would seem then that I must seek out a certain someone I used to know. Whether he is still around, or still alive, I do not know. But if he is and I can persuade him…"

"Persuade him of what? Persuade him to help? How do you know this person can be trusted?" Mr Bennet objected.

"Oh, he can be trusted, you know. He owes me... much."

Mr Bennet sighed. "Why am I not surprised?"

It was thus decided that Mr Bennet would remain in the inn, whilst Jacques made enquiries as to the whereabouts of his friend. Mr Bennet was not averse to this, as his enforced employment as a bootlegger had left him dreadfully tired. But before he could indulge in a day of simple rest, he had to first listen to many instructions from Jacques as to how to behave while he was gone.

"Do not talk. For the love of God, do not talk!" Jacques begged him. "If I am gone more than a day... ah, what to do? The food here in this inn is execrable, you will have the stomach gripes, most assuredly... Well then, we must take a small risk. If you must leave the inn to buy food, then do so only in broad daylight. Point at what you want, do not attempt to speak!"

Eventually, after many more such warnings and instructions, Jacques felt that Mr Bennet might not come to harm if he were left alone, even if overnight, so departed on his mission. Mr Bennet was glad of the respite, for his friend was very wearying. He looked forward to sleeping through the morning. However, once Jacques had departed, Mr Bennet found he could not go back to bed. The sun was high and bright, there were a myriad clamouring sounds coming from the street below his bedroom window, and intoxicating smells emanating from what looked like a *boulangerie* across the road. He sat at the window for a while, his weariness rapidly disappearing, simply absorbing all the sights and sounds. It was all so exciting, so alive and so very different from the sedate Paris he had visited many years before. Maybe he could take just a little walk without coming to any harm? Maybe if he went out for only fifteen minutes it would be safe? And surely if he only made left-hand turns during his explorations, he would inevitably come around in a full circle, and not get lost?

Accordingly, it was with trembling excitement that Mr Bennet ventured forth from the inn just before midday, when Jacques had been gone for two hours or so. He found the streets of Paris to be swarming with far more people then he had suspected from his safe vantage point back at the inn: far more than he had ever seen in one place in his life, including London. There were soldiers everywhere, some practising pack drills on any available square of land; people in coaches pulled by galloping horses careening down the street; street vendors calling out their wares in screeching voices; children playing war games with sticks and incredible dramatics; and the inevitable camp followers wandering up and down looking for a protector. Mr

Bennet thought that he would have many a tale to tell, should he ever manage to get home.

Making sure to turn only left, Mr Bennet wandered around the narrow, cobbled laneways, thoroughly absorbed in what he was seeing. To think that Napoleon might be only a few streets away from where he now stood! It was incredible how many adventures he had had since leaving Longbourn! With a little catch in his throat as he thought of home and family, he wondered what they were all doing, whether he had been wrong not to have written to them from London, letting them know he was all right. He only wanted to spare them anguish, he reasoned: that was why he did not write. He thought if he were only able to simply return home, triumphant, then they could continue as before. He sighed. The only possible way out of his awful predicament was to prove the legitimacy of his son.

As he ambled along the crowded laneways, his thoughts also turned to a letter which had been given to him — oh, so many years ago! — by the Comptesse the morning after he and his love had been hauled before her. He had been waiting in a noisome inn for his passage home, as commanded by the Comptesse, and enforced by heavy-set thugs, when the letter had been handed to him: a letter warning him in blunt terms of the consequences should he ever try to make contact.

With his thoughts churning over and over again, mired in the past, getting nowhere, it was inevitable that his mind should rebel and turn to more recent events. It was peculiar, as Jacques had pointed out, that Armand Picard had turned up at the Ball at all, but he was probably clutching at straws, and Mr Bennet agreed. The family was probably impoverished after having aligned itself to the wrong side during the Napoleonic Campaigns, and had probably seized upon Mr Bennet's past affiliation with one of their daughters as a possible avenue for monetary salvation. He supposed that Armand's intentions were to establish the claims of the boy, Thomas. No doubt he thought that his family could have a nice little nest-egg in the future, with Thomas being the rightful heir to Longbourn. Mr Bennet then quailed at the very thought of acknowledging the boy, trying not to imagine what Mrs Bennet would say to all this. A step-son! She would probably expire with conflicting emotions, even though the advent of Thomas meant that Mr Bennet's cousin, Mr Collins, would be disinherited and the family's future at Longbourn was ensured. She would, of course, be outraged that her husband had kept a prior marriage secret!

Mr Bennet's perusings and perambulations took him further afield than he had first intended. Rain clouds scudded across the now-lowering skies, and the sun disappeared behind them. Looking up with sudden apprehension, he was nevertheless unable to avoid a street urchin who bumped into him, whilst slipping a surreptitious hand into Mr Bennet's pocket.

"Stop that! What are you doing?" Mr Bennet yelled in surprise, forgetting he was supposed to be a taciturn French onion seller. As luck would have it, his outburst coincided with one of those inexplicable moments in a day when, perversely, all noise ceases for a few brief seconds, and his very loud and very English voice rang out across the square he was traversing. Several soldiers turned abruptly, and glared at him.

"*Merde*," Mr Bennet then said loudly, trying to retrieve the situation. "And... *Mon dieu*! Erm... *comment-allez vous*?"

It was all to no avail, however. Suddenly finding himself surrounded by up to half a dozen soldiers, all with bayonets pointed murderously at him, Mr Bennet had no choice but to surrender and go with them, as they bade him. The crowd jeered "Spy! Traitor!" and "To the guillotine!" and Mr Bennet was marched off.

Chapter Twelve
Bertram Bennet Behind Bars

Mr Bertram Bennet, lately of Longbourn, lay in his prison cell and waited for death. Although he was not chained, as were some of the other more unfortunate inmates, he was still incarcerated in a putrid place full of dank straw, rats, cockroaches and indeterminate forms lying on the floor, some of which were bodies, alive and dead. It was dark and cold, and he had already fended off one suggestion from a fellow detainee that he give up his coat in exchange for a bowl of slop. Mr Bennet declined. What was the point in eating? A day and a night had already passed and now it was probably well into the next morning, judging by the sunlight slanting across the filthy floor. The tiny window was too high up to see through, but Mr Bennet did not anticipate escape in that direction.

His one piece of active endeavour, since he had been incarcerated, had been to attempt to jump up and see out of the window in the hopes of finding out exactly where he was. Accordingly, he had backed away from the window as far as possible in the cell and had taken a few running leaps at it, trying to grab hold of the bars to swing himself up. After three attempts he managed to catch the bars, but unfortunately his momentum kept his body moving forwards and his knees collided painfully with the brick wall. Consequently, he now had scraped knees and wondered if an infection might start up in the broken skin. He welcomed it, thinking if he were delirious with fever he might not know or care about the guillotine's bite. And he had not managed even a glimpse of the outside. His brief flurry of activity had inspired interest in some of his less comatose cellmates, but now everybody had sunk back down again into heaps of despair upon the filthy floor.

After another interminable day, followed by a sleepless night, Mr Bennet was ready for death to appear and cart him off in a tumbril. He could sink no lower, he thought. During the course of his progress from Longbourn, he had slept in inns more suited for riff-raff than a country squire, in a swaying bunk bed aboard a smuggler's boat, in a cellar hidden beneath a stable housing a horse with a bladder problem, and now he was in a cell, sitting on straw, using a bucket for necessities and eating slop. His descent was complete.

There had not been much talk at first, there being only two topics of conversation: the food, and when one's execution time came. One of the other prisoners gave the opinion that the guillotine was out of favour, and it might be the hangman's noose or the firing squad that would do the deed for Mr Bennet, depending upon whether their captors decided if he were an English spy or a French Royalist. *A moot point*, thought Mr Bennet — either would put him out of his misery soon enough. His one major regret was that his family would never know of the method of his death. They would not know how he had tried to save the family, and how he had failed so miserably. He allowed himself a few moments of self-pity.

One of the prisoners kept up a running commentary under his breath about Field Marshall Blucher and the Battle of Leipzig.

"Those Prussians showed us all how to fight!" he repeated over and over, switching between two or three languages, and when Mr Bennet had made his futile assault upon the wall, he had roused himself enough to chant *"Ran wie Blücher!"* Mr Bennet thought he was mad, as he often made motions with his hands as if advancing with a weapon, stabbing at other prisoners as he saw fit.

Another prisoner took it upon himself to sing a very crude song about Englishmen, but Mr Bennet's French was not good enough for him to understand very much more than that it seemed to be about a young Englishman from some place rhyming with a part of the male body, who could not perform adequately with a young lady from Nancy. He surmised it was not complimentary about the English race, however, and retaliated with a popular song denigrating the "Little Corsican Emperor", which he had learned during his time as a smuggler. Surprisingly to him, this song was apparently very much appreciated by the other prisoners. He suddenly seemed to have made friends.

Despite the general air of despair and lethargy some of the inmates were more talkative than others. They were also of mixed heritage, being mostly French with a smattering of Spanish, Italian, Russian and German. There was no common *lingua franca* but those inclined to communicate seemed to know enough French to get by. A Frenchman named Gus had collected the bones of a small animal and was casting them around from one hand to another in a predetermined manner, as if playing a game. Mr Bennet observed him for a while and then suggested a game of knuckles. After some miming, the Frenchman agreed, exclaiming "Ah! *Astragaloi*!" and a small stone was found to serve as the jack. After a few preliminary games during which rules were established, they began to play with gusto, making wild bets with the onlookers egging them on.

It was a superb distraction and in this manner the games became rowdier and rowdier and the bets wilder and wilder. Mr Bennet won — and lost again — an entire French chateau, a vineyard and the complete contents of Versailles, whilst he himself put up the Palais Royale in Brighton, the Crown of Edward the Confessor and Alexander the Great's horse, Bucephalus. The afternoon passed swiftly as the game evolved into story-telling about each item of collateral, in particular how it had been 'attained'; Mr Bennet's improbable story of how his family had been keeping

Edward the Confessor's crown in hiding, ever since the dark days of the Cromwellian years, and of how no one had thus far suspected that the one in Westminster Abbey was a replica, was greeted with much appreciation, given the present political climate. When their evening bowls of gruel were brought in, the gaoler was a little startled to see almost merriment in the cell. Most of the other prisoners had got into the spirit of the pretence and one of them cavorted around pretending to serve the 'Royalty' with their 'repasts', making exaggerated bows and addressing Mr Bennet as 'Your Royal Highness'. Another picked up the water pitcher and expounded about the vintage wine he was about to serve, whilst another wore a bowl upon his head and demanded to be called 'Emperor'. It was a little oasis of sunshine in their dark, despairing lives.

The knucklebones were popular after that and caused a few fights amongst those who did not want to wait their turn. Mr Bennet was nowhere near up to the boxing weight of many of the protagonists, and neither was Gus, so they lost possession of their playing bones the very next day, uncontested. After that, the bones changed hands frequently through brief but intense tussles for possession, or natural attrition; a few deaths through natural or unnatural causes, or other owners being dragged off presumably to meet Madame Guillotine. It was peculiar, thought Bertram, how his world had narrowed down to this; the cell was now everything — his cellmates, his family, and the progress of the knucklebones his greatest interest.

Mr Bennet and Gus maintained a comradeship of sorts over the next week, for between them they had enough French and English to communicate. In fact, Gus had a French mother but an English father. It seemed he had been an honest shopkeeper until Napoleon rampaged across Europe. His dual nationality caused suspicion and he was arrested 'just in case'. His was a sad tale, for somewhere in Paris there was a family not knowing where he was, as with Mr Bennet himself. Gus had a wife, two sons and one daughter-in-law, and had been about to be blessed with his first grandchild when he was taken in for questioning. He was depressed that he would never see the child but seemed to be worried more for his family and whether they had escaped suspicion.

Mr Bennet also told his own tale; one which caused interest but no real surprise. Many of the other inmates also opened up and Mr Bennet was intrigued at how ordinary most of them were, for apart from a few members of the minor aristocracy, and a smattering of spies and rabble-rousers, they were, for the most part, honest folk with honest jobs: farmers, ostlers, bakers and the like who had fallen foul of Napoleon's megalomania and hatred of Royalists. These good folk were incarcerated, whilst cut-throats, murderers and deserters roamed the streets of Paris at will.

One day, just as Mr Bennet was enjoying a particularly good session of wallowing in self-pity, there was a slight commotion as another prisoner was brought in. He did not take much notice: their cell was already overflowing with humans and their effluent. One more tortured soul could not make any difference. There was some general shuffling as the new inmate was flung into the crowd, and then things settled down again, although the newcomer caused quite a few disgruntled comments as he shifted himself around the cell. *Probably looking for a good spot away from the dripping walls*, thought Mr Bennet. However, after a few minutes or so, he became aware that he was being intently scrutinised by the newcomer. He was used to it, for he did not exactly blend in. Any person with half a brain could see that his hands were soft under the blisters, his nails were still half manicured and he talked with a certain accent not in keeping with his persona. He prepared himself for the usual nosy questioning but did not fear it. Usually the newest addition to the family left him alone after a few moments of scrutiny. This time, however, he was not going to get away so easily.

"*Mon dieu!*" the newcomer exclaimed. "*C'est encroyable! Jamais, jamais jamais!*"

Mr Bennet did not look up but said wearily, "*Jamais* what?"

"*Monsieur Bennet*? Bertram Bennet?" the newcomer insisted.

Mr Bennet looked up and gasped. *What in the world...?* "Mr Picard? Armand Picard?" he exclaimed incredulously. He could hardly believe that Picard was actually standing right in front of him, when he had assumed, often bitterly, that the cause of all his problems was still safely in England.

"*Mais oui, c'est moi!*" The Frenchman was enthusiastic, for it was indeed the very same Picard who had invaded the Meryton Ball so very long ago and who had turned Mr Bennet's world upside down.

"Well, here is one for the record books," Mr Bennet proclaimed, sarcastically. "That I should meet the very cause of my present difficulties. An honour, sir," and he rose up, making an exaggerated bow.

"But this is wonderful! That I should meet you here! What... how...?" Picard was almost speechless.

"Well might you ask," Mr Bennet rejoined bitterly. "Were it not for you I would even now be comfortable in my own library, but instead I am chasing a will-o-the-wisp all over France in order to clear my besmirched name in order to save my family from ruin!" He was feeling both amazed and angry. That this scoundrel should be here, right now! He did not care to know why his nemesis had been arrested; he thought only that it would be marvellous were he taken out immediately to have his head chopped off, and then he should be drawn and quartered; or maybe drawn first and then publicly stoned.

"*Monsieur Bennet!* Do not say you are here to find me? You should not have come! I know that what I did was reprehensible, and I do regret certain actions on my part, but you will admit that I had the right! I wished only to see my nephew acknowledged and my sister Amelia avenged. For that was my prime concern, *tu sais*. How could I know you would follow me to France? Ah, that you had not, at such a time!" he burbled on in this way for some time, whilst Mr Bennet reflected that he was still as loquacious as usual.

Finally, Mr Bennet put a stop to Picard's oration. "I marvel at your effrontery in addressing me at all, sir. I also marvel at your arrogance in supposing I had come here to find you, of all people. You walked into my life and delivered the most damning news, which you had no doubt hoped would ruin my reputation and my family, and then you walked out again as if you had been delivering a laundry list. Well, the joke, as they say, is on you, for the boy is not my bastard, but truly legitimate! That is why I came to this God-forsaken place: to clear my name!" Mr Bennet clenched his fists and watched with some satisfaction as Picard flinched backwards.

"I... I know! I knew all along that Thomas was legitimate! I... I am so sorry! I only..."

Mr Bennet stared at the contrite Frenchman. "You knew...?" he half-whispered, passing a grubby hand across his eyes as if he had a sudden pain.

"Yes! I... I wanted to make you suffer! As my sainted sister suffered! I thought to make you squirm a little, and then to... I don't know what I wanted! I thought Thomas would not be accepted by you..."

Mr Bennet laughed, in a mournful way. "You are a bigger fool than I supposed." He was suddenly extremely tired and wanted nothing more than to slump back down onto his particular patch of slimy floor. "You thought perhaps to ruin me? Or maybe a little extortion was your plan? Well, you stupid man, you will get nothing from me or my family! You have actually done us all a great favour, you know."

Armand Picard, who had been alternately sobbing and wringing his hands, looked at Bertram, uncomprehendingly. "I have?"

"Yes. You see, thanks to you and your dramatics, I now know that I have an heir to my estates, and that the odious entail which has loomed over my family for the past quarter of a century has been nullified. As soon as I have proof of the marriage, I can overturn the entail. What do you say to that, you pathetic creature?"

By now a small audience gathered around them, and Mr Bennet thought wryly that he seemed destined to star in double acts with this ridiculous Frenchman, and to perform farces for the edification of mankind.

"You wish to acquire official proof of the marriage?" Picard demanded incredulously.

"Yes. I have only the marriage receipt, and my purpose in coming to France is to track down the actual certificate. You really did me a favour, you know! I do not suppose that was your intent, however," Mr Bennet riposted. "For no doubt you sought to advertise that I had been a libertine and had left a young innocent woman with child and then abandoned her. When I think of that, I…" And here Mr Bennet clenched his fists again.

Monsieur Picard continued his hand-wringing. "Ah, *non*! I never wanted to besmirch your name, only to make your son's existence known! I thought—"

"You evidently did not think!" Mr Bennet exploded. "You have put me and my family through hell. My wife is ill because of you, and I will probably be executed as an English spy!" At this point Mr Bennet really did advance upon Picard, the desire to punch the Frenchman's face evident on his own.

"But wait! There is no need. If it is the certificate you seek, why, I have — or had — your marriage certificate in my own possession! I have had it for quite some time!"

If events thus far had been farce-like, they now descended into Greek tragedy, as Mr Bennet allowed Picard to explain himself more fully. It seemed that Amelia's mother, the Comptesse de la Picardy, had come into possession of the marriage certificate following Amelia's death, although it had been hidden inside the pages of Amelia's diary. The Comptesse had locked this diary away without reading it and had thus not known of the certificate's existence. Why she had neither read nor destroyed the diary was easy to understand. To the Comptesse the diary represented a painful reminder of her lost daughter and she could not bear even to glance at it, but she also balked at destroying it. The Picardys, whilst being a noble family, had risen to their exalted heights through years of intrigue, and the Comptesse had always been loath to burn documents which might be useful in the future. Sometimes even the most insignificant slips of paper could prove to be of great importance.

Armand Picard further explained that the elderly Monsignor who had performed the marriage rites had mysteriously disappeared shortly after that day when Bertram and Amelia had confronted her mother. Following Bertram's enforced eviction, Amelia herself was bullied by her mother into lying about her alliance with "that pathetic English worm."

What Armand did not know was that Amelia had been petrified that her mother might have Bertram murdered; for underneath her silly exterior there lay a tender heart, albeit an avaricious one. The promise of a grand title for herself beckoned. Amelia had agreed to marry the Duke picked out for her by her Mama under the proviso that her family promise never to harm Bertram. To make him doubly safe, she also lied about his true name. Amelia had felt a little sorry for her erstwhile husband. *D'Accord*, he was no *Duc*, and once her mother dangled the prospect of marriage to one of the highest nobility before her, Amelia was just as anxious as her mother to make her brief marriage go away. *Assurément*, she felt a few qualms at what she had done, but deluded herself into thinking she could make amends by preventing her family from tracking him down in the future, should they ever decide that letting him live was too dangerous. No, she had decided: she would keep Bertram's identity secret, for she knew very well that her mother's promises were not to be trusted, and that it would take only one member of her large and influential family to decide that Bertram posed a threat to their name for the decision to be taken that he should be made to disappear. At this thought Amelia had dithered, sudden scenes of violence gathering in her head. He did not deserve that! Certainly a false name would protect him while she held onto the marriage certificate just in case, for who knows what lay ahead? There might come a time when an English connection would be useful. She decided to marry the Duke, but keep the proof of her marriage to Bertram as future insurance.

Armand Picard seemed to need to disgorge the entire sordid story of his sister's mendacity and downfall. He went on to explain that the Duc de la Roche, chosen for Amelia by her mother, was ugly, fat and well past middle age and certainly not Amelia's idea of a husband, but the Picards saw him as an easy mark for monetary gain and a powerful ally. All should have been well. The tragedy began to unfold when Amelia, not having ever been the most assiduous of record-keepers in certain aspects, realised she was expecting Mr Bennet's child — in fact, she had been nearly two months or more into the pregnancy before her marriage to de la Roche could take place. Naturally, her mother La Comptesse was incensed but very quickly came up with a plan to help pass off the child as her future husband's. The wedding was expedited, and subsequently, in order to keep up the pretence, Amelia was to announce 'the happily anticipated event' shortly after.

The plan was not without pitfalls, for it had been very difficult for Amelia to hide her nausea before the wedding, and she worried constantly that when the time came it would be difficult to convince everyone that she was delivering a very premature baby. As the pregnancy progressed, Amelia joked often about how large the baby was, lest her husband be suspicious. Others also marvelled at its size, and Amelia thought she might get away with it, were it not for the observant Duke himself, who began making cryptic remarks about cuckoos in nests. Amelia quailed at the thought of his finding out, and consulted the calendar often. As fate would have it, the baby boy was born nearly two weeks past the secret expected date; with each additional day Amelia breathed a little more easily, but was not so naïve as to suppose that the reprieve would last. Alas, when the child eventually made his inevitable arrival, he caused the death of his mother.

All of this, Armand explained, became known to him only when La Comptesse died and Armand came into possession of his mother's and sister's papers. It certainly explained a lot, Armand confided, as he watched Mr Bennet's face carefully for signs of renewed hostility. He had always known that de la Roche had been suspicious because of certain snippets of conversations he had overheard between Amelia and her mother. After Amelia's death, the Duke had questioned the servants and had spies sent forth. The truth never came out, for the Picards arranged an 'accident'. The Duke, who was apparently so distraught at his wife's death, rode his horse over a cliff.

Mr Bennet, at first aghast at the tale containing enough drama for a penny-dreadful opera, began to feel sorry for Amelia. He had never, in truth, felt any real animosity towards her, even though he had never forgotten the look on her face as her mother took her away, and how she had never looked back at him on that dreadful night of the Picard's Ball, while he lay bleeding on the beautiful Italian tiles and while hefty Frenchmen prevented him from following her. He now wondered if it was as Armand said; that they had all been terrified of their mother and what she would not do for the Picard name.

After some more questioning, Armand revealed more of the consequences of that affair. Contained amongst all the papers Armand possessed was Amelia's diary, wherein was hidden the marriage certificate of

Amelia and Bertram Bennet. It was still in an envelope sealed with wax. It was entirely possible that Mr Bennet's true identity might never have been discovered had Armand not given into a fit of curiosity and more closely inspected his sister's papers, many years later.

The story seems so incredible, it must be true, thought Mr Bennet. *No one could make up such a tale.* However, he could not feel sorry for Picard at all, although he now pitied Amelia.

"This is indeed a sad tale, but you will get no sympathy from me," Bertram spoke wearily. "Let us not forget that you knew of my son's legitimacy the entire time, and yet you chose to accost me at the Meryton Ball in such a manner as to make everyone believe I was a philanderer! That was deliberate! Do you have any idea how much that has cost me?" Mr Bennet worked himself up into a rage again.

Armand Picard flinched back again at Mr Bennet's renewed anger and stumbled against a prisoner lying on the floor, who threatened him with bodily harm if he did not get off his foot immediately. Mr Bennet was abruptly brought back to his immediate surrounds. He gestured around himself and said, with heavy sarcasm, "Well, look where it has all brought you. I hope you find your accommodations to your taste, for it is nothing less than you deserve!"

"Ah, *non, M'sieur Bennet*. I regret all of it! My intention was not to merely embarrass you in front of your friends! I… we… I wanted Thomas to be safe, to get him out of France! But I have no money! You cannot comprehend how dangerous it is for us here now! I thought if I could but shame you into acknowledging him, perhaps you might help. I did not think of the consequences…"

"Think on them now, Picard, for these might well be your last thoughts. We here in *Chateau Désespoir* await death."

Picard replied, with a choke in his voice, "Then I am glad to have met you here, to express my deep regrets before I meet my maker. I think it fortuitous that I have been granted such an opportunity. Perhaps the Good Lord smiles upon me and forgives me, as I hope do you."

Mr Bennet gritted his teeth. *What incredible arrogance. That the Lord would forgive him! What a primped-up, poncing popinjay!* He looked forward to the day when he was stripped by the gaolers, dressed in sack cloth and marched off to the guillotine. Maybe they would play knucklebones for his satin knee breeches and many-tailed coat of azure blue, and fight over his elegant shoes with those ludicrous high heels!

"I do not forgive." Mr Bennet turned away.

"*Mais… mais, mon ami, un moment*, I beg of you!" Picard clawed at Mr Bennet's tattered coat sleeve.

"I hope you suffer before you die, while you are dying, and after you die!"

"I have already suffered greatly," Picard moaned. Mr Bennet could not help himself and stopped to listen.

"My family! We are Royalists! Our houses burned, our wealth commandeered. The titles all gone! I have nothing left. I am destitute! My only hope was to go to England and maybe claim family standing with you for myself and Thomas! *Mon Dieu*... Thomas... Ah, I had hoped to bring him to you, but he has gone! I cannot find him! I should have taken him with me in the first place, but I barely had the money. Also, I was not sure: we hear such tales of you English and your barbarism."

Mr Bennet suddenly thought that Picard was an even bigger idiot than he had first supposed. Thanks to his poorly thought-out plans, his own son was hiding out somewhere in France right now, waiting for his uncle to return. What did Picard think he would have done had he presented him with his own son? Eaten him? Well, he could not help him now. Another regret.

"If you wanted only to make your claim for Thomas, why did you subject me to all those insinuations?" he continued berating the now sobbing Picard.

"Ah, *je ne sais pas*! It was, madness, *tu sais*? I wanted... wanted I know not what! To make you feel just a little of what I had felt all those years trying to find you!"

"So you indulged in amateur dramatics, for the show of it!" Mr Bennet suddenly grew tired, and sat down in his customary place between Gus and the wall.

"Yes." Picard hung his head in shame.

Mr Bennet closed his eyes and said wearily, "Very well. But I do not forgive." He would not allow Picard to talk to him any further, and waved him away.

After that, the day progressed as usual and the inmates slumped back into their usual apathy. The performance was over for the other inhabitants of the gaol. Those who had understood Picard's story translated to those who could not. There were many shrugs. *L'amour... ah, l'amour*. Mr Bennet was regarded with some renewed respect, while Picard was left to find his own spot on the floor.

Everything changed dramatically the next morning, however, when the usual clanking of keys and tramping of boots heralded the arrival of prison guards. Everyone braced themselves; the daily bucket of slop had already been previously delivered and everyone was thus anticipating either new inmates arriving or others being carted off. The door scraped open on rusting hinges. Mr Bennet closed his eyes - a vision of his family flashed into his head and he suddenly wanted more than anything else to live. "Not me. Not me today, please."

When he opened them, however, it was to behold not the usual sadistic and grinning guards but his friend and erstwhile fellow smuggler Jacques D'Aubrey, holding a cloak and a bunch of keys.

"Come on!" adjured Jacques. "Let's not wait for the grass to grow! Do you want to get out of here or not?"

Mr Bennet leapt up. "Jacques! How the devil...?"

Jacques shrugged. "Not quite the devil, but I do know friends in both high and low places. Your escape is at hand!"

Bertram fairly leapt towards the door. "No need to tell me twice!" he exclaimed joyfully, but then suddenly he paused, and looked down at Picard crouched on the floor in abject misery. He deliberated for only one second before saying "Oh, Jacques, this is my— well, apparently he is my brother-in-law, Armand, and that man over there is Gus, my friend. I would like them to come with us…" At the look on Jacques' face, he added, "If it's not too much trouble?"

With much eye-rolling and exasperated noises, Jacques nodded and led the way.

Chapter Thirteen
Mr Bennet's Breakout

Stumbling through the dimly-lit corridors of the French gaol, Bertram Bennet tried his best to keep up with Jacques, who set a cracking pace in front. Weakened from his incarceration, Bertram had no idea where he was, nor indeed how Jacques even knew where they were, as the corridors twisted and turned, seemingly without logical reason. In his wake also stumbled Armand Picard, who seemed to be in better shape than Bennet or indeed Gus, who kept glancing backwards over his shoulder and mumbling. At one point Mr Bennet tripped over the body of a guard slumped against a wall. As he let out an oath, Jacques turned around abruptly and signalled furiously for silence. Bertram needed no second bidding as they all stood silently, not daring to breathe, while two French soldiers suddenly appeared in the corridor ahead of them. Fortunately, their end of the passageway was in semi-darkness and the soldiers, looking the other way, had no idea who was lurking in the shadows. Mr Bennet was alarmed to note that Jacques had drawn a dagger. It was not needed, however, and after the soldiers moved off to a safer distance, the four men resumed their escape. Bertram hardly dared wonder what he would do if he lost sight of Jacques. Eventually, Jacques appeared to find what he was looking for, as he suddenly stopped and crouched down upon his heels. Bertram saw that he was grasping a large brass ring, which was set deeply into the filthy flagstones. With some effort, Jacques pulled on it to reveal a set of stone steps leading downwards into Stygian gloom. With a raised eyebrow, Bertram somewhat reluctantly allowed himself to pushed down into the hole. He was quickly followed by Armand and Gus, who suffered the same treatment at the hands of Jacques, who then had to struggle mightily to replace the flagstone from his new position halfway down the stone steps.

"Well, this is certainly an improvement on our previous accommodations," Mr Bennet whispered, as he glanced around himself and observed his surroundings. They were standing in a small cellar, damp and cold, which housed a few broken shelves, and ominously, some manacles bolted to the wall.

"What have I told you about whispering?" Jacques spoke in a low voice.

"Sorry," Mr Bennet complied. "What do we do here?"

"We just wait," Jacques replied.

"But wait for what?" Picard, shivering in the damp, sounded querulous as he spoke for the first time since they left their gaol cell. "Ouch! Get off my foot, you oaf!"

Gus shuffled sideways, apologetically.

"We are waiting for my friends," Jacques replied patiently. "They should not be too long." True to his word, after only a few more moments, a door suddenly opened at the other end of the cellar, and a dirty face poked through. After an intense conversation in very rapid French, Jacques turned to his companions and held out an assortment of filthy jackets.

"Put these on, quickly," he instructed.

"What are they?" Mr Bennet was not impressed.

"Uniforms, of course. What did you think?"

"But they are not very— er… uniform, are they? They are quite mismatched!" Bertram gingerly touched one of the malodorous jackets.

"And so are the many nations comprising Napoleon's Grand Army!" Jacques was terse. "What did you want? Matching red coats with shiny buttons and gold braid?"

Mr Bennet still looked dubious.

Picard, leaning forwards to take one of the coats, sided with Jacques. "Come, *mon ami*. Put on the coats. It is more convincing if we look as— er… eclectic as Napoleon's men."

Mr Bennet complied reluctantly, as his particular coat had lice wriggling in it. "Very well, my friends, but as soon as I get back to London I shall introduce you all to my tailor."

Wearing their new raiment, the four men passed silently through the back door of the cellar and emerged into a bright street, slick with rain and teeming with people. Mr Bennet was dismayed to see so many soldiers milling about, but Jacques blithely led the way, exhorting them all to keep up. Easing themselves as unobtrusively as possible into the crowd, they assumed the personae of itinerant soldiers; bedraggled certainly, but not out of place.

"The trick now, you see," Picard fell into step with Mr Bennet, "is to strut about as if you owned the place. Just… just swagger a bit, you know. You are a soldier; you have the right to be here. Don't skulk or stoop."

It was true: with so many people all about, with so many different purposes, it was not difficult to join in the throng and become one with it. With great bravado but with hammering heart, Mr Bennet followed Jacques and Picard across a large and very busy town square, and passed right by several groups of bona fide soldiers without incident, although Gus, bringing up the rear, kept up a nervous scrutiny of every face he saw.

After half an hour or so, they came across an inn, and Mr Bennet saw a couple of tired-looking ponies tied up outside. A giant of a man emerged from the inn and a very rapid conversation in French then ensued. Jacques appeared to have some difficulty making the man understand that he now needed four ponies and not two, as previously arranged. At one point, the man turned and began to lead the ponies away, but eventually

Jacques seemed to make enough promises to him, for not only were the two sad ponies relinquished to Jacques but another two were miraculously found. After only a few more moments of delay, while Picard commandeered some bread and cheese and a jug of wine from the inn keeper, they clambered upon their mounts and trotted off, looking as purposeful as possible.

They rode without stopping for several hours, leaving the busy city far behind them and thence traversing deeply rutted country roads. Scores of soldiers and heavy artillery wagons had used the road incessantly, and it now posed a real threat to their ponies' well-being, but the sure-footed animals did not hesitate as they negotiated pothole after pothole. Mr Bennet, feeling a cold breath on his neck, kept on looking backwards apprehensively, and wished for speedier steeds, but soon came to the conclusion that on these treacherous roads at least perhaps slow and steady would win the race.

After an hour or so they came to a roadside marker where the resourceful Jacques had hidden a cache of weapons wrapped in cloth. There was a handsome pair of Charleville muskets, which Picard was pleased about, explaining as he grabbed one of them that he personally could hit a man at one hundred paces although, as he explained, in the wrong hands the weapon itself was notorious for misfiring and taking off its owner's fingers. Mr Bennet, receiving only a rusty bayonet from

Jacques, sincerely doubted Picard's prowess although, as they mounted their horses once more, Jacques assured him that rumour had it that Picard was a very good shot. Mr Bennet, remembering that Jacques had indeed hinted at Picard being a "wanted man" in France, reflected that it seemed to be typical of the Picard family: intrigue followed them everywhere. Gus, following up the rear with his own short pikestaff, nodded agreeably.

The ponies plodded on until nightfall, when a great and golden full moon rose over the tree tops. The countryside through which they passed was lit up as brightly as a ballroom, and both Jacques and Picard were as jumpy as a kitten in a basket of puppies. Each shadow of every tree loomed menacingly at them as they rode past. Mr Bennet was so nervous that he jumped at every object: a small rock formation became, in his imagination, a contingent of *Carabiniers-à-Pied*, whilst a small clump of trees was surely some *Infanterie Légère*, and they were all about to be discovered and shot dead. He sincerely doubted he would be able to wield his bayonet with any force. Picard was just about to suggest that they hide out somewhere until the moon set, when Mr Bennet's fears materialised into an actual company of Light Infantry, riding straight towards them upon the country road. There was no way to avoid the twenty or thirty heavily armed men, and no way they had not been seen.

With some degree of farce, the two groups of men rode silently towards each other, neither group wanting to be the first to break silence. They halted eventually, facing each other upon the road, each group blocking the other's path.

"What do you do here?" Jacques D'Aubrey took the position of arrogant authority. "Let us pass."

"I might ask the same of you," the commander of the other group replied.

Jacques took a moment to sit back on his pony, and to stare insolently at the other man. "We are Hussars, of course. But undercover. That is all you need to know."

The Hussars of Napoleon's army were primarily used for reconnaissance, patrolling the countryside and keeping a wary eye on the movements of all and sundry. They had a reputation for being among the best horsemen and swordsmen of Napoleon's Grand Army, as well as for being the best dressed, and for Jacques to claim affinity with such an elite group seemed madness indeed.

"You will forgive me, Oh Exalted One, for not thinking that you look very much like a Hussar. Hussars ride steeds of unsurpassed swiftness and stamina... You all appear to be mounted on stunted ponies." There was a general tittering amongst the officer's men, but also a collective increase in alertness. "You also appear to have mislaid the magnificent uniforms for which the Hussars are so famous."

"As I said, we are undercover." Jacques was cool.

A moment passed as both men stared each other down.

"Your names?" the commander was insistent.

"Do you not hear well enough? We are undercover. We could hardly remain so if we advertised our identities."

Beside him, Mr Bennet could hear Picard humming softly under his breath, whilst Gus allowed his pony to take a few steps forwards.

"All the same…" the commander also rode forwards a little, holding his musket nonchalantly.

"Do you challenge us? General Lasalle, our commanding officer, has the ear of the Emperor himself and I personally have the ear of Lasalle. Perhaps I can convey to him your names?"

There was another tense moment, and then the commander of the Infantrymen suddenly addressed Mr Bennet directly. "You there," he pointed with his musket. "I repeat, what are you doing here?"

The absolutely terrified Mr Bennet decided to remain silent, and merely spat upon the ground instead, directing an insolent look at his interrogator.

"We are on a secret mission," Picard suddenly spoke up. "The countryside is teeming with spies. How do we know you are who you seem?"

"We appear to have reached détente." The Infantryman conceded.

"We do, indeed."

Very begrudgingly, and with an exaggerated show of respect, the opposing commander began to ride around the four men, his troops following suit. There was another frankly comic moment when it was obvious they could not pass comfortably on the narrow country road, and his horse stumbled into a ditch. With ill-concealed smirks, the four fugitives rode straight through the contingent of Infantrymen, which had almost dispersed in disarray in their anxiety to avoid following their leader into the same ditch. With many a sidelong glance being ruefully exchanged, the two groups disentangled themselves, and rode on. Mr Bennet finally let out his breath, and Gus resumed his whistling.

The rest of the night passed without incident as the four escapees slept in an abandoned manor house. When the dawn came, it revealed the full extent of the ruination of the once-imposing chateau, along with burned fields and charred bodies. It was obvious there had been a significant encounter there between Napoleon's Grand Army and the Coalition Army, with the house and attached farm becoming major casualties alongside soldiers of both sides. It was also patently obvious that one side or another had looted the premises, but Picard and Gus moved through the collapsed house carefully, hopeful of finding food.

There was not much left. All the furniture had been burned, there were gaping holes in the walls from heavy artillery, and many of the walls, tapestries and paintings had been defaced with crude slogans. Some were in English, some in French; silent testament to the sordid truth that neither side had been respectful. The four men did indeed find some sustenance: the well was still operational and the water still sweet, and Gus had found some cheese which proved to be quite tasty, once the mould had been shaved off. Bertram ate his repast sitting with his back against the remains of the wall of what might once have been a magnificent salle, regarding with interest the acres and acres of scorched vines filling his view.

"Seems ridiculous," he opined to no one in particular. "Why burn the fields? Isn't the whole idea of 'occupation' to 'occupy'? What is there left now to occupy? What gains have been made here?"

"You tell me, my friend," Jacques agreed. "But we have another little problem to contend with now. Our conveyances do not look too well."

It was true: the ponies they had acquired the day before had been a sickly lot to begin with, but they had performed admirably with no fodder for them at the end of the day. They had watered them, of course, but the horses were exhausted and were likely to starve. It was decided to turn them loose and let them forage where they could, and to continue on foot. They also decided to abandon their jackets, as they had been somewhat of dubious success as a disguise, and besides, as Picard pointed out, now they were out of the city they would blend in better as peasants, rather than soldiers.

It was thus with some reluctance that Bertram set off down the road with the others in the general direction of Le Havre. He had never, ever in his life been about in his shirt sleeves, and he marvelled both at how untrammelled and yet exposed he felt. It was set to be a hot day; there was not a cloud in the sky and already he could feel the heat rising off the dusty road. The only saving grace was that they encountered no one, as the entire countryside appeared to be abandoned. That night was spent huddled under a bridge which spanned a sluggish river, and the next day, they were all heartened to realise that they were but twenty miles from Le Havre. It looked as if the end was in sight. Bertram began to allow himself to think of Longbourn and his family, and after a pre-dawn start they reached the outskirts of Le Havre by mid-afternoon. However, instead of entering the town, they made their way to a small inlet some four or five miles further up the coast. Jacques explained that Le Havre was too busy, too well-patrolled, and that the insignificant little group of fishing huts they were bound for would be far safer. They did not even stop for provisions in Le Havre, which sorely tested Picard's equanimity.

As eager as Bertram was for escape, they then had to endure a long wait not only for nightfall, but for the moon to set, as well. Jacques was confident that his contacts would not let him down, and that the promised boat would appear as soon as it was dark enough. They therefore had no recourse other than to be patient.

Bertram attempted to snooze a little, propped up against a broken row boat, which lay upon the stony beach. Any residents who once inhabited the small cluster of fishing huts had long since vanished, or were hiding behind closed shutters, and so the men were quite alone. It was a warm night, thankfully, with just a slight breeze carrying with it the odours of salt and fish. The only sounds were those of the industrious crickets in the rough gorse bushes which littered the beach. It seemed to Bertram as if they were lulling him to sleep.

As the moon finally set, Jacques became fretful. There were now only a few short hours until dawn, and unless the promised vessel arrived within the next hour or so, it would be doubtful if they could get away that night. Picard also did not like their chances and stood peering out at the black horizon, as if he could will the boat to arrive. Gus had kept his pikestaff, and was now sharpening it with a stone. Bertram hummed a little tune.

"*Mon Dieu!* She is come at last!" Picard was the first to spot the small lugger creeping up on them with the tide. With agonising slowness and in almost surreal silence, the boat came closer and closer, and they all watched with growing impatience as a wherry was lowered over the side, with only a solitary man inside. Bertram was hopping up and down with excitement and began to wade out to the boat as soon as it was close enough. A rope was thrown by their unseen rescuer, and both Bertram and Jacques began to pull on it, drawing the wherry close enough for them to board. Bertram actually had one foot in it and one still in the water when Gus gave an urgent shout.

"*Regardez! Attention! Regardez!*" Bertram spun around in dismay to spy six armed men in the uniforms of the Coast Guard running across the beach towards them, shouting out for them to stop and stand still, or be fired upon.

"*Merde!*" breathed Jacques. "Not now! Quickly, quickly, onto the boat!"

They certainly needed no bidding. Now with frantic purpose, the four men climbed awkwardly into the wherry, exhorting the oarsman to get going. As the terrified oarsman changed positions in the boat, it rocked dangerously, and nearly overturned: it looked for one terrifying moment as if it would be scuttled and they would be stranded. By some miracle it righted itself, but Mr Bennet had been ejected over its side back into the cold sea. One of the Coast Guards then let off a shot. It landed in the water just ahead of them, and Mr Bennet staggered as he tried to regain his footing on the sea floor.

"Stand fast!" called out one of the guards, as Mr Bennet frantically grasped the side of the boat. "Stand where you are! In the name of his Most Excellent the Emperor Napoleon, I order you to stand fast!"

Jacques swore again. "They must think we are smugglers! Well, not this time! Come on, *mon ami*, come on!" He grabbed hold of Mr Bennet's arm and tried to haul him back on board.

By this time the guards had drawn up near enough to take very good shots at them, and several musket balls pinged into the water. They were still some way off though, and Bertram thought they still had a good chance. Just as it seemed as if they might succeed, however, one guard who was closer than the others put on an extra sprint across the stony beach and came splashing into the sea right behind Bertram at great speed, putting his musket up to his shoulder and taking careful aim. Bertram looked around at him. He could see his musket glinting faintly, but the face was blank in the darkness.

"Stand still!" the guard ordered Bertram in French, but he did not need a translator. "I am arresting you in the name of the Emperor. Stop, or I will shoot."

Bertram thought he meant it, but still hoped he had a chance. He continued to climb onto the boat, the guard began to depress the trigger, and suddenly there was a great splash as out of nowhere sprang Picard, wielding a piece of driftwood. There was no warning for the guard: he went down like a sack of wheat as Picard struck him across the shoulders with as much force as he could muster. The musket ball intended for Bertram's head flew off uselessly into the darkness, and the guard fell face forwards into the water. Bertram took one look at the man, and then with a terrified but grateful look at Picard, he made it into the boat. Picard then took a few moments to shove the boat further into the water and leapt aboard as the oarsman began frantically rowing towards the lugger. Gus found another set of oars and with shots whizzing by above their heads, the over-crowded rowboat inched towards the bigger boat. Some of the musket balls flew by awfully close, and Bertram wondered why there were no retaliatory shots from the men on the lugger.

It was a very close thing. After a few more extremely intense moments, they could all see that they were now mostly out of range of the guards on the beach. They came up alongside the lugger and were hauled somewhat roughly on board as the boat, by now unanchored, began to come about on the strong wind which had fortuitously suddenly sprung up. Slowly and laboriously, or so it seemed to Bertram, the lugger finally turned about and slipped away into the open sea, and thence into the Channel.

With heaving lungs and his heart hammering in his chest, Bertram sat down with a thud onto the deck of the coastal lugger, which was now getting underway with satisfying speed.

"We are lucky," one of the crewmen called out to him as he sprang to help with a recalcitrant sail. "The wind's come up nice. It were right flat before. Thought we'd never get 'ere."

Bertram allowed himself a deep breath. They had done it! Somehow, no doubt with the help of Providence and whatever sea-gods lurked in the waters below, they had managed to get away from the beach and coast guards. They had been so close to death; he was certain that every musket ball that had whined past his head was the one that carried his name. Now, in less than a day, he would be on English soil again!

With a deep sigh of exhaustion, Bertram felt himself become drowsy. He was nearly home again. Longbourn. His family. Matters still unresolved, of course, but he had survived the most extraordinary adventures. What stories he would tell!

****

Mr Bennet must have slept far more deeply than he thought, for when he awoke the sun was high, albeit playing hide-and-seek with heavy, black clouds. Looking around himself properly for the first time since being hauled on board, he observed that the ship they were in was far smaller than he had hoped, and with far fewer crew. If there was one thing he had learned during his days as a bootlegger, it was that in such a high wind there really ought to be a man on every sail. Instead, only one of the lugsails was getting any attention, and the other lay in a muddled heap on the deck, its ropes in a tangle. There was one man on the rudder at the stern, and one other battling with some ropes. As the little lugger was tossed about in the increasingly strong winds, Bertram heard the man swear before disappearing below deck. Now there were only two left on deck who were actually of any use; the rest of the crew appeared to be even less experienced than Bertram, as the boat began rising and plunging violently in the suddenly mountainous waves.

As the black clouds accumulated overhead and the winds increased to gale force, a cold and driving rain began beating down upon the deck. Bertram suggested they all go below to get out of the weather, but at that moment the crewman who had disappeared before now re-emerged from the depths, his face white with fear.

"We're taking on a lot o' water!" he shouted out to no one in particular.

At that same time there was a massive surge of water up over the deck, and Gus would have been swept overboard were it not for Picard who grasped the back of his shirt and held on for dear life.

By now the tiny lugger was rolling and pitching in a most alarming manner. Thunder boomed overhead, the wind increased in strength, and driving rain beat down upon their heads. There was a loud crack and the lugger's mast suddenly clove in two, sending lethal spears raining down upon the deck. The man on the rudder gave out a horrified yell as the entire steering mechanism broke apart under a particularly vicious wave and he was pitched into the roiling sea.

"Everyone below deck! Start bailin'!" screamed the man designated as captain. They all scrambled to comply but after only a few moments anyone could see this was useless. Deciding to take his chances back above deck, Bertram abandoned his task, along with most of the others. By now the lugger was listing so far to one side that everything on the deck was sliding off into sea. Men yelled and screamed in fear as they grasped at anything to save themselves from a similar fate. The seas churned and heaved, the rain lashed down upon the terrified crew and a howling wind tore their words out of their mouths and sent them flying uselessly into the storm. There was nothing to do but hold on to whatever could be found, and pray.

Eventually the storm played itself out. The wind decreased in intensity but still remained brisk, the clouds scattered and the rain ceased its relentless hammering. Soaked to the bone, Bertram relaxed his white-knuckled hold upon a railing, and looked around to count heads. By Heaven's mercy, he and his friends had survived the storm, but were apparently not completely out of danger. The lugger, having been obviously quite dilapidated to begin with, was struggling in the water even in the absence of those terrifying high waves of before. There were no sails left, the deck was crowded now with the land-lubberly crew who were so patently not sailors, and the ship was listing almost parallel to the water. As the last of the rain moved away, Jacques called out, taking a roll call. Satisfied that all his charges were still alive, he pointed to the horizon, where they could see the blessed outline of England.

"I am not sure where we are exactly," he shouted, "but it is land! We must hope we make it!"

Indeed, it was a race against time. On the one hand, the tide was in their favour for it was bearing them landwards at a great speed. On the other hand, the lugger was now breaking up very rapidly, and as they neared the shore several of the crew began jumping overboard to try to swim for it. Bertram was inclined to ride it out, but Picard pointed out that it was more dangerous to stay with the sinking ship. The captain and crew had by now all abandoned their doomed vessel. Bertram followed suit, leaping into the waves barely one mile offshore.

He thought himself quite a good swimmer, although it was not a skill he had recently employed and he was already exhausted. Struggling a great deal in the water, Bertram looked to the shore and nearly cried with relief when he saw they appeared to have fortuitously been wrecked close to a beach which was populated with many people who were even now organising themselves into a rescue attempt. Boats were being pushed out into the sea and on the shore he could see many gesticulating people. There were even several wooden floating devices also now within possible reach. Swimming now with renewed effort, he turned towards the nearest, and prayed he would reach it before his lungs gave out.

Chapter Fourteen
The Bennets Bathing

Two things were bothering Miss Mary Bennet: one was a letter she had recently received from her sister's husband, Mr Darcy, and the other was the behaviour of her sister Kitty, or Catherine as she now insisted upon being called. These things lay on her mind like a cloud over the horizon which no amount of sunshine, blue skies and sparkling seas could dissipate.

The letter from Mr Darcy contained all the usual greetings and hopes for their good health, which Mary found exceedingly tedious, fretting as they all were for news of Mr Bennet, but then her brother-in-law finally got to the point of the matter.

'I regret I do not have better tidings, but I must tell you what I have discovered', he wrote. 'After some considerable effort and after making the rounds of all the places I considered it probable your father visited, I decided to take a different approach and made enquiries of certain personages of doubtful honesty. I was thus able to track Mr Bennet down to a dubious-looking inn in London called the Duck n' Cider, where the innkeeper was persuaded to tell me that Mr Bennet had sold his horse to him, along with an ebony-tipped cane and a small gold ring. I do not need to tell you how bad this looks; your father divesting himself of all his property points to a man not expecting to return. However, the peculiar thing is that he did not visit his bank. All of the funds remain as they were. After having sold all his possessions, he left the inn in company of one Jack Dobbrey, and has not been seen since. All I know is that he was heard to be asking for a passage to France.'

Mary quailed at this. It looked very bad indeed, as if her father were absconding. And the ring had been an heirloom, more of sentimental value than monetary, so he must have been desperate indeed to have sold it. But if he had needed money, why had he not visited his bank?

The letter continued.

'In addition, the one named Jack Dobbrey is rather well known in certain quarters in London, such as St Giles, and is wanted by the authorities. I have made enquiries with the Watch, but and you will forgive my bluntness, no murder victims matching your father's description have been found, which we may count as a blessing. His whereabouts though now remain a mystery. I fear he has fallen into danger or bad company, but in either case he is almost certainly in France.

'Lord Castlereagh, the Commanding Officer of the Coalition Forces in France, is a personal friend of mine and I have sent him a despatch asking for any knowledge he or his staff might have, but I feel it is futile. To further complicate matters, if your father has indeed intentionally disappeared, then it would have been very easily achieved in France right now, with all the chaos present. We must assume that he has changed his name and may not wish to be found. The best recourse for us is to try and achieve normalcy. We must act as if your father is in Brighton with you all, recovering his health after a long winter illness. If he does not return within two months or so, then we must assume the worst.'

Mary felt a cold twinge of despair. Two months! She knew there was no hope of keeping up the recuperating-patient façade for that long, now that Brighton seemed to be teeming with their friends and acquaintances. It was already becoming difficult. Whenever the nosy Mrs Cowper asked after Mr Bennet, they had been fobbing her off with the story that he was above stairs in bed and was too weak to come down and then, when she had become insistent and had visited the house with the hopes of catching them out, they had said that he had been moved to a sanatorium in Hove, a small fishing village not more than one mile away. Oh, the lies! Mary abhorred her enforced mendacity. Mrs Cowper was very *au fait* with the rumours abounding concerning the Bennets, and sought to trip Mary up by proposing a visit to the sanatorium. Alas, Mary replied sweetly, her father was being kept isolated, to minimise anxiety.

The rest of Darcy's letter gave some news of Pemberley; expressed regrets at Elizabeth's not being able to join them in Brighton due to her condition; the news that Jane Bingley was also in a happy condition; and the assurance that he would continue all his efforts to track down their father. Mary sighed, reflecting that Darcy had managed to turn Elizabeth's and Jane's most exciting news almost into a footnote. But then, as wonderful as the news was about her sisters, she supposed they did rather have the Sword of Damocles hanging over their heads and that, quite rightly, any joy she felt for her sisters must be tempered with anguish over their father. She dithered as to which parts of the letter to read to her Mother, and whether or not Kitty — Catherine… was mature enough to hear the truth. In the end she shared the entire letter from Darcy with Catherine, as she felt she ought to know what was happening, and Catherine agreed with Mary that it was best to do as Mr Darcy asked and not let their mother know what he had discovered about their father's disappearance. They would, instead, make emphasis on the two happily anticipated events.

Catherine's acquiescence did not, however, allay Mary's concerns over her sister. She was certain that Catherine was up to something. She had several times come across Catherine and Betty-Letty with their heads together whispering, and had been greeted by many a guilty look on their faces when she had surprised them. She hoped it was not Mr Edgar Spencer who was the object of whatever mischief was brewing. This gentleman was a permanent fixture in the Bennet household, or so it seemed. Together with all this, Catherine seemed to be spending rather a lot of money and Mary did not know where she was getting it from. Catherine was always shopping with the Cartwright twins and seemed able to keep up with them as far as bonnets, lace, ribbons and whatnot were concerned. Whenever Mary accosted Catherine about this, Catherine merely answered, "Oh, tish tosh! It's nothing, a mere trifle! Things are quite cheap here, you know!"

Nasty thoughts sprang into Mary's head involving Mr Spencer, but she could not bring herself to voice any of her suspicions, as they were salacious indeed. Whenever Mary came across Catherine and her friends, they always stopped talking immediately, and then started up again, conversing rather loudly of the weather, or who was seen on the Promenade. At one point, Mary had actually startled Catherine and Edgar Spencer *tête-à-tête* and they had sprung apart guiltily. Mary felt sure she had seen a note passing hands, and was very cross about it, fearing that Catherine was heading for a dreadful scrape which would involve all the family again, as with Lydia. Mary was concerned that all her good works were going to pot with Catherine. Catherine's behaviour, her secrecy and her wastrel habits weighed heavily on Mary's mind. She knew her sister was fond of cards: she hoped she was not gambling or losing money to Edgar, for that would put her in a precarious position regarding her virtue. Mary was very well aware of how young ladies were lured into the most dreadful situations through gambling debts. But then, Catherine seemed to have money to burn. Maybe she was winning pots and pots of it? All of these worries made Mary very anxious indeed, and somewhat conscious of the fact that she was thinking such dreadful things of Mr Spencer, who really was not at all bad, and was at least a gentleman.

The only good thing of late was that Catherine had been at one with Mary in putting off her erstwhile partner in crime, Lydia, who had written to them inviting herself down to Brighton for the rest of the summer. That this had been achieved at all was really quite marvellous, for Lydia had been very insistent, but Catherine told her they had no money for parties or shopping, and that they spent their days in the library or walking. After another letter threatening a surprise arrival, Lydia dropped the subject and no more letters had arrived. Mary still lived in anxiety, wondering if each carriage stopping outside, or merely slowing down, would deposit their wayward sister upon the doorstep. What with all this, and worrying about her father, her sister and her mother, Mary felt nearly done in.

One good thing, though, was that their mother's health had improved dramatically. The Cartwright's seamstress had made up two new dresses according to Catherine's pattern, and Mrs Bennet loved to wear them. "I feel so cool and comfortable!" she exclaimed to them one day, after trying on one of the gowns. "And look, I am wearing this new type of stays which are much lighter! Oh, I feel as if I could walk for miles!"

Once some suitable walking shoes had been procured, instead of the flimsy satin slippers she usually favoured, she did indeed walk for miles with them almost every day. Her general demeanour improved a great deal and she was happy and content for most of the time when out, and only fell back into her usual megrims when they were at home, during those evenings when they had no engagements. She did not ever want to talk about Mr Bennet, or returning to Longbourn, and gave the opinion that they might as well stay in Brighton until October, as Mr Darcy had deep pockets and could afford to sponsor them for that length of time. Oh, if only they could procure an invitation to the Pavilion! One would think that Darcy, with all his money and contacts…!

Mary could not deny that Brighton was doing their mother good. If only Catherine would continue behaving and not be lured into a scandal of any sort!

Matters came to a head one day, when Mary had been extra vigilant and had intercepted another secret note passing between Edgar Spencer and Catherine. They were in the drawing room after dinner, and the tea tray had been brought in. Although Mary had been busy with setting cups and pouring tea, she had kept an eye on her sister in the corner with Edgar, and saw the exact moment when something was passed surreptitiously from one to the other.

"Kitty! What is that note? What are you doing? Show me at once!" Mary's voice was sharp with suspicion.

"Nothing!" Catherine jumped away from Mr Spencer, guiltily.

"What is it that you have there?" Mary demanded, advancing upon her sister with intent to wrest whatever it was from her hand.

"Nothing! What do you mean? I have nothing!" As Catherine's hand was clenched firmly behind her back at the time, it was blatantly obvious she was lying.

"Mr Spencer, if you mean to be a gentleman, you had better put a stop right now to whatever mischief you are indulging in, or planning!" Mary turned to Edgar, her face furious. "I will not have this family dragged down again by the thoughtless and imprudent actions of one of my sisters! Now, Kitty, give that to me!" And she snapped her fingers together imperiously, turning back towards her sister and advancing upon her menacingly.

"I shall not! That is… I do not have anything… do not threaten me!" Catherine squeaked, backing away until she nearly fell into the fire grate.

"Miss Catherine, the jig is up! Your sister has found us out. Better to acknowledge the hit gracefully," Edgar Spencer said ruefully, with a wry smile.

"Yes!" exclaimed Mary, glad her suspicions were correct and that she had evidently stumbled upon a dire plot. "You had better give it up!"

With a doleful yet rebellious expression, Catherine brought her hand forward, opened her fist, and held out large a wad of money towards Mary.

Mary was aghast. Oh no! This was what she had been dreading! She had hoped it might be a plot to elope, or at best a love note, as being the lesser of two evils, but this! Money! Why was Edgar Spencer handing her money? Was she, after all, in trouble with gambling?

"Explain." Mary's voice went quiet and cold.

"It's… it's mine!" Catherine declared defiantly. "It's all perfectly legal and above board. I earned it, and it is mine!"

Mary looked from her sister to Edgar Spencer, who was looking at Catherine and nodding encouragingly. "Come along, Kitty! Take your fences!" he adjured her.

"Well?" Mary was merciless.

"I… I… earned it selling dress patterns! My designs are unique, as Madame Colbert says, and she has the premier couturier's salon in town! I have sold nearly four dozen patterns so far!"

Mary was nearly speechless. "What! You actually sold one of your silly designs…?"

"They are not silly!" defended Catherine. "Everybody raves about them! And I get extra money for advising on fabric and trimmings! Oh, I know you don't care about such stuff, but everybody else does! I even design for older ladies, and even Mrs Cowper is wearing one of my styles, although she does not know it is mine!"

Mary took a moment to absorb this, and then said deprecatingly, "So that is how you are funding your mad spending sprees!" Half of Mary's anger was dissipated as she realised her sister was not gambling, but she was still furious with her. "Have I taught you nothing? Are you so vain and clothes-conscious that you must stoop to commerce?"

"It is a very genteel occupation," Mr Spencer butted in, but was silenced by a deathly glare from Mary.

"Why do you feel the need to earn extra money? Do you not have enough for your needs, or are you so besotted with fun and fashion that any amount of money is not enough? I suppose you spend it all on frivolity!" Mary paused to look at the wad of notes being held out to her by her scared but stubborn sister. "How much is there? Ten or twenty pounds, I suppose, which you will fritter away!"

"Two hundred pounds," Edgar Spencer stated loudly.

"Two *hundred*? Did I hear right?" Mary was astounded. "Two hundred *shillings*, you mean, not pounds?"

"No, it's pounds all right," Edgar verified.

Catherine gulped, but said triumphantly, "Yes! Two hundred pounds! There is nothing that the ladies of

Brighton will not pay for a new design made up with French trimmings! Mrs Cartwright helped me out by negotiating with Madame Colbert on my behalf, and my designs are displayed in a very elegant portfolio in her establishment. I go there nearly every day and supervise their making up, and ladies come to me for advice," Catherine continued. "Oh, Mary! Don't you see? In just a few short months, I have earned over four times my annual allowance! Should Papa not return... should he be... then I have a solution for saving us from financial ruin."

Mary suddenly had to sit down. Never had she felt so amazed and yet so aghast. She did not know whether to decry her sister's activities or to applaud them. More than four times her annuity! Incredible. And all Mary herself had done to secure her own financial future was to secrete her allowance in a box in her desk, begrudgingly spending a penny here or there in true miserly fashion. She had done nothing to make her money grow, had not even invested it, believing that usury was evil. Mary's quick mental calculations told her that, even after another twenty years, she still would not have enough for independence, whereas with hard work and good business acumen, Kitty — Catherine — would be safe. Matthew twenty-five, verse fourteen came to mind, and the parable of the servants with the talents struck her, and she laughed bitterly to herself.

"Well, I have never been so amazed or horrified in my life!" Mary exclaimed, leaping forward to clutch

Catherine's hands in her own. Her face contorted with the effort not to cry. "I... I have done you a terrible. I have not ever valued you as I should. You... you have shown great forethought, and industry, and you are clever... and... everything I am not!"

"Oh, Mary, do you really mean it? Do you really think I am clever?" choked Catherine, who had at first shrunk back at Mary's advance, but who was now grasping her sister's hands. "It means so much to me! All my life I have been 'Little Kitty', or Lydia's sister, or 'Silly Kitty-Cat'! Now I am Miss Catherine, and I own a business! Edgar has been invaluable in helping me set it all up, and Betty-Letty have all the contacts and put a lot of business my way. In a few years I can be reasonably well-off, and independent, all by myself!"

"I think you are one of the cleverest people I know," Mary admitted humbly, truly chastened and anticipating many hours spent on her knees with her Bible in order to shrive her tortured soul.

"You are cast down!" Catherine hugged her sister tightly. "Don't be! I want your help on this. Edgar says I am more creative than practical. You must help me! You can be my full partner!"

Mary was not certain she had heard Catherine's request. "Pardon? You want me as a partner? But why?"

"Because you are the cleverest of us all, dear sister. You must help me with the accounts, and advertising, and ordering supplies, and such. Edgar is trying to teach me but I have not much interest in it. Please say you will help me!"

Mary conceded, with humility and gratitude.

"But I thought you were going to run off with Mr Spencer," Mary explained, after they had finished another bout of hugging and tears.

Edgar Spencer snorted into his tea, and Catherine exclaimed, "Good God! Edgar? I am not that mad!"

"Thank you," said Edgar, only slightly miffed.

"Oh, I do not mean any insult, dear friend — you must know I could never look at you in that way!" Catherine explained, laughing. "I do not think I will ever marry, or certainly not for a very long time. It seems a very tedious institution, with no benefit for the wife! I mean, look at Betty-Letty! They cannot walk down the street for fortune hunters following them like little dogs! They laugh at the boys who follow them around, and are not so conceited they think it is because of their great beauty! Yet they know they must marry some time, and that they will never have control of their own fortunes! It is so unfair! Look at us — we can be thrown out of our home by our own cousin if Papa is declared— found to be... dead! We were paraded in front of that priggish Mr Collins like prize cattle when he came looking for a wife. Mama was treating him as if he were the Prince himself, and he acted it, too, so puffed up with his own importance. Ugh! Why cannot women inherit? Why must they be passed over for even the most obscure male relative? Edgar says the day those stupid laws will be changed will be the day we can vote! Never! And look at Lydia! A small baby already and another on the way! No, thank you!" And she gave a little shiver.

Mary's eyes gleamed with happiness. At last she had a sister who was like-minded! Together they could make their own fortunes! The evening ended with the sisters putting their heads together and making plans, whilst Edgar Spencer drank his tea and marvelled at modern women.

****

So happy and at charity with the whole world was Mary that she was inclined to look kindly upon Mrs Bennet's newest desire, sea-bathing. Mrs Bennet could talk of nothing else. It seemed that a certain Dr Richard Russell had devised a salt-water cure for almost everything and sea bathing thus became extremely popular. Mrs Bennet was sure it would cure her "leg ailment", as she put it. Since she really did suffer at nights with either real or imagined symptoms, including leg cramps and a feeling of "creepy-crawlies under the skin", Mary thought it was worth a try.

Catherine was scared of the water but Mrs Bennet poo-poohed this, saying that hundreds, nay thousands, of people every day went bathing in Brighton without drowning and why couldn't they, too? Catherine further objected by saying that she had read that the salt-water cure was effective only if performed during the colder months, but Mary insisted on that as being nonsense, asking who wanted to swim in the freezing cold? Edgar Spencer was despatched to reconnoitre the more-frequented bathing machines, and came back with the information that they looked perfectly safe and respectable. Betty-Letty were besides themselves with excitement at the prospect, and in the face of so much evidence as to its benefits, Catherine at last agreed to it, and thence became its greatest proponent.

There were two major operators of the bathing machines along the Promenade and the one felt to be more superior was that of Mr Smithers, who advertised "discreet changing facilities, linen or flannel shifts for those who wish to retain modesty, and female attendants for the ladies." Mrs Bennet thought that she could not go naked into the sea, for which her daughters were profoundly grateful, and decided upon a flannel shift. The others thought linen would be less cumbersome when wet. Catherine declared they would sew their own, as Mr Smithers was probably charging an exorbitant amount for inferior materials. Accordingly, she sewed up the shifts in quick time, and there was no more reason not to go and bathe immediately.

Mr Spencer declared he would drive them there in his own carriage and stand guard on the beach, lest they were in danger of being swept away. Betty-Letty giggled, and Mary said he would hardly notice, as they would be inside a great box on wheels festooned with drapes for privacy. Since men were not allowed within one hundred yards of the ladies' bathing area, he would need a telescope to see anything at all. Catherine stated that telescopes were banned anyway, as it had become a habit of young gentlemen to ride along the sea front on their horses or in their carriages brandishing these instruments, in the hopes of catching a glimpse of wet or naked women. Mrs Bennet tittered and Mary wondered how the boxes were pulled into the water: Catherine was able to inform her that horses did so. "In which case," Mary crowed triumphantly, "there must be men within the proscribed area, and can they be trusted?"

After another few days of planning and arguing, it was ascertained that Mr Smithers' own daughters, stocky farm lasses, were in charge of the horses in the ladies' bathing area. It seemed there were no more objections and Tuesday was chosen as the day, as it was Ladies' Day, when all men were banished from the Promenade, excepting those conducting business. However, the next Tuesday which came was wet and dreary, and it remained so for the following week. Their disappointment was great but they had no recourse other than to wait it out. The week after that they had another great disappointment, however, for although the day was hot and sunny, when they reached the bathing machine area, they found that they ought to have made a booking, as there were already up to fifty ladies bathing and many more besides waiting. The beach was scorching under the August sun and Catherine stamped her foot with impatience. The weather was predicted to turn bad again for the following week, and now they might never get to swim!

Mr Spencer came to the rescue. He knew of another but less popular bathing-machine area in Hove, only a mile away, and he was sure they could get a turn there. Accordingly, the little party boarded Mr Spencer's carriage and were driven along a picturesque route following the shoreline to the small village of Hove, which enjoyed much less patronage than Brighton on account of the Prince of Wales not ever wanting to walk further than fifty feet or so.

Hove did not disappoint them. It was only a tiny hamlet with just a few cosy tea shops and some retirement cottages, a small town square with an ancient ducking pond, and one inn. Its major attraction for the ladies was that there were not many people on the beach. In addition, not only were they able to immediately be taken into a bathing machine, but there were no predatory dandies lurking around. Mr Spencer offered to drive up the hill a way off and wait for a signal from them that they were ready to come home — Mary was to wave her red shawl - and with great excitement the Bennet ladies and the Cartwright twins entered the bathing boxes. It was all very discreet. There was a lady attendant who offered them the necessary bathing attire. However, the Bennets and Cartwrights produced their own costumes with a flourish as if to say, "We do this so often we had to make our own!" as it was obvious that other ladies who came often had their own made. Catherine lost a few minutes in surmising whether she could design something better for commercial production. Mary wondered if horses could swim.

As quickly and as modestly as possible, they all changed, with the attendant folding their clothing and placing it in little boxes up high out of danger of getting wet. The bathing machine was then dragged into the water by an obedient horse, and Mrs Bennet tied up everyone's hair with ribbons. Finally, with much squealing and shrieking, Mrs Bennet sat down upon a wooden stool and dipped her toe into the water. There were steps from the box which led down into the sea, and plenty of wooden bars to hang onto, so at no moment were any of them in danger of being swept away. Soon enough, they were all in the water, only waist deep, but very exhilarating and frightening all the same!

Mary had never felt so disencumbered! The cool water held her up nicely and she was daring enough to let go of the rails and wade out a bit further. She saw that other ladies had pushed back the drapes surrounding their own bathing machines entirely and were bobbing around at quite some distance, and she followed suit with her mother calling anxiously for her not to go out too far, and her sister squealing at the cold water. The seabed felt sandy with only a few pebbles, which did not really hurt her feet, and so with the water now up to her chin she attempted a few swimming strokes. Tentatively she grew bolder and bolder, putting her recently learned book theory of water sports into practice. She was a little disconcerted at the waves which buffeted her occasionally, but gradually felt her confidence grow, and dog-paddled out further. *This must be how fish feel*, she thought. Turning around she waved at the others. She felt free, rebellious, and revelled in the perfect congruence of sea and sky. She turned around again, and surveyed the horizon. Why, it was curved, she saw, and lay back to float freely.

She lay thus in the water for a while, hearing the giggles and squeals of those behind her, and thought blissfully of what a perfect day it was. The sky was azure blue with just a few little puffy clouds dotting it. The sea was a deeper blue, a shade her sister would certainly identify. Mary's hair had escaped its ribbons and was floating out around her head like a mermaid's tresses. She giggled to herself.

Suddenly, Mary noticed something odd. Out there on the horizon — a black dot. No, several black dots. What in the world...? Calling to the others to also take a look, Mary squinted at the objects. For one small moment she thought of whales, or giant squid, but then chastised herself for being silly. There was most definitely a boat, but at a peculiar angle. It listed alarmingly to one side: she could see the sails lying useless and sodden on the water. The black dots surrounding it were... good God! They were sailors! Drowning sailors!

Calling desperately to the others, Mary shaded her eyes to see all the better, but her short-sighted vision revealed not much more. Eventually, after much screeching from Mary, her sister and the other ladies also noticed the drowning men. Betty-Letty signalled madly to Mr Spencer up on the hill but he had apparently already noticed the boat-wreck and had begun to drive his carriage down towards them as fast as he could. Others on the beach and surrounds had also noticed, for there was now quite a large group of people gathering on the shore, gesticulating and exclaiming. One of the bathing-machine operators ran off up the road to fetch some fishermen to help. Mary looked on in despair. The men were swimming haphazardly towards the beach but as they got nearer, Mary could see they were struggling badly.

Although the tide was now rushing inwards, the water was still shallow for some way out, but these details were lost to Mary as she impulsively struck out in a kind of lurching run towards the nearest man, who waved his arm feebly in the air. She made some progress, until the sea floor suddenly disappeared from underneath her, causing her to panic. However, she then found she could stay afloat and make forward progress by kicking and moving her arms. She was not sure what she could do, she was no swimmer, but those people were drowning and it was her Christian duty to try and save them. Behind her, she dimly heard the shouts of other men who had now joined the rescue effort, and unbeknownst to her a small row boat had been launched.

She called out to one of the men who was now in her sights, thrashing madly towards him. "Hullo! Hullo there! Swim to me! To me!" And Mary tried gallantly to get closer. However, this far out from the shore, the waves were bigger, more unforgiving, and Mary felt a tidal pull backwards towards the beach which made her progress difficult. She began to get tired and panicked when she realised how deep the water was. Although her quarry was now no more than seventy feet away or so, Mary knew she would not make it. "Oh no!" she gasped, arms flailing. She was probably going to drown.

A wave washed over her head and she got a mouthful of salt water. And then another and another. Her linen shift was clinging to her legs and arms and seemed as it was pulling her down. *What a silly way to die,* she thought, commending her soul to the Lord and hoping for a good seat in the Hereafter, being as how she had expired trying to save others. She had a few more brief moments of regret, and then the waters closed over her head. As she lost consciousness she had a brief hallucinatory moment, or a glimpse of Heaven, as the last thing she saw was her father's face, swimming above hers and calling her name.

Chapter Fifteen
Bedlam On The Beach

The drowning sailors and Mary Bennet's heroic but ill-prepared attempts at rescuing them were at first largely unnoticed by Mary's sister and her mother. Neither was aware of this drama noticed at first by Betty or Letty, who were too busy splashing around and pretending to be shocked at how diaphanous their bathing costumes became, once wet. Indeed, Mrs Bennet had turned her face back towards the shoreline, and was thus unaware of the drama unfolding further out. She was squinting in the bright sunlight at a young lady in a rather overly-revealing bathing costume, who had splashed up to their bathing machine in an extremely rude and ungainly manner. Mrs Bennet regarded this newcomer with short-sighted indignation. "Well! Of all the nerve! Do keep your distance, young lady! Really, have you no—"

But Mrs Bennet's querulous remonstrations had no effect upon the newcomer, who splashed even closer and laughed loudly, calling out: "Mama! Mama! Lord, what a joke. Don't you recognise me?" And so saying, the young woman who was intruding upon their afternoon in such a presumptuous manner swam closer to Mrs Bennet, and thus came into proper view.

"Lydia! Good God! Lydia!" Mrs Bennet screeched, astounded. "Oh, my darling daughter! Oh, what a laugh! You are here? Catherine, look, here is your sister Lydia! I can hardly believe it!" And such exclamations and gesticulations as these managed to convey to Catherine that the apparition in the water with them was indeed her sister, Lydia Wickham, who seemed not to have the slightest care in the world regarding her condition.

Catherine squealed with disbelief and joy. Although she had only moments before been wondering what on earth Mary was doing so far out in the sea, she was now thoroughly distracted. "Lydia! Lydia! What felicity that you are here! But how…?"

"Lord! You should have seen your faces! I could have sold tickets! I came here with my friends, the Millers…" Lydia gestured vaguely at a nearby bathing machine which was festooned with about half a dozen ladies in various swimming outfits. "And imagine my delight to hear that you are in town!" Mrs Bennet was oblivious to Lydia's patent lies. "Lord, I nearly died!" Lydia continued. "And then I made up the plan to surprise you, you know…" with a half-defiant look at her mother, "…and the entire idea was made even more delicious when I found out you were bathing today! Of course, it's not nearly as nice as doing so in Brighton itself, and not nearly so exciting without the gentlemen lurking around trying to peep, but even so."

At this point, Catherine finally made it over to where Lydia stood, almost half naked in the water, and launched herself upon her younger sister.

"Lydia! Lydia! Lydia!" was all she could manage to say, albeit in a shrieking voice which demonstrated her excitement.

"Have a care, Kitty!" Lydia gurgled as sea water went into her mouth. Catching hold of her hair, which was wild and tangled around her face, she continued, "This is so marvellous! I say, Delia! Annabelle! Susan! Look! It is as I foretold! We have well and truly surprised them!"

Mrs Bennet, Catherine, and the equally vociferous Betty-Letty found themselves then quite besieged by a bevy of young ladies, who launched themselves into the sea and proceeded to laughingly introduce themselves, nearly capsizing the Bennet's bathing machine as they climbed aboard after Catherine and Lydia. Mrs Bennet was hauled aboard the front platform of the machine and sat between the ladies, alternately bombarding Lydia with questions and attempting to cover up her increasing nakedness with a shawl. Everybody seemed inclined to ignore the fact that their presence in Brighton was not such a surprise to Lydia, given her recent correspondence in which she threatened to visit, but since Mrs Bennet was ignorant of that information, the fib went unacknowledged.

"Goodness, Lydia, darling girl! That you should be here! What a joke! Oh, Kitty, look! Your darling sister!

And so tanned! Really, in your condition! Should you have travelled so far? Lydia, dearest, you look so wild! And... sort of... scandalous!"

"Oh, Mama!" retaliated Lydia, in between breathless attempts at explaining how she had cleverly planned the entire escapade. "Do stop fussing! I am a married woman, you know: you cannot disapprove of me now! My goodness!"

The platform of the Bennet's bathing machine was now perilously overcrowded, what with the Bennets, Betty and Letty, and Lydia Wickham and her cronies all clinging to it as if they were the sole survivors of a shipwreck. Mrs Bennet sat amidst all the young ladies with a silly, self-satisfied expression on her face. Her lovely Lydia returned for a visit! Oh, what stories they would have to tell her! All that business with the vicar and Cath— Kitty! Lord, how she would laugh with Lydia over the expression on the vicar's face when she and Mary had routed him so! And her triumph over Mrs Cowper! Not to mention the marvellous generosity of Darcy in giving them that envy-prompting townhouse right on the sea front! And now there would be another sympathetic ear for her ongoing woes regarding Mr Bennet's perfidy.

All of these thoughts dashed in and out of Mrs Bennet's mind, each one following the other with barely a pause between. The noise of the party on the platform became intermingled with the sounds of the crashing waves and screeching seagulls, which began to sound uncannily human. The hot sun beat down upon her uncovered head, the platform rocked up and down in a most soothing manner, and she fell silent, blissful at her reunion with her youngest daughter, but becoming less and less aware of the half a dozen or so conversations all being carried on at the same time. The rocking of the bathing machine and the hot sunshine lulled her senses to the point where she almost dozed off, and she did not hear more than half the noise around her.

"So when she said she was going to Brighton, I said…"

"Where is your sister Mary…?"

"And he said, 'You are not going!' And I said, well pooh to that…"

"Is your sister here, too? Oh, careful, you will make the tear even bigger! Oh, la, you can see my…"

"I say, we must all go to the tearooms tomorrow! The Prince will be there…"

"But where IS Mary?"

At the sound of her other daughter's name, Mrs Bennet suddenly snapped her head around, as if she had heard a loud noise. Mary? Mary? Yes, where WAS Mary?

Almost gently, as if all the world had slowed down to an impossible crawl, Mrs Bennet became aware of other, more distant sounds overlaying the deafening ruckus on the platform. There seemed to be male voices shouting… She seemed to be surrounded by loud male voices. Why, there were men on the shoreline, waving and gesticulating madly at them. *How rude!* Where were the attendants? Were they to have no privacy? And why were they all pointing out to sea? Slowly, she turned her head, and slipped into the water to get away from the press of bodies all around her. What on earth was the matter with everyone? *Goodness!* Why was Catherine now signalling to Mr Spencer? She wasn't ready to go home, not by a long shot. And look, some of the men were even now splashing out into the sea, fully clothed. Heavens! Were they to be attacked and violated in the middle of the day? Oh, woe was the day she had ever had the idea to… And what was that in the water just ahead of her? Some dread sea creature about to devour them all? Where was Mary? Mary! Oh, merciful heaven, was Mary already eaten? Those men, the noise: was that a boat?

With great suddenness, the world sped up to its usual speed. The girlish squeals emanating from the bathing-machine platform became genuine screams of terror, and several things happened all at once. There suddenly appeared before them, or so it seemed, a large piece of a boat wreck, borne rapidly in with the onrushing tide, to which were clinging several exhausted sailors. Men were shouting from the beach and some were wading out with ropes towards them. The bathing machine, overwhelmed, overturned and deposited the screaming ladies into the sea, where they flailed around crying that they were drowning, too terrified to realise they were only waist deep in the water. Mrs Bennet cried out in anguish for Mary, who was lying at the bottom of the sea, but no... who was apparently being held in the cruel grip of a monstrous being from the deep: she could not comprehend which. The creature was festooned with seaweed, and was advancing upon them rapidly. No! Whatever it was, it would not take her daughter! Grimly but ineffectually, Mrs Bennet struck out at the kraken-like creature, sobbing as she did so. "Let her go! Evil creature! Leave my daughter alone!" she beseeched it piteously, beating at its tentacle with her bare hands. In her terror, she thought she heard the monster laugh at her.

By this time, the sea was a churning mass of panicked bodies. The men from the shore were striking out past them towards the remains of the boat, which was now being borne inwards on the tide towards them at terrifying speed. Other men were trying to assist the ladies, some of whom had gone under the water completely and who were now greatly hampered by their wet bathing outfits. There was suddenly a pressing urgency to get out of the water, lest they be crushed by the boat wreck as it rushed on top of them. All of the ladies were torn between crying for rescue and protecting their offended sensibilities, with their bathing costumes clinging revealingly to their bodies. Catherine was sobbing and clinging to Lydia who had finally, finally, realised that the entire situation was not a joke. In a wonderful display of sisterly love, Lydia practically shoved her sister back under the waves as she lunged for the outstretched arm of a man who was attempting to get hold of them both.

"Help me! Oh, help me!" she cried in desperation, even though she was already upright again. Catherine, not to be left behind, clung to the rescuer's other arm.

Mrs Bennet did not know what to do first. She was, quite literally, in a blind panic. She thought all her daughters were about to be eaten by a sea-monster, or had already drowned, even though she could see that Kitty and Lydia were in the arms of a burly sailor, who was hauling them unceremoniously towards the shore. Catherine was struggling with holding her bathing outfit together, and Lydia was crying with panic and clinging to their rescuer in such a manner as to nearly pull him under, too. Such a scandal should they be seen, half naked as they were, but really…who cared? Mary! Mary was in the clutches of a vile leviathan which, even now, was dragging her back to its watery lair.

With renewed courage, Mrs Bennet lashed out at the sea-monster with a piece of the foundering boat which came suddenly into her hand. "Let her go!" she screamed, striking a good couple of blows upon the creature. "Let her go! Oh, why won't someone help me? Mary! Mary, please don't be dead…!" A crashing sound filled Mrs Bennet's ears, sea water filled her mouth and the salt stung her eyes, blinding her. She sobbed for mercy. "Please, please… please…" and with each syllable, Mrs Bennet landed increasingly weakened blows upon the tentacle nearest to her. "Let… her…

go..." she pleaded, staring up into the monstrous, seaweed-covered head.

The kraken stretched out one of its tentacles towards her, and Mrs Bennet knew she was now also one of its victims. She moaned, dropped the piece of wood she had been using as a weapon, and sagged in the water.

"My dear Mrs Bennet," said the sea-monster, clawing seaweed out of its eyes with the tentacle not engaged in clutching the body of her daughter. "I realise you must, of course, be still quite angry with me, but could I trouble you to put that aside for now, and assist me in carrying our daughter back to the shore? You may, of course, resume your remonstrations once we are all safely upon dry land." And with this, Bertram Bennet, erstwhile bootlegger, accused English spy and suspected philanderer, put his arm around his wife and hauled both Mrs Bennet and his daughter back to the shore.

***

The tiny hamlet of Hove, far less fashionable than Brighton and thus infinitely quieter, had never seen so much excitement before. The usually quietly peopled promenade was teeming with men, women and children, all shouting, and exclaiming, and jostling one another for a better look. Horses whinnied in frustration as their forward progress was made impossible by the crowds, despite the urgings and proddings of their riders. Carriage wheels became entangled. Tempers flared as fishermen tried to launch boats out to rescue the drowning sailors. Other, less philanthropic persons, also tried to launch their vessels, but theirs was a mission bent on pillage, as the rumour that the stricken ship had been carrying brandy and wine from France swept across the beach faster than the incoming tide. Consequently, the would-be rescuers found themselves constantly thwarted in their attempts, and the fate of the sailors looked grim indeed.

Together with all this ruckus, all of the bathing machines were being hauled back up the beach by panicked operators; there was a monster out there, a terrible beast which had scuttled a ship and was advancing murderously ashore. Ladies in various stages of undress were squealing and attempting to relocate clothing; and three dandies, either already drunk or still drunk from the night before, were openly ogling them.

If the scene upon Hove beach had been bedlam before, it was now seven kinds of hell combined. There were up to two hundred people on the beach, comprising rescued sailors, bedraggled women, fishermen, men absconding with casks of brandy washed ashore from the stricken ship, the town watch, and many useless onlookers who could do nothing but stare and gawp at the scene. Tragically, there was also a growing number of bodies lying on the sand, covered with whatever could be found.

Amongst all this tragedy and mayhem, there strode a haughty woman dressed in a rather old-fashioned manner. As she picked her way disdainfully across the sand, with a lace handkerchief soaked in cologne held up to her beak-like nose and a look of disgust across her discontented features, her eyes gleamed a little when she spotted her quarry. Coming upon a bizarre grouping of half-naked people crouched over a coughing and spluttering woman, the haughty lady sneered down at them. Raising an antiquated quizzing glass up to her right eye, she raised her cane and poked one of them in the shoulder.

"I knew," she began in a voice dripping with scorn, "that the Bennets were no better than common farmers. But this..." and she swept the cane around in an arc encompassing the entire beach, "...is beyond anything else. To see, with my own eyes, the orgy in which the Bennets are indulging! To think that they have knowingly placed themselves in such a nefarious position, taken part in such a salacious activity as this is more than I could predict. The Bennets have sunk as low as they possibly can, and there can be no amelioration of their... their... disgusting behaviour. To think that my nephew actually married one of them! However, the marriage will not last much longer, I can assure you!" With triumph in her voice, Lady Catherine de Bourgh, for it was indeed she, swept away imperiously before any of the astonished Bennets could reply.

One must not suppose that Lady Catherine was upon that beach through chance alone. That lady had been following the Bennets for some time, albeit by proxy through hired agents. She had hired a house in a lesser-known area of Brighton and had stayed out of sight, merely waiting for that family's inevitable debacle, which would promote her cause. The news that the Bennets were sea-bathing was too good an opportunity to miss. She hoped for impropriety: what she saw was wanton nudity! She hardly noticed the wreck and the struggling survivors as she left the beach, arm-in-arm with her companion, the equally as scathing but infinitely more influential Countess Lieven. With a backward and condemning glance, Lady Catherine said, "We must set things in motion at once!" and she strode off, with malice gleaming in her eye.

"Well, I see Lady Catherine is her usual sanguine self," quipped Mr Bennet, the first to realise the imperious lady's identity. And then, as Mrs Bennet grasped his arm and began to sob, he said, very gently, "There, there, my dear… You see? Not dead, after all!"

Chapter Sixteen
Everything Explained

The following days saw even more excitement. The weather turned stormy and cold but that did not deter the hordes of sightseers descending daily from Brighton, and all points surrounding, in order to see the wreck with their own eyes, and also to perhaps discover some of the scattered cargo for themselves. The bodies of the unfortunate dead had been removed as quickly as possible; the remnants of the ship that had washed ashore and the smashed bathing machines disappeared just as thoroughly. Free firewood was, after all, free firewood.

With each passing day, hyperbolic stories of the boat wreck became more lurid. It would seem that a giant whale had surfaced and scuttled the ship; the reported number of the dead increased daily, so that it had been a huge cargo ship carrying all the wealth of the Indies, or of Africa, that had been scuttled. Others understood that the ship had been carrying secret documents containing information vital to the War, or bore Napoleon himself. There were also increasingly heroic stories of rescue, and many a townsman greatly embellished his own role on that particular day. The Bennets, after having managed to locate several capes and cloaks to conceal their bedraggled and near-naked appearances, had retreated to their house on the Promenade in Brighton and ventured out only when necessary, taking their time in recovering from their individual watery ordeals. Having their own tales to tell of all their recent adventures, it seemed they could not get enough of each other, could not gaze upon beloved faces often enough, and they had no desire to go into society.

It often seemed to them, in the weeks following the wreck, that the world had turned upside down. Mr Bennet was not an absconding philanderer after all but a hero, having rescued his drowning daughter and several sailors from the ravaging sea. In addition to this, he seemed to have had the most romantic adventures in France. His family were in awe when he told of how he landed in Paris, even though he made light of his incarceration. Mrs Bennet, regarding her once-boring husband with adoring eyes, declaimed to all who would listen that she never doubted her husband for a moment. She had known all along he was not a womaniser!

In every recounting of his adventures, Mr Bennet exercised extreme caution. Not wanting to either exaggerate his deeds, nor alarm his family with some of the dangers he had faced, he drew a compromise by downplaying most of the events as much as possible. Accordingly, the smuggling expeditions became tame fishing trips with worthy, honest fishermen; the horse-urine-riddled smuggler's hole under the stable became a clean but humble inn; the streets of Paris had been teeming not with French soldiers and pressgangs, but with ordinary Parisians merely rebuilding their lives, and the noisome French prison in which he had been incarcerated became a mere inconvenience, a short spell in some official's office wherein credentials had been checked.

As Fortune would have it, Mr Bennet's companions in adventure had also been spared from drowning. Taking up residence in a nearby inn, they spent many an evening recounting their own roles in their escape from France to all who would listen, and discovered that ale and steaks were free-flowing in exchange for their tales of adventure. Things began to get out of hand as fact and fiction became more and more interchangeable, and an emergency meeting saw them all perforce coming to agreement as to which version of the 'facts' they should all adopt. It was agreed that the ladies should be spared some of the more gruesome details.

The mostly silent Gus did not have much trouble with remembering the details of the heavily censored misadventures, as his lack of English skills rendered him even more taciturn than usual. However, Armand and Jacques very often accidentally let slip a few hair-raising details which had then to be glossed over as quickly as possible. One evening after dinner, Bertram Bennet was recounting the tale of when, having been liberated from his cell, Armand, Gus and he were led along the corridors of the Paris gaol at a rapid pace by the resourceful Jacques, but not so rapidly that Bertram had not been aware of several bodies slumped against the walls or on the floor. On the telling of this chapter in their adventures, Armand had become philosophical, expressing the opinion that Jacques had had to do what he did, in order to secure their escape.

"Had to do what?" the sharp-eared Mary, now fully recovered from her near-drowning, was suspicious.

"Er— no," Bertram Bennet interrupted quickly. "Armand means... that— I mean, the expression Armand used, 'dead to the world'... He was confused. He actually meant the officials — their silence had cost the earth... um... *mort au monde* and *couter le monde* are similar, are they not? Ha ha!"

"Hmm," replied Mary. "And how much of '*le monde*' did your passage home on that 'fishing boat' cost? '*Tout le monde*'? Or just a bit?"

Since there was no way of denying that their boat seemed to have broken up very rapidly in the storm during the night before his family's fateful bathing expedition, Bertram acknowledged they had been duped with regard to the seaworthiness of the vessel on which they trusted their lives. He also made little of their agonising wait on a stony beach at Le Havre for the promised boat to arrive, and played down the heart-stopping moment when the French coast guard turned up, just as they were rowing out to the promised vessel.

All of these facts were glossed over, but there was one thing which needed no dissemination, no embellishment, and that was the crack in Bertram Bennet's voice when he told of his amazement when he was struggling in the water and saw what appeared to be his entire family sitting in a bathing machine, and Mary risking her own life by attempting to save what she had perceived to be a complete stranger.

Mr Bennet himself was also well supplied with amazing tales, for here was silly Kitty, suddenly grown into an astute and talented businesswoman, whose fashion designs were hotly sought after, and who was now known as Miss Catherine. He was shown her portfolio, and was impressed so much that he abjured his lifelong abhorrence of descriptions of lace. As for Miss Mary, he saw her now as someone softened, chastened, but not diminished by her new humility. He marvelled at how she had held the family together and how she had managed the house. He laughed out loud, for the first time in many weeks, when he heard how Mary and Catherine together had routed the insidious vicar who had been bullying Catherine into marriage. *Yes*, he thought, *Mary's new humility suits her well, as does Kitty's new confidence.* He knew not what to make of either Edgar or Betty-Letty, beyond reflecting that Edgar seemed rather rakish and slightly dissipated, but worthy nevertheless of gratitude for assisting Kit— Catherine, rather, in her business endeavours, and that Betty-Letty were too silly for their own good. He wondered fleetingly if Edgar might marry either Betty or Letty, and then his brain segued unbidden into speculation as to how Edgar would know which twin he had wed. He decided it was none of his business. He had seen enough, and done enough, in the past weeks to understand that some things were best left alone.

Indeed, in those weeks following the Great Happening at Hove it seemed to Bertram that the only constant was his daughter Lydia, who remained her usual self, piqued at not being the centre of attention as she had hoped, and annoyed that her sisters would not go out on the town with her. Once Lydia discovered that the Bennets were residing in one of the most superior addresses in Brighton, she cavalierly abandoned her friends and moved in with her family as fast as she could. She brought with her the young baby Wickham and a nanny of dubious skills. Alas, Lydia's plans of swanning around town as the superior married sister and playing the sophisticated woman were put to naught. No one wanted to hear her petty posturings or engage with her daily dramas when there were real tales to tell.

Mr Bennet was very naturally overjoyed to hear that Elizabeth and Jane were both expecting their first babies, but although Lydia was also in the same 'delicate' condition he was not so pleased with his youngest daughter. He did not presume to know much about the entire business, but he was sure that Lydia was taking her second pregnancy all too lightly, and thought she was probably endangering both herself and the baby with her hoydenish gallivanting around town. He was roused enough by her shenanigans to remonstrate with her, calling her to account over the latest episode in which she had arrived home quite drunk at past three o'clock in the morning.

"Really, Papa, I am a married lady, you know. You cannot remonstrate with me now, as before!" Lydia was defiant.

However, Mr Bennet replied that since she was living under his roof (albeit a borrowed one), she could jolly well exercise a little more decorum. Furthermore, since he deemed himself to have authority over her in Wickham's absence, he felt it was within his right to expect her to behave. He then demanded to know just exactly where her husband was. Lydia, not liking the interrogation, at first dissembled, but then cried out suddenly.

"Well, if you must know, he has gone off! Left me! I do not know where he is, and I do not care!" Lydia then burst into real tears and was enfolded into her mother's bosom. Her mother, naturally, exclaimed over her and petted her greatly, letting all who would listen know that she had never liked George Wickham, never; and now see what had happened!

As the hot summer marched on well into September, the newest additions to the family circle, Armand Picard, Jacques D'Aubrey (or Jack Dobbrey, as he was once more) and the enigmatic Gus, became restive as their positions grew increasingly problematic.

They had sat through Mr Bennet's watered down re-telling of their adventures with Jacques kicking Armand underneath the table to maintain his silence, and Gus being wise enough to just nod agreeably, but now all were unsure of what the future held for them. Armand, in particular, was at a loose end. Having struggled ashore alongside Mr Bennet on the day of the wreck, Armand attached himself to the family as a barnacle on a boat. Ever conscious of the wrong he had inflicted upon the Bennets, and that his dramatic declaration on the night of that Yule Ball had been the start of the entire escapade, he wandered around feeling like an inconvenient interloper. His discomfiture led him to make plans to leave as soon as possible, but his lack of funds forced him to first enquire of Mr Bennet whether he could suggest some employment for him, which would enable him to afford a passage back to France as soon as possible. Thomas was still missing.

"Well, Monsieur Picard, it is true that I have often thought of you as the devil incarnate, but I feel it my Christian duty to assist you. I have, in fact, been thinking of where there might be a suitable position for you, and as soon as I discover one, I shall inform you," Mr Bennet said, in reply to Armand's query.

"You are so kind!" Picard exclaimed, breathlessly. "Your consideration for one who has wronged you so much is prodigious! I—"

"Don't be so quick to attribute me with noble sentiments! I have also spent many a long hour wishing ill upon you and devising plans for revenge. However," Mr Bennet flung up a hand to reassure the stricken Frenchman, "your actions in France no doubt saved my life."

"Monsieur Bennet! You are too kind! I did nothing," Armand protested, wringing his hands.

"Not true," Mr Bennet stated bluntly. "Jack— Jacques would not have been able to carry off our escape without your assistance, and bravery. There were so many soldiers upon that beach at Le Havre! No, I will not allow this circular argument to continue. If you had not invaded my life with your salacious accusations, I would not have gone to France in the first place, but you did say those things, and I did go to France, and there you helped to save my life, so we are even — you understand? You have made more than enough reparation. And let us not forget that you also, in a manner of speaking, gave me a son."

"I... I do not know what to say," stammered Picard, for once bereft of words.

"Then say nothing," Mr Bennet advised. "In another world we would have been friends, but in truth we are brothers-in-law. Let us, at least, work on that."

Whilst Picard wandered around inhabiting his precarious position in the Bennet household, Edgar Spencer and Betty-Letty, the only visitors the Bennets would admit, did their best to put him at his ease. However, although his English was good, it was not at a level that enabled him to grasp subtle nuances of meaning, and their quick repartee often left him bemused. He could not decide more than half the time if the Bennets were joking, or were deadly serious, when one of them made such remarks as "Oh yes — Armand, our family's nemesis."

The Bennets themselves were extremely confused about their feelings towards Picard. Mr Bennet's unfolding story of the reasons for his ill-advised dash to France, together with the confirmation of their having a half-brother, was the only possible topic of conversation for many an evening to come. Although their father had been downplaying the dreadful peril in which he had been placed, they all suspected that matters had been more dangerous than they had been led to believe. Mrs Bennet had a vague notion that her husband might have fallen foul of French authorities in his quest for the all-important marriage certificate, but Mary and Catherine had a very good idea of the true story and through artful eavesdropping on Mary's part, they gleaned that at one point Picard had indeed been extremely active in saving their father's life. They therefore dithered between regarding Picard as a hateful interloper, and a saviour. In addition, although they naturally at once believed Mr Bennet when he informed them of the legitimacy of their as-yet unmet brother Thomas, none of them was naïve enough to believe that the world would accept him as such. It could neither be proved nor disproved, pieces of paper notwithstanding. So, Armand was there in their house, either an uncle to them, or an imposter, as far as the world was concerned.

Mrs Bennet's initial raptures in having her husband restored to her gave way occasionally to hysterics and recriminations. If Mary and Catherine were ambivalent towards Armand, she fluctuated between downright hostility and haughty disregard. Her hostility was easily explained: Armand, after all, was directly responsible for all of their woes ever since that Yule Ball. Her haughtiness was more difficult to understand. The fact that she now had a stepson older than her own eldest child was amazing to her, and she was fully cognisant of the fact that, were it not for Armand, they would have never known about Thomas. She therefore realised, in some rather dim way, that some good had come out of it all, so at times her hatred of Armand was tempered. She could not bring herself to like him, of course. She therefore spent many a day alternating between cool politeness and downright rudeness towards Armand. She also vacillated between berating her husband for having concealed a previous marriage, praising him for his heroic efforts, and in scheming how best to get the troublesome Thomas declared legitimate.

Indeed, proving Thomas' legitimacy became the only topic of conversation. Round and around the arguments went. The entail would still hold unless they could find that all-important piece of paper. Jack Dobbrey, finding himself at a loose end and eager to go off on another adventure, took on board the task of retrieving the very vital record from the ruins of the Picard family home. In his usual cloak-and-dagger way, he set about meeting with people of dubious character and loose morals. He became very well acquainted with public houses and alleyways. Money often exchanged hands. There were also a few threats.

Unsurprisingly to Jack Dobbrey, Armand Picard proved quite useful in this quest. Of all the Bennet household, save Bertram, Jack alone knew that Picard had been a spy of sorts for the English: he had hinted as much to Mr Bennet when he first heard of Picard's appearance. It was therefore no great wonder to him that Picard should know someone who knew someone, in Brighton of all places. Since things were still very perilous across the water in France, and since their recent adventures had made it somewhat impossible for them to travel there, Armand had tracked down a person who was willing to take on the task themselves. More money exchanged hands; delicate negotiations ensued, followed by a long wait which passed unnoticed by all but Jack and Armand. In due course there was a knock at the basement door one night; a hooded figure handed over a small packet, and disappeared silently into the darkness. The certificate had been found where Picard had said it would be: in a desk in the library of the Picardy's chateau, which was now unfortunately a smoking ruin.

The Bennets read that piece of paper over and over again, and all came to the same sad but inevitable conclusion: it was worthless. After all the trials and sufferings endured by Mr Bennet, it had all been for nothing, for the paper was badly burned in one corner and the date was illegible. It could either vilify Bertram Bennet as a bigamist, or vindicate him as an innocent bridegroom who had been tragically bereaved. It mattered not that, by all calculations, the ill-fated Amelia de la Picardy had been dead at least two months before Bertram's marriage to the young Jane Gardiner. As far as Bertram knew, that marriage had been annulled anyway.

It was Lydia, in her thoughtless way, who pointed out the obvious. Marriage certificates notwithstanding, how could anyone prove that Thomas was the son of their own father? As far as the world was concerned, he was the son of Amelia's second husband, the ageing Duke. This then caused a very circular argument which went on for days. Nothing could be proved. The only person now who could say for sure was long buried.

If Bertram Bennet had had any time to spare, he would have reflected upon the futility of his recent quest. It would seem that even if he had personally been successful, the outcome would still have been the same. Thomas would remain illegitimate in the eyes of the lawyers. However, since the Bennet family now felt it was nearly time to leave Brighton and return home to Longbourn, Bertram was much too occupied in planning the journey home to spend more than a few hours each day worrying about this. There were many delays; they couldn't possibly leave before they had done this, or that, and so it was several more weeks, when the weather began to cool and the leaves to turn golden, before the actual date of their departure was set. Eventually the household was packed up, servants sent on ahead, and goodbyes were said to all their friends and acquaintances, with many promises of keeping in touch and catching up in the future.

Jack Dobbrey declined to go with them. He felt certain that he would go insane if he remained inactive for very much longer and so, in order to stave off his increasing boredom, he decided to risk it and return to France to help track down the missing Thomas Picard. He felt sure that the increasing dangers in France would actually aid his mission, as by now surely his own notoriety would have faded a little. The family had become quite fond of him by this time and begged him not to go — it was still so dangerous over there — but he replied that he needed to be off again. Life *en famille* was *trés charmant,* but he was becoming as jumpy as a horse kept too long in a stable. He would take no payment from them for his services, he assured the family. He had some lucrative prospects ahead of him, and would seek out his smuggler friends and take passage back to Paris. He felt optimistic regarding finding the missing Thomas, whom he felt should be returned to his family, whether that be Armand Picard alone or the Bennets as well. All were in agreement eventually. Bertram Bennet repeatedly offered to cover Jack's travel costs, but was denied.

Bertram's erstwhile cellmate, Gus, also looked relieved at the prospect of being active again, and wanted to accompany Jack. His own agenda, of course, was to find his own family, and thus the two adventurers found mutual purpose and support in each other. Gus was not alone in his separation from his family. Napoleon and his manic lust for European domination had split up countless thousands of French families in a similar manner, but at least Gus now had a companion in his search, and a stand-in family to return to, should he need it. Gus himself was moved to tears by the offer from Mr Bennet of a future home among his family, who were all so loud, lively opinionated that they ought to have been French, and promised to return some time in the future and hopefully bring his family to visit.

Mrs Bennet, patting her husband's arm and grasping it intermittently, a new habit she had acquired, only nodded her agreement to her husband's offer in an absent-minded way.

Chapter Seventeen
Still The Storm

Unfortunately, while the Bennets sojourned in Brighton, recovering from their ordeals and recounting their adventures, another storm was brewing outside their very door. Unbeknownst to them, amongst all the stories of the Day of the Wreck circulating around Brighton and filtering up to London, there was another wonderful piece of gossip doing the rounds. It would seem that the Bennets had been caught in yet another scandal. It would seem that they had been seen bathing naked in mixed company, for all the world to see. This story was instigated primarily by that paragon of virtue and propriety, Lady Catherine de Bourgh, having ensconced herself in London for that very purpose, and was seconded most willingly by her friend Countess Lieven, the powerful and well-known society snob.

Lady Catherine was most adept in spreading her story, and in ignoring whatever facts did not sit well with her fiction. There was no denying the wreck, of course, but as Lady Catherine put it, "The real pity that day for the Bennets was that it resulted in them being caught out in their highly immoral activities. Of course, what could one expect of such a family? I have often said that they are nothing but mere commoners, and now we all see that they are licentious, as well!"

Lady Catherine's antipathy towards the family that had thwarted her plans to found a Darcy-de Bourgh dynasty through the marriage of her daughter Anne and her nephew, Fitzwilliam Darcy, grew with each passing week. Her censure of Darcy's wife Elizabeth was unabated, and recent news from Pemberley of Elizabeth's happy condition inflamed her anger further. She was determined to see the marriage annulled, Elizabeth's pregnancy — if it were true! - notwithstanding, and Darcy freed up to marry her daughter. Her campaign to besmirch the Bennet name and cause disgust for his wife in Darcy's heart was conducted with military efficiency. Such a campaign, of course, needed allies, and Lady Catherine had a very powerful alliance indeed in Countess Lieven.

There was no such antipathy towards the Bennets on the part of the Countess, who hardly knew nor cared about such nobodies from the country. Rather, her willingness to participate in the vilification of that family sprang from self-preservation. Some years before our tale begins, Lady Catherine had suspected that her friend Dorothea Lieven was having an affair with the parliamentarian Lord Palmerston, who had political aspirations out of line with his current status. Of course, the entire world, as well as her husband Prince Khristofor, already knew of Dorothea's rather open liaison with the Austrian Chancellor Prince Klemens, but not many knew of her other secret affairs, and Dorothea herself was at pains to keep them secret. She was extremely loath to give up the prestige and wealth of being married to Prince Khristofor, who had told her in no uncertain terms that having one affair was tolerable but that two or more was execrable. It was suspected by many but not proven that the Countess was licentious, and Lady Catherine's methods of discovering the sordid truth about her friend were nothing short of inspired.

"So tell me, dear Dorothea! Have you managed to break off your association with Lord Palmerston yet? Or is he still being tiresome?" Lady Catherine had asked, rather innocently, of her friend one day.

Somewhat startled by the boldness of the question, Dorothea Lieven could only murmur, "No, not yet. But how did you know…?"

"Oh, I didn't really know," smirked Lady Catherine. "I merely suspected it, along with everyone else. You have, of course, just confirmed it." And from that moment, Dorothea Lieven was beholden to Lady Catherine de Bourgh. With her privileged, exciting and influential position in London society in jeopardy, she found it extremely prudent to humour Lady Catherine; she did not need to be told that she had better act as though they were close friends.

Mrs Bennet, with her husband now restored to her, was very keen to return to Longbourn. She held fantasises of parading her husband as a local hero and of rubbing Mrs Cowper's nose well and truly in it. The Bennet family then became fully occupied in planning their travel homewards, and since it was a very long journey indeed, a sojourn in London was agreed upon, despite Mrs Bennet's chagrin at having to delay her planned revenge upon her nemesis. Miss Catherine was extremely excited at the prospect and was, in fact, the primary reason for the family's decision to break the journey in London. Her fashions were now being displayed in at least one London establishment and she could hardly wait to see for herself, to supervise and advise on trimmings and colours, and to perhaps enjoy a little fame. Thus, they were all eager and excited and busy, and oblivious to the scurrilous rumours about them which were now being circulated throughout London.

The long-suffering Mr Darcy was prevailed upon to lend his London home for the purpose and by the time the oblivious Bennets arrived, together with Edgar Spencer and Betty-Letty, who could not bear the thought of being left behind in Brighton, all of town was abuzz with speculation. One might think that one more silly story about a bunch of provincials was small change compared to the intrigues and scandals abounding in town, but there was an added cache to this story which sped it along its way.

Miss Mary was the first of the family to become aware of it, once the Bennets had established themselves in London. Ensconced one rainy day in a comfortable armchair in the lending library of Lackington Allen and Co., she had been alternately leafing through the dozen or so volumes on the table beside her (alas, it was only permitted to borrow three at a time!) and marvelling at the library itself, which was several storeys tall, when she became aware of a conversation being held at the table across from her. She did not know the young ladies partaking of the conversation, and they themselves did not know her, and so with the disguise of anonymity, Mary was able to hear every word spoken.

"My dear," thus spake one. "You have, of course, cancelled your order?"

"Of course, my dear, as have you?"

"Naturally! To think I very nearly wore one of her gowns to the Assembly!" The young lady shuddered as she spoke.

Her companion gave a false shiver, by way of support. "So wicked! Nude sea-bathing!" She covered her mouth with her hand, as if she might be ill at the thought.

"Shocking!" the first speaker sympathised. "Of course, you know, the father had been in Brighton all along, cavorting in some kind of... men's club activities... before the rest of the family joined him?"

"I had been told! So dreadful! And you know he himself is a libertine of the most dreadful kind! It all came out at some country ball or another! He was confronted by the brother, or the father, of a French lady he had seduced and left in a delicate way! Such…!

"Oh, I know! But you know, God has his ways of exposing sinners, and the wreck could not have happened at a worse time for that family! They had though to conduct their disgusting nude activities well-hidden from public eye, for that is what those bathing machines are primarily for, you know, but the happenings of the day exposed them in more ways than one!" tittered the first lady, fanning herself vigorously.

"Such dreadful behaviour. Of course, sea-bathing itself is quite the thing, but this…!"

"Oh, I know! Of course, no lady of quality will now be seen wearing that Miss Catherine's designs! To be associated with that family!"

"And yet she still has the nerve to show her face in the salons, looking over her patterns as if she were innocent! She and her entire family must be boycotted!"

"Oh, my dear, I could not agree more…!"

And thus went the entire conversation. Miss Mary could not move from her seat lest she be recognised by some small chance, or lest she not hear the end of it. Outraged as she was, she kept still and quiet with her nose in the book and ears wide open, and returned home only after the two gossipers had left. With heavy heart she ascended the steps to Darcy's town house, not sure how she was to tell her sister that her dreams were now in tatters. Poor Catherine! She had been so excited when they had arrived in London and seen, for herself, her designs being taken up by quite a few fashionable London salons! She had such dreams of expanding her business! And now all would be ruined, for there was no denying it: as little as Mary herself cared for the opinion of the public, she was not so removed from the fashionable world that she did not know that for Catherine to succeed as she hoped she must first conquer London.

Things got worse. Not only was 'Miss Catherine's Couture' suddenly anathema to all young society ladies, nearly all but one of the London salons that displayed her portfolio had sent Catherine a note, relating how sorry they were but they must remove... they had overstocked... not quite the thing... you know how it is, and it is with regret...

Mary seethed with anger but lost no time in acquainting her family with the unjust situation. Catherine bewailed, wringing her hands in anguish at her shattered dreams, and Lydia saw an opportunity to grab hold of the excess stock and outfit herself for nothing. Mrs Bennet, fussing around her husband, abruptly told her daughters to stop moaning and do something about it. Greatly surprised by her mother's display of practicality, a new development of late, Catherine agreed to go into town the next day with Mary and confront the proprietor of Madame Maxine's, the latest establishment to suddenly find itself unable to continue with her portfolio. Edgar and Betty-Letty, naturally, at once offered to go with them for moral support. Lydia could not forgo an opportunity to shop, and thus it was agreed that they would waste no time and do the deed on the morrow with stout heart.

Left alone, no amount of resolve in the world would have induced Catherine to enter Madame Maxine's the next day, for it seemed to be teeming with haughty young ladies. However, Mary grasped her arm and encouraged her to look up and smile; Lydia rushed in, heedless of the crowd; Edgar held the door open gallantly and Betty-Letty, enacting their own conjured-up scenario, waltzed into the room, declaring loudly, "I must see what Miss Catherine has to offer! I adore her styles, you know!"

As they advanced into the room, they immediately perceived a gaggle of women clustered around an older woman who commanded attention by her very height and presence. With her was a younger but even more commanding woman, who was mid-sentence.

"I do not know," the younger of the two women sniffed deprecatingly, "why my eyes must be assaulted at the sight of these… these… so-called designs. Why are you so tardy at removing them? Not only are they an abomination to my senses, they have been perpetrated by a woman of the loosest morals! Indeed, to purchase one of these designs would result in being forever tainted by the immorality of that entire family!"

The proprietor of the establishment herself, the haughty Madame Maxine, was being confronted by two women who exceeded, in every way, her own sense of superiority, and was attempting to explain why she had not had enough time to remove the offensive, immoral and salacious drawings, which still graced her display shelves. As Madame Maxine attempted to soothe the offended sensibilities of her illustrious visitors, Mary and Catherine realised, with sinking hearts, that the elder of the two imperious women was none other than Lady Catherine de Bourgh, a lady who was rapidly becoming their nemesis.

"Indeed," Lady Catherine was saying, holding a lace handkerchief to her nose as she spoke. "This is true, for I know for a fact that this so-called Miss Catherine is one of the Bennet menagerie. You know the Bennets, don't you? They are the ones who cavort naked in public on beaches. The father is a libertine of the most shocking kind."

There were gasps of shock and titillation around the salon as all the young ladies drew nearer to Lady Catherine and her companion, Countess Lieven. Mary felt like sinking into the ground. This could not be worse!

"Oh yes!" agreed Countess Lieven. "So shocking! These abominations must be removed from this establishment at once!" And she snapped her fingers.

Madame Maxine's sense of superiority had by now completely evaporated, as she fully realised who her interrogators were. She curtseyed forward, bowing most abjectly at the two very frightening ladies, and murmuring placatory remarks.

"Of course. At once. I do not know how... did not realise there were any left. Is there anything else I can show you...? Rest assured—"

"I do not know," yawned Lady Catherine. "One feels rather besmirched. I do not know if I can possibly patronise this establishment any more..."

Madame Maxine was in the act of further grovelling when she was abruptly shoved to one side by a furious Mary Bennet, who strode forward angrily and glared boldly up at Lady Catherine.

"You do not speak the truth, Lady Catherine! You have been sadly misinformed. My father is not a libertine, and my family certainly do not partake of licentious behaviours! To speak such untruth is to commit libel!"

Gasps of shock spread across the room as Lady Catherine turned slowly to regard Miss Mary. With excruciating deliberation, Lady Catherine raised a quizzing-glass to her eye, sniffed loudly into her cologne-soaked handkerchief and regarded Mary Bennet with a glacial stare.

"What is this? Some woman of the lower orders mistakenly blundered into this establishment? But no, I am mistaken. Behold, it is one of the very family of which I speak. And lo, alongside her is one of her sisters, infamous for an elopement of the most salacious kind." And thus saying, Lady Catherine allowed her gaze to sweep insolently over Lydia, who stood there, mouth agape and body a-tremble.

"That... that's not true!" spluttered Mary.

"Not true?" queried Lady Catherine, turning to Countess Lieven. "Assist me. Is this not the Bennet company? And is that not the woman who cohabited before marriage with a man?" She gestured at Lydia.

"Well, no... yes... We are the Bennets, of course, but it is not true that..." Mary tried in vain to explain. "We—"

"You have no doubt come to remove your sister's vulgar attempts at *haute couture* from this respectable, Christian establishment. It is the least you can do." Lady Catherine was inexorable.

Murmurs of condemnation and outcries of anger swept across the room. Many young ladies backed away from the Bennets as if they carried the plague. Edgar gazed at the ceiling, Betty-Letty's little act came to an abrupt end, Lydia almost swooned, and Mary realised they were ruined. Not content with besmirching their name, Lady Catherine seemed determined to destroy them financially. Not able to fully grasp her motives, Mary could only stare at Lady Catherine as if she was mad.

Slowly, with leaden feet, Catherine advanced towards the display tables and began to gather up her slim portfolio. "Of course. We will go at once. So sorry to have intruded. I will remove them at once." With tears streaming down her face, Catherine continued muttering half-sentences of apology. "I did not realise. Of course I am not—"

But Catherine was suddenly interrupted in her abject apologies by a loud commotion at the door, as the gathered crowd parted suddenly, swept aside by an unstoppable force.

"But *vy*..." demanded a heavily accented German voice, "...*vould* you remove *zese* patterns, *ven I haf* come here particularly to see *zem*?"

All heads looked up sharply, and all heads immediately bobbed down, as the bodies they were attached to curtsied to the owner of the German voice, who was none other than the Prince of Wales' wife, Princess Caroline. A heavy silence descended upon the room as Princess Caroline and her large retinue of ladies-in-waiting advanced into the salon, regally giving the briefest of nods to Countess Lieven.

"I must ask you again. *Vy* are *zese* patterns being removed? I *vish* to see *zem*!"

No body moved or hardly dare breathe. Then Lady Catherine, rallying bravely after the shock of seeing the Prince Regent's wife in person, attempted to regroup. "I was just saying the same thing myself, Your Highness. Why are they being removed, indeed!"

Princess Caroline directed a bored and disdainful glance in her direction. "Do I know you? I think not. Move aside, if you please." The Princess proceeded to look about her in a most interested way. "*Vy* are there so many people in this salon? It is very crowded!"

Immediately, Madame Maxine, so anxious before to bend as low as possible to Lady Catherine and

Countess Lieven, abandoned her two erstwhile objects of admiration and came cringingly up to Princess Caroline. "Your Highness, if you would step this way?" and she made a gesture attempting to include both the remaining patterns on the table, and those now clutched in Catherine's shaking hands.

"I *vould*, because I *vish* to see *zese vonderful* styles of which I *haf* heard so much. Are *zese* the ones?"

"They are, Your Highness, and might I say—"

But whatever it was Madame Maxine was about to say was abruptly cut short by Mary Bennet, who suddenly had a thought inspired by either madness or cunning, she knew not which. Shoving herself and the trembling Catherine forward, Mary spoke.

"Your Royal Highness, not only are these the very designs you seek, but here also is the very talented designer of them!" And poor Catherine suddenly found herself propelled forwards to stand, front and centre, fully in the gaze of the terrifying Princess Caroline.

"Indeed? *Zis* young lady here before me? Are you *ze* young lady of whom I hear so much?" Princess Caroline turned her basilisk gaze upon the speechless Catherine, who could only squeak.

"*Vot*? *Vot*? I cannot hear you. Speak up."

"Um... yes, Your Highness. These are my little... patterns... um..." Catherine gulped and tried to make her legs and arms work.

"*Zen* show me, and be quick! I *haf* many engagement coming up, and I *haf* a need for an entire new wardrobe. *Ja, ja. Zis* one is *sehr gut. Und zis* one also. *Zis* one… maybe not. But *zis* one… Tell me, young lady, do you *sink zis* one suits?"

In what seemed no time at all to Miss Catherine and the entire gathering, Princess Caroline had ordered nearly a dozen ball gowns and day dresses, all of which were styled after Miss Catherine's drawings. Madame Maxine, foreseeing an avalanche of orders as most of London attempted to follow what Royalty was wearing, recovered her wits enough to order refreshments, to evict from her premises those deemed not able to keep up financially, and mentally resolved to hire more staff. There was one sticky moment when Princess Caroline turned to the agog audience and demanded to know whether these *"wunderbar"* styles would be enough to negate her notorious reputation as a dowdy and frumpy dresser. To assure the Princess that Miss Catherine's Couture was just the thing she needed to lift her public image would be to acknowledge the cruel stories circulating about her renowned poor dress sense. However, the Princess herself obviated the necessity for reply by chortling, "I make *choke*! I make *choke*!" Once the assembled ladies realised they were required to laugh, and that no one was about to be strangled, the mood lightened somewhat.

"Ha ha. Very droll indeed. Your Royal Highness's sense of humour is well renowned," came a voice from the back of the room, and Lady Catherine de Bourgh once more attempted to push herself forward. "As I have often said—"

"Once again I ask: who are you? No, *vait.* I do not care. Please do not approach me again." And so saying, Her Royal Highness Princess Caroline turned her back and effectively removed Lady Catherine de Bourgh from society's list of contenders and pretenders. With burning cheeks, Lady Catherine retreated, conscious of titters, haughty looks and murmured witticisms. The astute Countess Lieven had absconded five minutes before.

Chapter Eighteen
Epilogue And Exeunt

The Bennet family, Edgar Spencer, and Betty-Letty stayed in London for most of the Season, spending Christmas in the perforce generous Mr Darcy's town house, and New Year as well. It was nigh on Easter time before the family removed to Longbourn, so busy were they with social engagements. Everything was so perfect, the winter was so mild, London was so delightful... How could they tear themselves away so soon? They were a very lively party indeed and were much sought after: scarcely a day went by without some card or invitation or another appearing on the little hall table.

Mr Bennet found himself somewhat of a celebrity and was constantly being called upon to recount yet again the tale of how, despite his being only recently arisen from his 'sick bed', he had heroically waded into the sea to rescue the shipwrecked sailors (for that was the story being put about, and one the family thought wise not to gainsay). Indeed, he was almost in a jolly mood, and found himself so much in accord with his wife, after his prolonged absence, that he was continually seeking out her company and escorting her to whatever amusement she desired. Although his acerbic tongue often still found employment, particularly when his good wife rambled on about lace and shoes, he found himself checking his temper with her more than was usual. He was ever conscious of the terrible wrong he had inflicted upon his family by his sudden decampment.

Mrs Bennet herself was also in total accord with her husband, and many were the long walks they had taken together during that mild London winter; she in her new walking boots, and he admiring her new walking outfit. She had much to tell. He was a willing listener, and they therefore spent many a pleasant hour rambling through Hyde Park and feeding the swans, as she spoke at length of Kitty's remarkable success, Mary's business acumen, or Lydia's precipitous return.

Dances, parties, suppers and balls notwithstanding, there was another, more important reason for staying in town so long, and that was Miss Catherine's House of Couture, a new development over which Catherine, Mary and Edgar presided as partners in commerce. Indeed, the business grew so rapidly and went along so nicely that Mary found herself not only managing the salon, but also becoming the chatelaine of yet another new venture, a Home for Young Women in Distress. This worthy establishment was formed primarily to rescue women who had found themselves in difficult circumstances, but it soon evolved into an establishment wherein such distressed women were trained in needlecraft, thus supplying skilled workers to sew up Catherine's designs. In this extremely charitable work, Mary found she was able to soothe her conscience over her commercialism, and consoled herself with the thought that such good works as she was performing would surely sit well in her ledger when the Good Lord inspected it.

Consequently, neither Catherine nor Mary stayed in Longbourn over-long when the family eventually did return to their childhood home, merely returning there long enough to pack up prior to moving permanently to London. As Catherine said, it made more sense. Mary consoled their mother with the promise that it was not to be forever, predicting that fashions being fickle, she and Catherine would most likely get out of the business within five years or so, having by then put by more than enough for their futures. Although saddened at the loss of his "two now most sensible daughters", as Mr Bennet now often called them, he was philosophical, reflecting that in one year Catherine had earned far more than he had ever dreamed she could, and he was glad to see them thus freed up from the spectre of poverty.

Indeed, the sisters' newfound financial independence also negated that other spectre, the one of their continuing spinsterhood. With a steady income and the opportunity to build a sizeable nest-egg, the dread of being left on the shelf became a matter of no consequence to either Mary and Catherine. The sisters agreed wholeheartedly with one another that marriage was not for either of them. Why should they marry, when a husband would only spoil things, presume to take over the business, curtail their independence and generally be a nuisance? Who wanted a husband who would constantly demand his rights, expect them to be silent on important matters, and want them to produce babies *ad hoc*? Lydia had been less than discreet in some of her lurid tales of marriage, and neither Catherine nor Mary fancied any of that at all. Since Jane, Elizabeth and Lydia had by now produced four boy babies between them, Mary and Catherine felt that their parents were well-supplied with grandchildren. No, they were better off single.

Jack Dobbrey and Gus eventually arrived at Longbourn with the missing Thomas in tow, after several hair-raising months sneaking through France. Thomas was welcomed into the family, Mrs Bennet now having had time to inure herself to the idea. Thomas spoke not a word of English, and there were some hilarious times when Mr Bennet's French did not quite come up to scratch, as when, infamously, Mr Bennet had innocently asked of Thomas whether he had found his bed quite comfortable, but had instead unwittingly asked him something completely different and a lot ruder. Laughter ensued, and much embarrassment.

Indeed, laughter and noise were plentiful commodities those days, what with Lydia's two babies ruling the roost above-stairs, Mrs Hill chasing after the eldest who was off and running at an early age, demanding he be brought to book for some misdemeanour or another; Armand attempting to ride a horse and look like a gentleman farmer; and Mrs Bennet walking around with a permanent smile upon her face.

Jack came and went often, always shadowed by Gus. Where he went and what he did were questions never asked. Suffice it to say the Bennets were well-supplied in French brandy and lace from Brussels. Whenever Jack returned to Longbourn, he was always sure of a welcome and indeed had his own room, albeit over the stables, at his own request. Apparently it made slipping away in the dead of night much easier.

Once, by secret agreement with Mr Bennet, Jack and Gus set off to find Lydia's missing husband, George Wickham. It was not too difficult a task: they had only to follow the trail of bad debts and wronged women. They returned in short course somewhat successful, as they had indeed located the errant husband, but the news was grim: Mr Wickham was deceased. Bad eggs will always find a bad end, and Wickham's end had been bad indeed.

Lydia cried not, having already decided that she was very comfortable at her father's table, thank you very much. She found it altogether quite delightful to have servants again, to have the babies looked after, and to not be afraid that every knock at the door was a bailiff come to demand payment of some tradesman's debts.

Indeed, although she had quickly made up her mind not to return to her husband even if he had been found, she now found herself suddenly in the position of being the widow of an army officer, rather than a deserted wife. She thus decided to play on this turn of fortune and for a while was doing a good job in her new role as respectably bereaved woman. Certainly she behaved so sensibly that her family felt she was completely changed, but she subsequently reverted true to type soon after by setting about the countryside for a new husband for herself — *plus ça change*.

Eventually the gossip and rumours surrounding the Bennet family subsided for want of feeding. Thomas was accepted by society as Mr Bennet's son from a previous but brief marriage, although the legal problem of proving his legitimacy still remained. As far as the lawyers were concerned, the entail still stood in favour of Mr Collins, Mr Bennet's irksome cousin. The all-important marriage certificate was useless as most of it was illegible. Public opinion was, of course, in favour of Mr Bennet, the Hero of the Hove Calamity. Certainly, the sordid details of the annulled marriage to Amelia were not widely advertised, and it was agreed by all that Mr Bennet was the victim of legal contortion. Instead, all sympathy was with Mr Bennet and his long-suffering family. How tragic that Mr Bennet had never known about his son! How wonderful that they had been united at last! Mr Bennet was regarded with sympathy and Thomas as quite the romantic figure, newly escaped from Paris ahead of Napoleon's ravening hordes, and now very sensibly having come home to Longbourn in order to learn how to become English.

This new 'truth' led many to regard Armand Picard as a mere bumbling fool whose poor use of English, the night of his dramatic announcement at the Yule Ball, had led to misunderstandings all around. Of course everyone in the surrounding countryside had always known that Mr Bennet had never been a bigamist, nor a philanderer — where on earth had such stories come from? In addition, everyone suddenly purported to have known all along about Mr Bennet's heroic trip to France to rescue his son. No, wait — hadn't he been ill or something? No, of course he had not deserted his wife and children, what nonsense!

Edgar Spencer married either Betty or Letty, no one could remember which. Their wedding and subsequent *ménàge a trois* was the cause of so much gossip as to totally eclipse the old scandals involving Lydia's elopement, the Bennet's new French son, and the highly unlikely adventures of Mr Bennet. Edgar's aunt, Mrs Cowper, on the receiving end of Mrs Bennet's condescension and barely disguised triumph, was hard pressed to downplay the rumours. Betty-Letty did not help matters by deliberately continuing to dress exactly alike. Edgar always avowed he knew the difference, but this was said with such a twinkling eye as to make even the most ribald, young buck grow pink around the collar.

The activities of Edgar Spencer and his new family, once they were ensconced in their new home in London, were so avidly reported and maliciously embroidered upon that one would suppose them to be ostracised from polite company, but the reverse was true. The stories did not preclude society from calling on them often in their new home in London — rather, it was the opposite. Their house became one of the main attractions of town, and the rumours and gossip filtering back to Meryton almost eclipsed the new and highly salacious stories that sprang up surrounding the odious vicar, Broughton, and his cook. The goodly people of Meryton, not being as modern and understanding as Londoners, insisted on retribution, and Broughton was removed from his post. It was understood he was to make his case before the Archbishop of Canterbury. It was hoped he would be de-frocked. The vicar was indeed subsequently replaced by a sandy-haired, young widower with an Irish accent, for whom Lydia had great hopes.

The Christmas following the Bennets' return to Longbourn, two years almost to the day of Picard's fateful announcement, saw a full table at the Bennet home. Mr and Mrs Bennet happily presided over Mary and Catherine, who had returned briefly from London for the Yuletide. Darcy and Elizabeth were also visiting, as were Charles and Jane Bingley. Lydia was, of course, there together with Thomas, Armand, Jacques and Gus. A feast was eaten, toasts were proposed, and the family retired to the drawing room to exclaim over gifts.

Shortly thereafter, several nursemaids entered the room bearing sundry babies and toddlers: Master William Edward Darcy, Master Charles Reginald Bingley, and Masters John and Peter Wickham.

But perhaps the most feted child present that Christmas, the most precious, was also the youngest of them all. All of six weeks old, the newest baby made his family debut — Master Bertram Robert Bennet, much-loved male child of the Bennets, greatest surprise of their later years and undisputed heir to Longbourn. As the entire ensemble surged forward to claim first nursing rights, this paragon of all infant beauty and virtues, this triumphant ouster of all pretenders, blinked in surprise at all the noise and hubbub, and then yawned, contentedly.

Mr Bennet, cradling his newborn son in his arms, looked around himself at all his daughters, at his sons-in-law, at all the babies, at his guests and at Thomas, who hovered, uncertain in the background. Beckoning him forward, Mr Bennet placed the baby in Thomas' arms, saying, "Hold your brother for a while, will you? I am fatigued." He added, "From a dearth of sons to a surplus!" And then, at the stricken look on Thomas' face, he said, "I meant only that now there is a new legal matter to disentangle. But never mind; things have a habit of working themselves out as they should." Mr Bennet then paused to look around at the table laden with treats, and at the babies being passed from one set of arms to another. He gazed at his wife, looking tired but well, and at his daughters, blooming with happiness. "You know, Thomas," Mr Bennet continued, "this house was full for a very long time. I thought, too full, and I craved peace and quiet. Then it sadly emptied out, but I had not much peace. Now… now it is full again, and — do you know, I am very content."